SKIN DEEP

STORIES OF BEAUTY AND BODY IMAGE

EDITED BY STEPHANIE SANDERS-JACOB

Copyright © 2026 by Stephanie Sanders-Jacob. Featuring contributions by Chloe Spencer, Amanda M. Blake, Paul Lonardo, Basile Lebret, J. Neira, Samantha Alis, Briar Hyssop, Sam Logan, Mark Pariselli, Catherine Crow, Hannah Baxter, Pete Jacob, Sutton Harris, Kay Hanifen, Julian Nopakun, Vanessa Leonardo, Whitney Trang, Dawn Winters, Leon Lavender, Solstice Lamarre, Valerie Hunter, and Jude Deluca.

Cover by Sarah Brown (@willowandroxas).

Edited and formatted by Stephanie Sanders-Jacob.

ISBN-13: 979-8-9933182-3-3

Contents

An Introduction   1
from Damien Casey

Strawberry Skin Scrape   4
Chloe Spencer

Changing Room   13
Amanda M. Blake

Size Matters   22
Paul Lonardo

The Technomancer's Body   34
Basile Lebret

Germaphobe Girls   44
J. Neira

Not Pretty   58
Samantha Alis

Sucker   64
Briar Hyssop

Catalytic Converter   78
Sam Logan

Facing   89
Mark Pariselli

Love the Skin You're In 98
Catherine Crow

Fleshbound 115
Hannah Baxter

Perfectly Preserved 130
Pete Jacob

Cutting Season 138
Sutton Harris

The Medusa Serum 148
Kay Hanifen

Boys Will Eat Boys 157
Julian Nopakun

Mirrors 163
Vanessa Leonardo

The Beauty Tester 176
Whitney Trang

First Day of School 188
Dawn Winters

Inside Outside 201
Leon Lavender

Mirror Girl, Hungry Gods 211
Solstice Lamarre

Monsters 226
Valerie Hunter

Pearls for a Swine 235
Jude Deluca

An Introduction
from Damien Casey

WHEN I WAS A kid my face was really flat. I don't know how to explain that because, sure, I had a nose and a mouth and eyes and all that business... but my face was flat. My friends used to make up stories about me; I got smashed in the face by a frying pan trying to steal pie, someone taped a bag of Cheetos to a brick wall and I walked into it... that kind of thing. Always on something about my weight problem and my fat face.

We all made fun of each other for this stuff; big ears, weird nose, gapped teeth. If it wasn't physically "good" you better believe it's free game. I have a pretty good feeling it's that way where you are too, and always has been.

We've put people on the moon, yogurt in a tube, and invented the Predator franchise.

Humans have done some really cool things.

One thing we seem to not be able to let go of though: judging people based on their looks.

My young mind tried to process all of this through the lens of horror. Usually, the message came up short. Stories like *The Haunted Mask* sent the message that being ugly means you were also going to be evil; no chance of getting that thing off your face, uggo. Stories about a young woman who uses a cream that puts spider eggs in her skin telling me that if I try to fix anything, I'm going to have tarantulas climbing out of my cheeks. I can't even count the amount of kids eating chocolate in horror movies getting called names like "Hoagie" or the clever and well thought out "Fat Kid."

Sure doesn't feel so hot being the flat faced tub-o-lard when the only things you see in media are people who are evil because of an ugly face, fat kids who get killed because they couldn't leave a Whopper behind (burger or candy... it doesn't matter), and people being punished in horribly painful ways for trying to fix their physical ailments.

The message I received was clear: Don't even try it, tubby.

In a genre that thrives on cheering for the nerdy guy, immediately knowing who the "final girl" is because she's being billed as the "ugly duckling", and a place where we all wanted that Frankenstein action figure... Why do we feel so maligned for our looks?

It's an easy target.

Go online and look at any celebrity's post, especially women, and you'll see how easy it is to throw out a "you're ugly" or "she isn't pretty" at someone. We use it as a crutch to climb up a mountain of our own insecurities on a stair set we've made from other people's hurt feelings. It's the first insult we throw when we don't like someone, and it's the first insult that sticks when it comes our way.

I remember showing my friends *Aliens* with Sigourney Weaver and trying to explain to them why she was way cooler than Arny in *Predator*. She fought like forty times more of her monster than Arny; therefore she's cooler. My friends all agreed that she just wasn't very pretty. I assume that was based on the obsessive crush with the pink ranger everyone had at the time. But, why did it matter? Did they think Arny was pretty? Why does being pretty matter when you're being the coolest person in the galaxy?

I can write a whole book about how this has to do with the way society expects women more than anyone to maintain a level of attraction while doing anything; but I'll save that for another intro somewhere.

I want to say that Squirm has done something special here. This is a book for young readers that sends a message of empathy. It encourages young men to ask the young women around them what their lives are like because of beauty standards. It encourages young women to stop being their own worst enemy and feel confident in themselves and be who they want to be for themself. It encourages all of us to be a little nicer to ourselves and the world around us.

The girl with the mask learned to love herself and reject her bully, the "fat kid" in the monster squad saved his bullies, the spider girl... well that one's just a tragedy; but we can learn to love ourselves none the less.

My face started to curve out, I lost weight, and still never felt better about myself. Being force fed the idea of the perfect body image still haunts me and other people my age to this day.

I have confidence that the young people who read this book will take away the messages they need to. They will refuse to make the same mistakes as my generation and generations before.

I believe they can save the world.

Strawberry Skin Scrape

Chloe Spencer

BUTTER. THAT WAS THE best word that I could use to describe the texture of Kenna's skin. So soft, so smooth, with a sheen to it, courtesy of the suntan lotion I had rubbed into her shoulders. Her golden-brown skin shimmered in the sun like a topaz that had been freshly unearthed from a mine, but any gem would pale in comparison to her beauty.

"Thanks, Cass!" she chirped, leaning into a butterfly stretch. Some of the muscles and joints in her back audibly popped, and she groaned. "I can't believe I had to haul around so many boxes. I'm going to *kill* Ayden."

Yesterday, Kenna had been roped into helping her brother move into his new apartment. Her father had told him to pack everything in small boxes, so that they'd have lighter loads to carry, but that had resulted in them running up and down the stairs more than they had planned. When I picked her up from her house this morning, she had whined about how sore her body was, but despite the amount of pain she was in, there was no way she was giving up today's beach excursion. We had so few days of summer left, after all. Even fewer, now that we were heading into our senior year of high school. I didn't want to think about that for too long.

"Do you need me to do your back?" Kenna asked as I squirted more sunscreen into my palms. She played with her necklace, her fingers rubbing the little spiral-stomached woman that dangled from the center of the silver chain. Wearing jewelry to the beach seemed silly to me, but I've never seen her without it. It was a keepsake from her mother, passed down through generations of women in her family. And Kenna was sentimental like that. She held onto every birthday card she had ever received, and was one of the few people I knew who printed physical photo albums.

"Not yet," I replied, and winced, dragging my hands over the surface of my legs. My pores were hard, ruby red seeds against the surface of a bleached white canvas. Strawberry skin. I had shaved my legs in anticipation for this day, but as I massaged my hands over the bumps and nodules, I regretted that decision.

Kenna lowered her sunglasses. "Ooh."

"I know. It's bad."

"Do you use any kind of moisturizer after you shave?"

"Yeah, but that doesn't help much."

"What about an exfoliator?" Kenna unscrewed the cap to her water bottle, taking a sip, a few droplets rolling down her chin and dripping onto the floral beach towel we sat on. "Do you have one of those African sponge nets?"

"I've tried everything." My eyes roamed over her perfectly smooth body. I don't think blemishes have ever graced the surface of her skin.

"Even waxing? Sometimes waxing is better because it rips the hair right out of the pore."

"Waxing makes it a little bit better, but it takes too much time." Not to mention it hurts more. There's only so many times I can grit my teeth in anticipation of the violence to come before I start to worry about breaking down my enamel. I didn't need dental problems on top of my skin issues. "I wish I looked more like you."

"What? What do you mean?"

"Are you kidding me?" I gestured to her, all of her. "What's not to love about all of this? You make it look so effortless."

"I know I do, but it's not. Trust me." Some sort of uncertain expression stumbled its way across her face. I rarely saw Kenna look like that. She was normally so self-assured.

"I'd give anything to have your skin."

"Anything?"

I nodded.

Kenna's shimmery hand touched my shoulder, rubbing it. "Don't worry. I got you."

"What?"

"I got you," she said, a smile tugging at the corners of her glossy pink lips. There was nothing about her that didn't sparkle or shine. "Give me a couple of days and I can get you what you need."

She sprang to her feet, wiping off some remaining flecks of sand. I watched as she pranced across the beach, her footwork fast and delicate so as not to scorch the bottoms of her feet, before she plunged below the waters of Lake Harriet.

Days later, I forgot about our conversation. The ACT prep books I ordered came in, and I sat down to do a few more practice tests. I had already taken the ACT once before, and scored a 28, but I was trying to get a 30. From my research, you could take the test up to three times before colleges would start to look negatively at your scores. Apparently, there was such a thing as being a try-hard, at least when it came to college admissions offices.

For hours, I pored over the workbooks, the TV playing *Love Island* on low volume in the background. The mathematical word problems in these workbooks were always written in the most difficult, annoying ways possible. *Fatima hauled boxes of apples to the market for 3 straight days, and the count of each box was 30, 75, and 40. What is the mean number of apples she brought to the market?* Why did we even use the word "mean" when we meant "average?" What was the point of using synonyms in math?

A knock startled me out of my frustrated calculations. Kenna's face squeezed in the small oval window of our front door. I bookmarked my place in my workbook and opened the door. She stumbled inside on her chunky heeled sandals, a plastic bag in hand.

"I got it!"

"Got what?" I muttered, trying to peek inside the bag, but she squeezed it together, hiding the contents from me.

"The stuff for your legs," she replied. She squinted as she peered up and down the hallway. "Are your parents home?"

"No. They're not going to be home for a few more hours."

Kenna nodded, squeezing my hand and tugging me upstairs, but to my surprise, we didn't enter my bedroom. Instead, she pulled me into my bathroom, shutting the door behind me and locking it. Anxiety bubbled in my chest like a pot of hot water on a stove. Not only was she acting weirdly, but I hadn't had the chance to clean my bathroom yet. Strands of wet hair traced their way across the shower tile wall like some bizarre and disgusting watercolor. Body soap gathered in clumps at the base of the drain cover. But Kenna didn't pay any attention to this. She crouched on the mat, peeled away the drain cover, and plugged the tub. She tried to pull on the handles, but the water shot out of the shower head, not the bath faucet. She shrieked with surprise, springing backwards.

"What are you doing?" I crouched beside her, and pulled on the handles, not to turn it off, but to switch the water flow from the shower head to the bathtub faucet.

"Running you a bath, obviously."

"It's 86 degrees outside."

Kenna shook her head. "This is only going to work if you're in the bath."

"What is?"

"This."

She reached into the plastic bag and withdrew a small circular orb. No, not an orb. A bath bomb, shrink-wrapped in plastic, glass-like and almost transparent if not for the streaks of pink that twisted their way through its visible core. I've seen my fair share of bath bombs in all sorts of shapes and colors, but never one like this. The packaging had strange words scrawled across it in white letters, none of them legible in the English language.

"Is this some sort of Korean skincare product?" But I've bought Korean skincare products before, and these letters didn't resemble Hangul. Those letters were smooth, rigid, and as strict as branches on leafless trees. These letters were silly circles and loops, twisting through each other in an endless legato rhythm, as though someone had penned music but couldn't be bothered to separate one note from the next. It didn't look like any language I was familiar with.

Kenna chewed on her bottom lip. "Not exactly."

"Where the heck did you get this from?"

"Not important," she replied. "What's important is that if you want to get rid of the strawberry skin, you gotta get in the bath. We gotta do it now, before anyone comes home."

"What? Why?" Heat flooded my cheeks, and the roar of the faucet behind me did nothing to quiet the tremors in my chest. Kenna expected me to take a bath in front of her? She couldn't be serious, right?

"There're some side effects. But don't worry," she said, squeezing my hands. "I'll be with you the entire time."

I'll be with you the entire time. Kenna always said this before dragging me into some sort of crazy situation. Like when we went to the haunted house at the Minnesota State Fairgrounds, or when Kyle Morton threw that rager last year where the cops were called. Whatever was in this bath bomb, it wasn't good.

"I'm not getting naked in front of you."

"You gotta be naked for it to work. Can't wear a swimsuit."

"And *you* have to be here for me to use it?"

"I don't want you to be in here alone when it starts to work," she whispered. "I can leave the room and you can get in the water and add the bath bomb, and then I'll come back in? The bubbles might, um, hide your body?"

"What the hell is this bath bomb?"

She took a deep breath. "It's the ultimate exfoliator. It's going to get rid of your strawberry legs once and for all."

"Yeah, right." I snorted, shaking my head. "What business plan involves creating a product that doesn't ensure repeat customers?"

"It's not a business," Kenna whispered. "It's something I made myself."

"You made a bath bomb?"

"Look, Cassidy." Whenever she used my full name instead of my nickname, I knew she meant business. "Do you trust me?"

My heartbeat roared in my ears, drowning out the sound of the water behind me. I nodded. We didn't need to say anything else. She exited the bathroom, leaving the door ajar, her body rigidly facing the opposite wall like a soldier standing at attention. Swallowing, I peeled each layer of clothing from my body. Steam streaked its way across the mirror, obscuring my reflection. The heat of the room clung between the folds of my body, sweat dripping down my forehead and legs. Still, I stepped into the bathtub, allowing the piping hot water to envelope me like a blanket. I reached for the bath bomb, punching a nail through the plastic and peeling it back. Sitting in the palm of my hands, it felt unusually smooth. Bath bombs were normally little chunks of brittle moon crater. But it felt... like butter. Like Kenna's skin. My whole life I thought that her beauty was a natural gift, but was it possible that this little thing was responsible for it? All of it? Exhaling, I dropped the bath bomb in the water. Wisps of white rose up from its now bubbling surface. The bomb turned the water from transparent to opaque milk, smooth and silky.

"It's in," I told her, and she stepped inside, closing the door and locking it behind her. I folded my arms over my chest, trying to hide my breasts. Water continued to pour from the faucet, but Kenna made no move to turn it off as she crouched by my side. "It seems... normal?"

She shook her head. "Just wait."

For a few minutes, we sat there in silence, her fingers combing through my hair. Then she reached over and turned off the water. Even though I should have felt nothing but warmth, ice crawled its way through my veins, and goosebumps rose on the surface of my skin. Soon, my teeth were chattering. I looked at her, chuckling at the ridiculousness of the situation, but she didn't smile.

Pink seeped into the whiteness. Blood infecting the milk. We had to be down to the core of the bath bomb now, not that I could see it. The water sloshed as I shifted, trying to make myself more comfortable, but then I felt it. It was like when you're chopping vegetables with a sharp knife, and you nick the tip of your finger. And then it's like when you take that little flap of bloody skin and peel it off.

"*Kenna.*" I gasped, trying to stand.

She squeezed my shoulders, forcing me back down, brown eyes bearing into mine. "You have to stay here until it's done."

"Or what?"

"Or you'll die."

"W-what?!" My feet slipped on the bottom of the surface, and I could feel it, chunks and chunks sloughing off my muscles, the raw muscle beneath colliding with the heat of the bath water. Every time I moved or so much as brushed myself against the sides of the bathtub, the skin peeled away in shaky strips of gelatin. It was coagulated, like remnants of chicken fat that had been left to soak in a pan. It didn't look human. It didn't even look like my skin anymore, if it had ever been a part of my body to begin with.

"You have to relax," Kenna insisted. "Remember that you're the one who wanted this."

"I didn't want to remove my skin!"

I lifted my arm out of the water to examine it. Fatty white tissue clung to the bone, curved and sloping. Clumps dropped into the water. *Plip plop plop!* Kenna grabbed my arm and plunged it below the waters once more, her grip iron tight. As she removed her hand, I felt more tissue peel away in ribbons. The water had gone from pink to a strawberry red, glimmering and effervescent.

"You don't feel pain, do you?"

I sucked a shuddering breath into my lungs. "N-no."

"That means it's working."

She stood up, leaning over the tub, and snagged the African sponge net from one of the shelves. Crouching back down again, she got to work, running it over my shoulders and exposed parts of my upper arms, scraping away every layer. I was human soup, quivering and peeling apart at her mercy. But with each stroke she painted across my body, somehow, I felt less afraid. She gazed upon me with the determination of a sculptor, chiseling and scraping to make her next masterpiece. I couldn't let her do the work all by herself. I dug my nails into my body, scratching and scraping, until I could feel the heat of the water flowing through me, filling me, consuming me.

Setting down the sponge, she gripped my shoulders. "Are you ready?"

I nodded. She pushed me below the surface of the water, and I was reborn.

If before my body had been a canvas, starchy and stretched, it was now porcelain, smooth and flawless. I traced my fingers over my clavicle and shoulders over and over again as though to memorize the new texture. Kenna wrapped her arms around my waist, squeezing me tight as I examined my dewy face in the mirror. I glistened and shimmered like a freshly waxed muscle car.

"I look... glowy," I told her. "Like I've got my own personal sun beneath the surface of my skin."

She nodded. "You're as gorgeous as you've always been."

Heat flooded my cheeks. "Gorgeous?"

"I wanted you to see yourself in the way that I've always seen you." Her voice was soft. Gossamer.

Butter.

About Chloe Spencer

Minnesota native Chloe Spencer (she/her) is an award winning writer, indie gamedev, and filmmaker. She is the author of multiple sapphic horror novellas, novels, and short stories. In her spare time she enjoys playing video games, trying her best at Pilates, and cuddling with her cats. She holds a BA in Journalism from the University of Oregon and an MFA in Film and Television from SCAD Atlanta.

Changing Room
Amanda M. Blake

THERE'S A CERTAIN FEELING when one is adjacent to greatness, especially when you don't deserve to be near it.

Melanie didn't even have to sacrifice her dignity. They laughed at her jokes, not at her. And maybe some of those jokes were self-deprecating, but Becky always told her she was too hard on herself, and no one snickered behind their hands or abruptly stopped whispering after she walked into a room.

Bewildering, to have been mocked all through elementary school and middle school—for everything obvious, but also as though they *knew*, before any of them even really understood what it meant. Then she hit freshman year and, boom, suddenly the cool girls wanted to hang out with her.

At first, even they seemed surprised how much they liked spending time with her, but in a whirlwind, she got invited to all the parties, trips, sleepovers, and study sessions. She sat at their table during lunch. Every day, she couldn't believe that she was the one they chose.

Becky taught her how to do her hair. Marcia and Layla taught her makeup, set her up with a skin routine, and recommended their dermatologist to manage her acne. Constance and her both helped everyone with their homework. Some combination of the girls always came to her volleyball games to cheer her on, sometimes in their pleated cheerleading uniforms but sometimes just as themselves. They took her out to Whataburger or Waffle House when their team won, because they were proud of her.

Melanie didn't understand it, but she wasn't about to question it.

However, she did often question how, if they all ate the same things when they were together, she was still the big one of the group. Like her, they seemed to eat whatever they wanted, neither too much nor too little, but here at the mall, the girls tried on double zero, zero, two, and Melanie couldn't seem to fit into anything right—eight, ten, twelve, large, extra large... Becky stroked her hair when she came out of her changing room without anything and reassured her that sizes in these places ran small and clothes sizes in general were deliberately unstandardized to make girls feel fat and inadequate.

These skinny girls telling her that they felt fat, too.... So what did she seem like to them? A fucking manatee?

But they weren't cruel, and Becky sprang for smoothies for everyone. No one told Melanie not to get peanut butter in her smoothie. No one told her she needed to watch her figure, like her mother did whenever they shopped together, which was a good part of the reason why she liked shopping with her friends instead. Not the only reason, of course, not the most important reason...

It was just so embarrassing that she couldn't fit into things like they did, though, which was why, after the first few times of cramming everyone into one dressing room, Melanie had started splitting off and dressing on her own. She could judge herself just fine without imagining them judging her, too. They were too nice to do it to her face, but she knew they were thinking it. She didn't want them looking. She didn't want them seeing. Not when she knew whose eyes were on her and her face would flush hot and she'd be even more ashamed than when she was alone.

"If you want jeans, you should try here. My older sister gets all of hers from this place. They last forever." Becky nodded at the Blue Jean Barn, which boasted jeans in all shapes, sizes, colors, and styles.

"Ew. Hard pants equals hard pass," said Constance, who preferred her vast array of yoga leggings and athleisure.

Melanie hesitated, but she really wanted some blue jeans that wouldn't friction-wear so fast at the crotch and thighs.

"At least you know that every size will probably be the same, since it's all the same brand," Becky said.

As opposed to stores with five million different brands and five million different ways to define sizing. And since jeans were pretty much the bulk of what they offered, maybe they'd acknowledge the existence of an actual ass and not just a flat extension of thigh. Maybe they'd accommodate belly fat and hips. Weren't most of these stores supposed to be for young *adults*? Why did they insist on making clothes from curveless patterns, then just expand out the patterns for larger sizes without acknowledging change in proportion?

If it wasn't a button digging into her belly fat, it was a gap above her butt or a pinch in her knees, leg holes too small for her calves, crotch too short for the length of her hips, legs too long for her height. If only there were a way to shop by multiple measurements and not just some generic 'size.' Men shopped by waist size and leg length. Women shopped according to numbers devised by goblins to inspire anyone who wasn't skeletal to give themselves impromptu liposuction just to fit into the goddamn things.

"I suppose it wouldn't hurt to try." Melanie threw the rest of her shake into the trash can outside the denim boutique. She regretted eating anything that would bloat her before trying on more clothes. She'd thought they were going to do something less demoralizing the rest of the afternoon, like catch a movie or ice skate.

Becky immediately headed for the blue jean wall and investigated the different styles for different body types—every pair artfully worn and torn, technically against school dress code, but that didn't stop anyone. "Size ten, right?"

"A little louder, would you?" Melanie looked around to make sure neither staff nor strangers had heard.

"Melanie, you're gorgeous. Beauty at every size, right, girls?" Becky said to the others as they dug through piles close to their eye level.

Everything double digit required a crouch, and there were never as many. The sizes here only went up as far as twelve, so Melanie had to hope that they ran big, not small, or else she was at risk of sizing out.

She accepted the several curvy and straight-legged pants in sizes ten and twelve that Becky selected for her. She couldn't say thank you when Becky was this close, looking straight into her eyes, or whenever she stroked Melanie's hair or rubbed her back or shoulders after a game, or whenever she slept just an arm's length away on the floor at a sleepover. Melanie struggled to breathe, much less talk, her tongue a heavy thing in her dry mouth. For a moment, everyone and everything else diminished in insignificance. Melanie wished she could, too.

Becky carried size fours and twos on her other arm.

"Let's go try these on."

And because Becky said it, everyone grabbed their one or two pairs of jeans and followed her to the changing rooms. Most boutiques like this used curtains, especially when all the clientele were girls and women—easier to go in and out to try on new clothes, new sizes. But there were actual doors here.

Becky and her friends took the corner changing room, which looked like it was bigger, with a more expansive mirror. Melanie was relieved to take the smaller room next to them.

The doors locked automatically.

Usually, they'd talk over the changing room walls, but these rooms were completely enclosed. Melanie heard them through the wall, but faint, like they were several rooms away instead of just one.

Their muffled laughter was the loneliest sound in the world.

Melanie unslung her purse and shucked her high school sweatpants. Even keeping her shirt on, she didn't like that a whole wall was mirror. And changing rooms seemed to either be the most flattering light and the most slimming mirrors or the most horrible light and funhouse mirrors—no in between, although sometimes mix and match.

This one was flattering light and funhouse mirrors that made her thighs look like columns of veiny cottage cheese. They were strong and served her well on the volleyball court, as did the rest of her, but in comparison to the other girls, even when they weren't next to her, she seemed like some kind of beast.

She missed her body before puberty hit—not that it had saved her from bullying, when kids had found other things to hate, like her big nose and freckles and how pale she was, who and what they thought she was. She knew intellectually that none of these things were actual disqualifiers from the game of life. Celebrities had the same attributes, and other people in her classes with the same attributes weren't bullied. Her qualities in and of themselves were fine; she was the one who made everything mortifyingly monstrous.

Melanie stuck her tongue out at the reflection, then pulled on the straight-leg jeans, size ten. If everyone followed Old Navy sizing, these should have fit. But she couldn't get the placket together enough to zip, much less button, and the thicker material strangled her thighs.

Fuck. She worked the jeans off and picked up the size twelve instead.

No such luck. She could get the zip up, but she couldn't button it without sucking her belly in more than she could maintain—never mind sitting down, when the waist of any jeans that didn't fit perfectly tried to slice her in half.

This was all such an exercise in futility. She ripped off the jeans, barely managing to not tear them in the process.

She covered her belly with her hands and glared at her reflection, angry at herself, angry at the mirror, because the closer she came, the more her muffin top swelled under her fingers like an inflated balloon.

The laughter in the other room had subsided, giving way to hushed conversation instead.

Though she feared they were talking about her, Melanie cupped her hands between her ear and the wall. She almost wanted them to be saying all the terrible things she'd ever imagined them saying. She would be devastated. There would be tears. She'd consider walking off the mall roof. But the world would stop tilting and everything would make sense again. Reality couldn't be so kind when the mirrors weren't.

"Damn it, I went up another size. I was being so careful."

"God, look at how much fat in this pinch. Fucking disgusting."

"If I don't lose some of this, they're going to kick me off the squad."

"It just keeps coming back, Becky. If I get any bigger, Jason's going to leave me."

"All I have after I go through my fat clothes are my sister's clothes and she's a cow."

"Enough," Becky snapped.

Melanie expected her to do what she always did when Melanie put herself down for her size or complexion: tell them that they were beautiful and they couldn't let the capitalistic bastards win by thinking they were anything less. Melanie's dreams rang with Becky telling her she was beautiful, sometimes whispered in her ear, and meaning it every damn time, before taking off her clothes and making Melanie feel as beautiful as she said.

"Everyone gets their turn. But you know how this works. We can't give too much. Callie tried, and now she's in a recovery center in Georgia. Maintenance, ladies. That's why we're here. And to look damn good in a good pair of jeans. Now, if you want this to go faster, bitches, then chant with me instead of making me do all the work. Hating yourself isn't going to make you lose more. We're just lucky we have someone who can afford to take what we lose."

Melanie jerked back, not sure if she was hearing things right or whether the wall distorted Becky's words so much that she couldn't trust what she heard.

She pressed her ear itself against the wall this time.

"Mirror, mirror, make me less of myself. Take this offering for Melanie, the recipient of our sacrifice, to become fruitful and full."

They tried to stay quiet, but with more than just Becky speaking, it was easier to understand them. Each word intensified and reverberated through her ear, her skull.

She recoiled again from the wall.

And when she caught her reflection, it wasn't just her imagination, she was sure of it. Her belly bloated. Her boobs pressed against their cups. Her thighs jiggled with more jelly as she turned around to look at her fatter ass.

"What? What?" She grabbed for the size twelve again and yanked it on. This time she couldn't zip the jeans, no matter how she sucked her tummy in.

"Mirror, mirror, make me less of myself. Take this offering for Melanie, the recipient of our sacrifice, to become fruitful and full."

And this wasn't the first time something like this had happened, was it? No, almost every time she went out with them, ever since she'd started going into changing rooms alone, she'd returned home hungry as hell, but her pants would feel tighter than when she'd left. She'd blamed chips and soda, an extra slice or two of pizza.

She'd thought it was all her.

"Mirror, mirror, make me less of myself. Take this offering for Melanie, the recipient of our sacrifice, to become fruitful and full."

She threw the jeans on the changing room bench and grabbed her own pants, with their elastic waistband that made her think less about her stomach. Her body pushed against the front and back of the pants now, with prominence and protuberance of rolls over her belly and hips that surely hadn't been there before.

She stared at herself in the mirror as she got bigger, bigger…

Except this was impossible. It was just the mirror. It was just her. She just shouldn't have had the peanut butter.

She pulled her t-shirt down. The shirt had been a size too big before but now seemed to fit perfectly, cradling the belly she'd wanted to camouflage.

"Is everything okay in there, miss? Do you need another size?" the attendant asked.

"I don't need anything. Thank you."

I don't fit in here was what she didn't say.

"Mirror, mirror, make me less of myself. Take this offering for Melanie, the recipient of our sacrifice, to become fruitful and full."

Melanie thought she might to throw up. Was this why they'd become her friends? She'd thought they were having a good time with her, but they'd only kept her around because they considered her fat beyond hope and it didn't matter if she got fatter?

Was any of this possible? Was any of this real?

Becky had never insisted that she change with them. Despite Melanie's insecurities, Becky always insisted that she participate with the group, stroking her ego and sometimes her cheek until Melanie would do anything for her and the word 'no' fled from her vocabulary with the rest of it. But in this, she'd never insisted.

It was ludicrous. A carnival trick of mirror, mixed with paranoia about the fabulousness of her friends and the distortion of her own self-hatred. Her therapist would have a few things to say about this episode in a few days.

Body dysmorphia: a focused delusion mixed with a fatphobic society afraid of its own helpless growth. That's what she suffered. Not being fat. Not gaining the fat of her friends.

Melanie rested her cheek on the cool mirror glass, struggling to see herself for what she was, instead of I Was a Teenage Blob.

Eventually, she had to close her eyes and hold her breath.

Melanie pushed away from the mirror and burst out the door to gasp fresher air.

All the girls were admiring themselves in an alcove of mirrors, inspecting their asses and legs and flat, flat bellies at the altar of silver and infinite reflection, with the sacred cow in the background and her patron goddess Becky in the center, stunning. She lit up when she saw Melanie emerge behind her. That she didn't seem cruel was almost the cruelest blow.

They'd never looked thinner.

About Amanda M. Blake

A mass of tentacles and rose vines masquerading as a person, Amanda M. Blake is the author of horror titles QUESTION NOT MY SALT and DEEP DOWN, dark poetry collection DEAD ENDS, and the Thorns fairy tale mash-up series. Alt-historical plague novel MASQUE has been acquired by Quill & Crow for publication in 2027. For more, visit amandamblake.com.

Size Matters
Paul Lonardo

THE SHOW WAS JUST two days away and Antoine was at his peak size. As he studied his physique in the mirrored wall of the gym with a critical eye, he groaned and considered dropping out of the event to spare himself the humiliation of not placing at all. There were going to be some real monsters at the Bay Area Amateur Body Building Invitational, and barring some miracle that would help him gain a significant amount of size in a short period of time, he stood no chance of finishing high enough to qualify for the regionals at the end of the year.

This early in the afternoon, with a big show coming up, Antoine normally would have stayed to bang out a few more sets, but he was feeling sufficiently discouraged and all he wanted to do was go home to spend some time with Atlas, his Australian Shepherd, who was always happy to see him no matter how big he was.

He was about to hit the locker room for a shower when a shadow engulfed him along with half of the gym. He thought the place might be closing for some reason and the owner was shutting the lights, but then he saw the most enormous man he'd ever seen in his life, a walking mountain with a chest of chiseled marble, legs like boulders, and arms as thick as the trunks of giant sequoias. He made Arnold Schwarzenegger look like Pee-wee Herman.

A perpetual smile was fixed above a square, rigid jaw. His blond hair was thin and long, flowing to his shoulders and accentuating an enormous neck and traps that any bodybuilder would envy. Antoine self-consciously brought his right hand up to his own neck, one that he'd once been so proud of, and it felt like he was gripping a pencil.

The giant was wearing a tight tank top that was stretched so thin it looked like it might rip apart at the seams. It was black with red block lettering that read, "BODY BY BRANKO." On the back was the definitive bodybuilding and all-purpose male maxim, "SIZE MATTERS."

Antoine couldn't take his eyes off the guy. It took him several moments to notice that there were two people in tow behind him, a woman with an expensive camera and a man carrying lighting equipment. They were like twin moons pulled into the orbit of an immense planet.

Antoine was watching the crew set up their equipment in front of the T-REX BODYBUILDING sign at the back of the gym when the owner came out of his office. Rex, a former bodybuilding champion himself, looked like a child next to the colossus in the tank top. As the two shook hands, Rex handed a folded sheet of paper to the massive stranger, who stuffed it into the black fanny pack around his waist.

Antoine strolled over and stood beside Rex, who observed the photoshoot with a prideful grin.

"Who the hell is that guy, Rex?" Antoine asked. "He's unbelievable."

Rex didn't take his eyes off the muscle man as he posed and flexed for the lens, curling the heaviest dumbbells like they were nothing. "That's the guy who's going to put T-REX'S JURASSIC GYM back on the map," he said. "It cost me quite a bit to get him to come in and sit for a couple photos, but this ad campaign could put me in position to open up that second location I've always dreamed about."

"Yeah, but who is he?"

"His name is Branko Zoric."

Antoine scratched his head. "I never heard of him."

"Well, he's not exactly from around here."

"A guy that big wouldn't go unnoticed. Not in the bodybuilding world."

Rex leaned in close to Antoine and spoke in a conspiratorial whisper. "He's supposed to have come up with some new training method. You should meet him. I'm sure he could do something for you if you ask him." Then he walked away.

This immediately got Antoine's attention because it was exactly what he needed. At nineteen, he was just starting out in body building, but he wanted to make a name for himself, and he was hungry for the respect and adulation that, for him, could only be achieved by standing on the top tier of the stage after winning an event. Having Branko walk into his life at that time was a sign of better things to come, Antoine thought, and he had to go for it.

Antoine waited until Branko was through and the small crew had everything packed up before making his approach. He stuck out his right hand and introduced himself. "Antoine Rivera."

"How do you do?" The man spoke with a heavy Eastern European accent and took Antoine's hand, along with part of his wrist as he shook it. "Branko Zoric."

"I'm sorry to intrude," Antoine began. "Forgive me, but as an aspiring bodybuilder, I have to say that your physique is amazing."

"Thank you, Mr. Rivera, but I have to correct you and inform you I do not complete professionally."

"Please, call me Antoine. And on behalf of bodybuilders everywhere, thank you, because you would win every competition you entered."

Branko laughed good-naturedly.

"What I mean is you deserve a lot of credit and respect for your work ethic," Antoine continued. "I appreciate it, and that's why I must ask if you can teach me how to develop my body the way you did."

Branko sighed deeply. "I'm afraid I cannot do that."

"I tried everything, and I can't seem to get to the next level no matter how much time I spend in the weight room. You've obviously come up with a phenomenally effective workout regimen; I want to try it."

Branko shook his head definitively. "I just couldn't in good conscious recommend it for anyone." He turned to leave. "I'm sorry."

In a bold move that surprised himself, Antoine stepped directly in front of the enormous man, blocking his path. "Please. I beg you."

Branko sighed again. "It's not that I don't want to help you, but my training method is... how you say... unorthodox. It's not for everyone. You'll gain the extra size you want, but at a considerable hardship."

"If I could get anywhere close to your size, it would be worth it, no matter what I had to endure."

A smile played at the corners of Branko's mouth. "I really shouldn't do this," he said as he removed a business card from his fanny pack and handed it to Antoine.

It read, "BODY BY BRANKO," and listed a downtown address, but no phone number or email. "Meet me tomorrow at 1 PM." He walked away and the floor seemed to tip in that direction.

Antoine was so excited he almost fell over.

The next day, Antoine arrived at the location ten minutes early. He thought he was in the wrong place because rather than a gym he found himself in an abandoned industrial park. There were no signs indicating an occupying business of any kind. He walked up to a random door and peeked inside. To his surprise, it opened when he tried the handle. He entered and wandered the maze of corridors until he spotted Branko inside one of the suites. He was wearing eyeglasses and a white lab coat. If this was some kind of disguise, it wasn't working, Antoine thought. He was simply too big to be mistaken for anyone else.

The colossus saw him and waved him in.

Antoine entered and looked around. "So, where's the weight room?" he asked.

"There's no gym here," Branko disclosed. "I offer something completely different. As I told you yesterday, I'm not a professional body builder."

Antoine gazed at the lab coat and nodded in understanding. "You're a scientist, aren't you?"

Branko didn't say anything. He just smiled.

"Let me guess, you've probably done work for the government."

Branko wagged a finger and offered a conspiratorial smile. "That's not something I can talk about."

"I knew it," Antoine said. "All right. So, maybe you were involved in the secret experiment for muscle gain that you're not supposed to share. Don't worry, I won't tell a soul."

"Covertness is very much my stock in trade, Antoine. And while I do believe you, I'm afraid I must ask you to sign this." Branko produced a folded document and presented it to Antoine.

"Is this one of those nondisclosure agreements?" Antoine asked as he unfolded the single sheet of paper. The cursive handwriting penned in leaky red ink made it nearly impossible for him read.

"It's a standard release form," Branko told him.

"Where do I sign?"

"Anywhere is fine."

Before Antoine could ask for a pen, Branko had one in hand. It produced the same leaky red ink, and it seemed to absorb directly into the paper upon contact.

Branko scooped up the document, blowing on the signature to hasten the drying process, then stuffed it into a pocket of his lab coat. "Just one other thing, Antoine. You also need to know that while the results are guaranteed—you'll achieve all the size you desire, and then some—it's not going to last forever."

"Well, nothing lasts forever," Antoine said with cheery acceptance.

"Follow me." Branko led Antoine into a room around the corner where everything was red. The floor tiles were a slightly deeper shade than the painted plaster walls and ceiling. The light from the overhead fixture was dim, making the average-size room appear even smaller than it was. The only items inside were a small cot adorned with red bedding and a mop sitting in a bucket of water. There was a drain in the middle of the floor. Collectively, these elements evoked a primal fear reaction in Antoine and, for the first time, part of him began to question if what he was doing was worth it. Then he looked at the incredible size and girth of the man in front of him and his doubts evaporated at once.

"For true growth, it's not only muscle that you must tear so that it can repair and grow, but you must also break down bone. That's the secret to achieving ultimate size and strength."

Antoine snorted in amusement. "How do you break down bone?"

Just then, a bald man, almost equally as large as Branko, entered the room. He had light brown skin, almost every inch of which was covered in tattoos, including his neck. He was holding a sledgehammer in one hand.

"What's that for?" Antoine asked nervously.

"Don't worry," Branko said with a cocksure grin. "When you heal, you'll be bigger and stronger than you ever thought possible."

"What do you mean, *when I heal*?"

"Is there any area in particular you want to work on?" Branko asked, ignoring Antoine's question. "If you don't mind me saying, your calves are a little disproportionate to the rest of your body. But we'll fix that."

Suddenly Branko grasped Antoine, wrestling him into a chokehold.

"What are you doing?" Antoine shrieked, completely immobilized.

"Just relax," Branko said.

Tattoo Man approached and stopped in front of them.

Antoine's eyes went wide with terror as Tattoo Man raised the hammer over his head. All Antoine could do was scream as the steel head of the hammer came down.

The initial impact on Antoine's upper right arm shattered his humerus bone. The pain was unlike anything he had ever experienced before. The intensity was savage, and it radiated around his entire body.

Tattoo Man wasn't done. He continued to swing the demolition tool, striking Antoine in the chest, upper and lower legs, and shoulders. His screams for mercy came unbidden from his lips.

With a sound like tree branches snapping in half, chunks of splintered bone burst through the skin all over his body. Cartilage and tendons were pulverized. The blood that spilled from the open gashes, spattering the walls and puddling on the floor, seemed to disappear at once, absorbing into the interior of the room like the red ink into the paper that Antoine had signed.

After the first couple of blows, Antoine's nerve endings reached a point where they could no longer transmit all the information to his overloaded brain. It wasn't that he no longer felt the impacts, he just wasn't sure where he was being struck.

"Be sure to get those calves good," Branko instructed Tattoo Man.

Antoine heard snippets of other comments made by the two men as he was being bludgeoned, but their voices slowly faded. His suffering became overwhelming, and his body mercifully began to shut down. As he drifted into oblivion, the last thing he remembered was Branko dropping his pants and urinating on him while laughing heartily.

Antoine didn't expect to survive, and in his last fragments of consciousness, he prayed that he wouldn't. But he did awaken, and to his surprise there was no pain or discomfort whatsoever, though he did feel profoundly different. He knew he was in the same room, lying on his back and staring up at the red ceiling. He didn't want to initiate movement, fearful that he was paralyzed. He had to gather the courage to look down at his lower half, expecting to see a mangled, broken body. What he saw instead made him wonder if he was dreaming. He was wearing a black singlet, and not only was he unmarred, but his legs were easily double the size they had been.

The door to the room opened and Branko entered, a big smile on his face.

"Is this heaven?" Antoine asked him.

The big man just laughed. Only Branko was not so big anymore, at least by comparison. Antoine was almost his equal.

"You can move," Branko assured him. "Go ahead."

Antoine slowly lifted his torso upright and eased his bulk off the cot. He gazed in wonderment at the bulging veins in his arms, his chiseled abs, his pecs, and quads. Turning his right leg out, he flexed his calf muscles and cackled with delight at their incredible size and definition.

"You're pleased, I take it."

"I'm sorry I doubted you. I feel like a million bucks."

Branko nodded in satisfaction. "Hopefully, at the very least, your new body will earn you the $20,000 prize money at the Bay Area Amateur Body Building Invitational tonight."

Antoine snapped his head up at Branko, looking away from his body for the first time. "That's tonight? You mean I haven't missed it?"

"Not yet," Branko told him. "But you better get going."

There were many big guys at the competition, but none as big as Antoine. Everyone was amazed by his size and definition. He won easily, and as a result he was eligible to compete in the Eastern Regionals.

Just like that, everything changed for Antoine, not just his body but his entire life. He enjoyed his newfound celebrity, and all the perks that went with it, including dating a handsome Bahamian fitness model, Jayden, who he met at the competition.

Antoine became the instant favorite to win the Regionals and eventually go on to compete for Mr. World in Las Vegas the following spring. Then two days before the show, he woke in a cold sweat. He sat upright in bed for a moment, feeling strange but unsure what was wrong. He was alone. Jayden wasn't there. He was due to return from a photoshoot that night. As Antoine's gaze fixed on his championship trophy sitting on the dresser, he caught sight of himself in the mirror.

"Oh, my God!" he gasped.

Antoine didn't recognize the person staring back at him in abject horror, but when he moved, so did the skeletal figure in the looking glass. He lowered his head to peer down at his body, hoping it was an illusion of some kind, like those mirrors in a funhouse that distort the way you look. But it was even worse to the naked eye.

It was his body all right, but without any muscle mass to speak of. Panic gripped him and his heart began to race. "This can't be," he cried out. He jumped out of bed and just stood there for a moment, not knowing what to do. His first thought was of Jayden and what he would say if he saw the shriveled husk Antoine had become.

Antoine was glad Jayden was away, but he knew he had to do something fast. His only chance was to find Branko, and he quickly scrambled to get dressed. None of his clothes fit, and he left swimming in a T-shirt that was ten sizes too big for him and holding up the waistband of the smallest pair of shorts he could find. He raced to the industrial park hoping Branko would be there. He managed to locate the same suite, but this time it was completely empty. The red room looked the same, only now the sledgehammer was resting on the floor. He wanted nothing more than to tear the place apart, and in a fit of rage he reached for the handle of the mallet. To his profound dismay, however, he found that he was unable to lift it.

"Branko!" he screamed in frustration.

"Back for more?"

Antoine turned around quickly, shocked to see Branko standing in the doorway, grinning.

"What the fuck happened?" Antoine fumed. "Look at me!"

"I told you it wouldn't last," Branko said. "And you signed the contract." He produced the document out of thin air and flipped it at Antoine.

"What's this?" Antoine asked after examining it more closely. "I can't read this."

"It would be surprising. It's Latin," Branko informed him. "And that's your signature. *Antoine Rivera.*"

Antoine's frail body stiffened with rage. "Who the fuck are you?"

"You know who I am," Branko said with a sinister sneer.

The paper burst into flames in his hands and was gone. At the same moment, Tattoo Man entered the room with an even larger sledgehammer than the one Antoine was unable to heft.

"No." Antoine shook his head in defiance, refusing to endure the pain of the hammer and indignity of being a toilet for the devil for the fulfillment of a short-term favor. "I won't do it."

"It's the hammer or me," Branko said, and then his body began to transform before Antoine's eyes. His flesh became black as soot and brittle, like it had been baked in a furnace. His eyes were dark, empty black holes. As Satan began to laugh, a sulfurous stench was emitted from his gaping maw. Then the Beast disappeared and it became clear to Antoine that Satan wanted something from him in exchange for the substantial muscle mass that he had been bestowed, however briefly.

This gave Antoine an idea.

***

Over the next couple of months, Antoine worked hard to gain back some of the size and strength that he had lost, though he wasn't able to get anywhere close to where he had been even before his pact with the devil. Jayden had left him, but that was all right. He still had Atlas.

Then came the day that Antoine walked into an empty T-Rex's shortly after closing. He was carrying a gym bag at his side, but he was not there to work out. His stride was awkward as he struggled to maintain his balance due to the weight of the bag. He headed straight to Rex's office.

The owner was sitting behind his desk in front of a laptop. He looked up in surprise when he saw Antoine enter.

Antoine closed and locked the door behind him, then strode up to the desk and placed the gym bag on top.

"What the hell are you doing?" Rex asked.

Antoine unzipped the bag and pulled out a sledgehammer. As he raised the twelve-pound piece of steel on a stick, Rex pushed his chair back against the wall behind him and stood up, but there was nowhere he could go.

"Are you fucking crazy?" The alarm in Rex's voice was sweet music to Antoine's ears.

It took all the strength Antoine had, but he managed swing the weapon and wield it with enough force to strike Rex. The first blow made a dull, popping sound as it impacted the victim's head, cracking it like a coconut. Blood speckled the wall behind Rex, turning it into a Jackson Pollock canvas. As Rex cried out in terror and agony, the next strike caught him in the back of the neck, shattering his cervical spine in multiple places and silencing him at once. He was already dead as Antoine stepped around the side of the desk and continued to bash Rex's head and face until there was nothing left but pieces of skull and brain matter.

Perspiring and exhausted, Antoine straightened up and looked down with a sense of triumph at what he'd done. As far as he was concerned, the diabolical ledger was balanced.

Antoine dropped the hammer into the pulp that had once been Rex's head and walked out of the gym feeling a whole lot bigger in stature than ever before.

About Paul Lonardo

Paul Lonardo is a freelance writer and author with numerous titles, both fiction and nonfiction books. Paul has placed short stories and nonfiction pieces in various genre magazines and ezines. He is a contributing writer for several publications, including *Tales from the Moonlit Path*, and an HWA member.

The Technomancer's Body

Basile Lebret

RIGHT NOW, THERE'S A genitor, somewhere in France, writing a binary text message to his estranged progeny. The house he resides in is as cold and damp and wet as the void in between distant stars. A television yells in the background, the machine is always working. Water heater is down, but the father would die before the screen turns black mirror.

It is through this symbiosis the elderly learned of NASA losing contact with Voyager. The lonesome adult knows what happened, can picture it on the cathodic tube of his eyelids. And so, he writes to his life-away lineage, for the stern man possesses some arcane knowledge whispering in his ear there isn't much time.

The father starts his palimpsest in hopes of finally meeting his granddaughter, forgets about it after a few words, already spreading his life thin across the immensity of the email. Explaining himself. The old man in his frozen abode weaves a tale of madness.

The encoded letter now speaks of high school, of an era passed and already dead. Still and preserved.

Story starts with a boy called Thomas. Teenage loner, a new face in a sea of already known, already proven people. The hooded young man is seventeen, this is his senior year. The old man was then fresh and more mobile, bearing an identity known as Serge, for there existed entities to call him this in those days.

Thomas picked Serge's curiosity, not because he was tech savvy—this the father would later learn—but for his sheer size. A giant is always a useful companion in an age when fights break out in the blink of an eye.

The mastodon had some problems at home with his dad. Or his mom. Serge would never know. Soon they befriend one another. Thomas repairs smartphones, this is routine to fuel his tobacco addiction. He soon makes a habit out of sleeping at Serge's. As a tribute, he will fix his friend's broken screen. For free.

A mystery surrounds the boy, his body, and the lack of repair kit. Serge never notices. Too self-absorbed. His mate, Anne, always says so.

Fury devours the genitor once his nudes are leaked on the internet. An acquaintance hacking his Facebook account, stumbling upon his Messenger antecedents. Serge can deal with his ashamed girlfriend leaving him, but he cannot bear the jokes about the size of his genitalia. Late at night, in a moist and tiny room, Serge confides in Thomas.

Weird series of events on the next day. Anne embraces Serge as if nothing ever happened. No laughter follows his footsteps through the always-clean halls of the high school building. Scrolling through any social network feed, you'd be embarrassed in finding any trace of the incident. All that exists seems to be the older man's faulty memory.

This is the first of Thomas's powers. Father, the boy known as Serge, thinks to himself: *that's weird*. But the blaze and the haze and the noise of his life swallow his doubts as an overpowered bulldozer would do of a pile of electronic rubble. Calmly, in a steel-like fashion.

In his letter, the father states that on one foggy afternoon, while a pink sun was slowly laying behind the horizon, tinting clouds purple and golden and shades of grey, Thomas joked about extracting part of his own brain to do so. The giant had smashed his skull with a hammer and a pin before extracting a maggot of grey matter as small as a node. Serge never buffered this precise souvenir.

Yet he remembers asking, "You into self-mutilation or something?" The boy is wondering, for he has never seen Thomas' flesh, save for his face.

The giant laughs it off.

Doesn't answer.

There is an angler fish which is a car crawling its way towards us and you don't know it is the next sentence, yet it makes no sense.

The genitor in his damp and cold house, his burial ground, tries to explain as best as conceivable the day Thomas showed him the trick.

He describes the bedroom as yellow and plague-ridden and messy. There's a lone light bulb buzzing overhead, but the always-turned-on computer muffles it as some unheard nuisance. Thomas is sitting cross-legged on the small bed frame. The giant, he is showing one of his meaty arms. There are missing patches of skin on the exposed body part. Concentrate hard enough on something other than the streaks across his muscles, you might notice the shapes cut in there resemble the size of smartphone screens. Closer inspection would teach you the ones closest to the wrist possess ragged edges, implying this is where Thomas started, implying he got upward and better.

With an accompanying kind gesture, the long-haired giant tells Serge, "Hand me your phone." The father-to-be is still looking at the naked muscles with disbelief and a tingling sensation he hopes not to interpret as arousal.

"Hand me your phone, I know you've broken it." With a tired smile, Thomas confidently adds: "I know everything about you." The giant grabs the communication device, tells Serge: "Now go fetch me some nail polish."

The teenager, who exists solely in the memory of an old man stuck in a crumbling house, hesitates. Finally goes.

When he gets back in his room, Thomas grips a sharp scalpel. Serge skips a breath, for the blade is shiny and long and clean, so much so it could be some Catholic's saint remnants. The thin piece of steel reflects the lone bulb, the greenish OLED screen, the blue glow of the overheating computer in the fashion of those *Days of Our Lives* TV shows.

The giant is now gently pressing the medical instrument to the right of his belly button. He possesses some fat there, the smooth form of his torso makes him appear brisk and strong. Happy patches of hair lead erratically to his nipples, still hidden by an eternal black hoodie.

"I don't know how to make protection. I can grow back screens." The colossus, he jabs the triangle of metal slightly into his flesh. An inch, maybe. "I don't know how to make protective glass." He doesn't suffer.

Serge gazes intently as the other man is tearing his belly up. Serge doesn't notice that he, at least once, passed a moist red tongue upon his lips. There is not as much blood as he would have thought. Thomas is now sweating rivulets. He glistens, but still makes no noise.

"Grab a bowl, wha'ever," exhales the one in bondage.

Swiftly, Serge empties a Tupperware full of rotting chips onto the always-dirty floor. He extends it as a child would an offering towards Thomas. The sparkling giant.

"Now, you pour the nail polish in the box," says Thomas. With his right hand, he is now slowly peeling the skin, which is thin and rosy and veiny in the dim light. Scalpel lies on the floor, immaculate; the droplet of blood dripping off it only adds to its enthralling charm.

Abrupt for the first time, Thomas grabs the Tupperware from Serge's hands. They remain still, wondering and silent for a moment. With minutiae, the hulk lays the screen made of skin onto the opaque liquid. The patch rests lightly as if it were some naked man doing the plank on a silvery sea. Then it plunges into the grey mist. Silvery bubbles hawk around as alien grey fish.

For the first time, Serge opens his lips, all red and shiny and moist. "What the fu... ck?"

"We wait," answers Thomas, touching his friend's left pectoral muscle in the same movement.

Both boys sit cross-legged, facing one another. Between them, Thomas' repair kit is chemically hardening. A border in formation. The giant smiles, less interested in the carcinization than his friend. "You wanna see it?" he asks.

"Wh... What?" responds Serge, breathless. Nitrogen narcosis.

"The hole I made in my brain for you."

The giant doesn't wait for any answer and turns around. With his large back to his mate, Thomas takes a hold of his long auburn hair, pulls them upwards.

The opening seems like a beauty mark you'd find on some French aristocrat. All small and dark and almost classy. There's a hypnotic quality to its lack of any bleeding. Serge drowns in the cut, the emptiness, the sacrifice. Facing the other way, Thomas hushes in a pressed manner: "Touch it."

Serge does not want to, yet his fingers are already flying towards the orifice. His dirty nail presses on the perfect void circle, then a tiny part of his fleshy digit enters the aperture. Not by much.

Inside the tunnel which Thomas dug, devoid of self-esteem, a small creature jerks. Serge takes off his appendage but he'll always remember on lonesome thundery nights, the feeling of a maggot making walls of flesh tremble under its imprint.

"You take the skin and you put it onto the broken screen," is what Thomas says in order to break the unease.

Serge, still shaken, watches the technomancer spreading the flesh across the shattered glass.

"Then you pick some paper," says Thomas, grabbing some homework sheet laying on the dusty floor. "You fold it four or six times. You don't go for five. Never five," says the giant, making sure his friend prints the information. "Once you're done, you lick the large side of the square, and the side which presents two folds."

Serge watches Thomas's soft red tongue lapping the dirty paper, gulps.

"You then use this round smooth side to pressure the skin into the cracks." Thomas then presses the paper and, in an arcane, antique, accustomed manner, swipes the flabby translucent skin towards the charger opening. "Oh, oh, I forget. You gotta move it from the top of the screen to its lower part. Okay? It doesn't work any other way."

Across the white matter of the paper, the decaying blob of flesh now lays useless, wastes of a surgical performance already undergone. Without a second thought, Thomas discards his epidermis.

"If you did good, it shall be repaired in, like, two hours."

Overhead, the light still buzzes. In a dark corner, the computer still overheats. The television is always on.

***

The abode is creaking with the almost certainty of old bones. The genitor hopes this'll convey his message, his knowledge to his estranged son. In some other room, the Hertzian communication device is spewing landslides of news. "Haven't some space anomalies been reported recently?" and "What do you think happened to Voyager?" are asked to dead-eyed pedestrians.

There is an instant the father will not speak about. A fragment he deems unnecessary and non-existent on his binge-drinking days. Blurry remembrance of a Christmas vacation. In the old man's mind, he and Thomas never had sex. For they never touched. The shards of lust he ever felt resided solely on his friend's submission.

Nobody needs to know.

Came the night which broke both boys' existences.

Thomas had been sleeping less and less at Serge's house by this point. The end of the school year and tests and diplomas were coming fast, a decisive moving train crushing children's skeletons with ironclad wheels. Serge knew the technomancer was working on another ritual. Thought it would be related to the exams.

Hence why the boy didn't flinch when the giant gently led him by the fingers towards the hill over in Morsang. It was a steep bulge that existed for no apparent reason in the otherwise plain landscape of their home county. The night sky glimmered as vividly as mating fireflies. The air was hot and damp with pollution, and you could witness the tentacles of the Parisian metropolitan area crashing into disparate, regressing woodwork.

Both boys would blaze on the crushing grass, dried up by the June sun, would finally get hungry; for neither had prepared for such an eventuality. Through the smoke, the pair would grab McDonald's, although Serge preferred Quick, but the Belgian fast-food chain restaurants were becoming a rare breed.

Back up the hill, while kneeling and unpacking his bag, the giant asked: "You good? You gon' stop complaining?"

The machine appeared complex and Serge was almost sure its structure was made of human bones, although he dared not ask. Munching on the double buns, the boy wonders if his pal had found a way to hack into the global WIFI connection. The router looked like a small canine once it was assembled. A satellite dish stemmed from the left side of it, as some exotic flower.

"I really need to show you this," said the giant, his lips half-clamped around a bent cigarette. His eyes were as shiny as the summer sky on a cloudless day. Serge took notice of this, forgot it. The giant, he stared at the globe of ether, at his mate. "Okay," he simply said before baring his chest. There was almost no skin left under his dark sweater. The genitor took in the raw flesh, so wide it now seemed a plague conquering entire continents. Serge thought of drawing maps with his finger across the fleshy circuit board, would never admit it.

"I found it while trying to hack through a satellite," said the giant, proudly. "It's weird. It's like... some' you never seen."

Sat atop the warm swirling grass, the machine had begun to croon. It reminded Serge of first-generation computers, when every sound seemed not to come from the speaker but a failure of the motherboard. Yet, the slow wavelike echo appeared relaxing to him.

Thomas, starry-eyed, hushed: "Witness!"

In the galactic void which should have been the firmament, now rests a vague shape of imprecise, somewhat moving borders. A wormhole. Staring through it felt like drowning in some cyclopean silicious screen. The image was purple and pale yellow and ochre and almost green, reminding the teenager of those colours you have to add to cells before trying to decipher their pattern through a microscope, or those surreal pigments NASA likes to paste on their extra-terrestrial photographs. But it wasn't the rainy pastels that caught Serge's eyes, it was the angler fish who was a car currently ripping at the purple clouds surrounding him.

"I don't know what this is," said the giant on a plane where an object could only be perceived through one form. "It just comes there every two months, and it eats."

The sudden realization caught Serge off-guard. A sucker punch. The creature wasn't somewhat big. It. Was. Far. Away. A distance so wide, four generations of human beings couldn't have thought to close in on its scaly, wheeled flanks. Noticing the Lilliputian size of his existence, of ours, Serge fell to his knees. He was crying. Would never admit to it.

"It's beautiful. I wanted to show it to you. Like it'd be our little secret."

"There is no *us*, there's no *our*," asserted Serge while getting up. Cold. Eyes all dried up and puffy red.

"Ain't what I meant," said the giant apologetically.

***

On Serge's computer screen, the letter reads: There exists this very distinct moment when one decides to use a weapon. Feels like you're standing on top of this colossal diving board and you're deciding. Either you get back down the ladder or you jump. I drowned.

Swiftly, Serge had closed the distance between him and his friend. His right-hand whitening around a medium-sized rock. First hit only tilted the giant's head sideways. In the time it took for the victim to readjust his sight, a tendril of blood shot from his temporal lobe. Took four more hits to take his carcass to the ground. Bashing someone's skull with a rock, it is surprising that the first dropping membrane is the cheekbone. Then the nose diving deeper, deeper into the cranium. Thomas never fought back. He looked solely surprised. As if in reality, the system inhabiting it had already taught the teenager he was expandable. After fifteen swings, the genitor should have stopped. Saliva drooling from his mouth, the father would beat the boy, the body at least another forty times. Before trying to recoup his breath, seated on the giant's zipper, both soft and hard.

Overhead, the car eating the clouds who was almost certainly an angler fish whose teeth were tendrils asserted the pettiness of the show, the meaninglessness of both Serge's existence and crime.

The murderer got up by pressing his hands on the still hot, almost firm torso of the corpse. It was nice. Serge kicked the machine, which yelped as it fell.

A rumble hissed through the blackened universe and when he raised his eyes to witness the closing of the portal, Serge saw the entity crawling towards him. It was difficult to notice, yet he knew that the beast had seen him and was now rolling with hungry eyes.

The creature was farther than he'd thought.

The connection broke.

***

Right now, there is a father who is also an old man and a teenage murderer. In here. In France. His house is dark and damp and cold and silent except for the television, which is always on. The message he is writing, he is writing for his estranged son. It explains how he hid the technomancer's body. In his decaying mind, it explains why he has a problem with his progeny's coming out.

The old man doesn't remember his son's partner's name, has never cared for it, yet knows they have a daughter. And he knows an angler fish who's also a car is crawling towards us. Fast.

It already ate Voyager.

All the father writes about is himself.

About Basile Lebret

While he's French and lives south of Paris, Basile Lebret writes in English. Since it first sprouted in 2022, his work has now spread to over twenty publications in the US, the UK, France or Canada. The most recent include The Horror Zine Spring 2026 Issue, The Alien Buddha Zine 85, God's Cruel Joke, Squirm Books' Skin Deep and Lowell & Benson's The Dichotomy of Love. Soon in Life, Death, and Rebirth by Dark Moon Rising Publications. His first collection Welcome to Valenton is being published by Carnage House. Find him on any network: @evoripclaw

Germaphobe Girls

J. Neira

"Come on, almost there," I muttered to myself, my thumb hitting the A button repeatedly until **TIME UP** flashed across the screen in thick red letters, displaying my final total.

I set the controller down with a heavy sigh, my body rocking backwards until I was partially slumped against the sofa behind me. After three attempts, I still hadn't been able to beat Jacinta's score.

My friend sat next to me, a small smirk dancing along her lips. "Almost," she said, patting the air just above my shoulder, knowing I didn't appreciate unsolicited touches. "A bit more practice and I'm sure you'll get there."

"Yeah, yeah, we both know you're much better at this than I am anyway," I said, lifting my arms over my head with a grunt, trying to ease the cramp out of my shoulders. I'd been sitting like a gremlin for the past five minutes, and it had put a lot of strain on my neck and arms.

The two of us were sitting on cushions on the floor of my basement, our backs leaning against the base of the sofa so that we could be closer to the television. I'd made sure to thoroughly sweep and clean the floor before we'd sat down, even laying a blanket beneath the cushions to protect us from any dirt.

I'd been germophobic my whole life. Even as a child, dirt and dust had bothered me far more than any other kids. At school, I'd hated getting my hands dirty, hated playing outside with my friends, who seemed to have no problem sticking their fingers in the mud or playing with random objects they had found on the ground, with no idea who had touched them previously.

Growing up, this had only gotten worse. Learning about germs and bacteria in biology class made me even more wary of the risks they carried, and through childhood to teenagerhood, I'd always been careful about what I touched, aware of where germs were most prevalent. Excessive handwashing, avoiding public places and anxiety about contamination were all signs of my obvious mysophobia. Just the very *thought* of germs made me want to scrub my hands until they were raw. I was meticulous in keeping my surroundings clean and avoiding anything that might contaminate me, and now that I was in college, these were just normal parts of my daily routine.

My friend, Jacinta, was of a similar mindset, though she was much laxer about her germophobia. Only some things bothered her on an extreme level, while other things she could deal with much better than I could.

"Wipes, please," I said to Jacinta, who wordlessly reached for the pack of disinfectant wipes that were sitting on the sofa behind her head. She passed them to me, and I began to laboriously wipe down the controllers we had just used, making sure to get between the buttons and around the joysticks.

Although there were no windows in the basement, it was already past 8pm, and it would soon be getting dark outside. Jacinta had been here for a few hours already, playing video games and generally hanging out.

"This isn't over yet," I said as I binned the used wipes. "Next time, I'll *definitely* beat you."

"Mhm," Jacinta said with a teasing smile.

"I do appreciate you coming over though," I said, my tone turning serious as I faced her. "And thanks for not saying 'I told you so' about my date being a terrible person."

Jacinta shook her head, her dark ringlets falling across her eyes. "I'd never do that. We all make mistakes about people's character." She hesitated, shooting me a lopsided smile. "Listen, I know I'm aromantic and personally not really interested in romance at all."

"What about Joseph?" I asked, thinking of Jacinta's male feminist friend; I'd caught them kissing.

"He's just a friend. A kiss buddy sometimes," Jacinta said in such a 'duh' way that I knew she was telling the truth. "Aromantic doesn't mean asexual, you know that. Anyway, date who you want. But next time, just make sure he's not some incel, or 'based' loser."

I grimaced, but nodded. "Yeah, I promise I'll be more careful. It was a serious lapse of judgement, I'll admit."

I glanced at Jacinta's shirt. It was long, black and baggy, with the short-sleeves coming all the way down to her elbows. But that wasn't what I was looking at. I was looking at the cloth covering her chest, where the words YOU'RE LIKE FIREWORKS. BEAUTIFUL, BUT I WOULDN'T WANT YOU NEAR MY GENITALS were written in the colors of the aromantic flag. To me, it sounded more like an asexual message than an aromantic one, but I knew it wasn't my place to point it out. After all, Jacinta was sort of asexual – she never had sex and was disgusted by the idea of having it. But she did get "turned on" by other leftist activists and loved passionate kissing and foreplay, which was why she identified as aromantic instead of asexual.

I climbed to my feet, still feeling achy from sitting too long. "Can I get you another drink? Some more snacks?"

Before she could answer, the doorbell rang, the melody drifting faintly down the basement steps towards us.

I exchanged a surprised glance with Jacinta. My parents were away on a trip, and I wasn't expecting anyone. I lived on the rural outskirts, far from any other houses, so it couldn't be a neighbor. And it was a long way for a late-night cold caller to drive.

"Want me to come with you to see who it is?" Jacinta offered, but I waved her off.

"It's okay. I'll handle it."

I left my friend where she was and climbed the creaky steps of the basement, my brows furrowing when the doorbell rang again.

"I'm coming, I'm coming, jeez," I muttered. Had someone broken down on the road or something?

The house had grown dark while we'd been downstairs, and shadows stretched out from my feet as I stumbled half-blindly through the living room towards the front door. In the hallway, I switched on the lamp, a warm orange glow spreading around me. The front door didn't have any frosted glass or a peephole, so I wouldn't know who was on the other side until I opened it.

I grabbed one of my reusable facemasks from the sideboard and put it on, making sure it was tucked comfortably around my mouth and nose with no gaps. Then I unlocked the door and opened it just wide enough to peer out.

When I saw who was standing on the doorstep, my mood immediately soured. I was almost tempted to slam it closed without a word, but decided against it. I opened it wider and took a few steps backward, making sure there was an appropriate distance between us.

"What the hell are you doing here?"

Lucas, my ex, stood smirking at me from the doorway, the evening breeze tousling his dull brown hair. Behind him, silhouetted against the dusky sky, his black Tesla sat idling in the driveway. The headlights were still switched on, two sharp beams cutting across the gravel and highlighting part of the house. I noticed a shadow inside the car, and realized there was a figure sitting in the front passenger seat. A woman, most likely, with blonde hair. A new girlfriend already?

Beyond the house, the road was dark and empty, the view vanishing, descending into wheat fields and empty plots of land. The nearest house was miles away, so not many cars passed through this way. I had never managed to get used to city life. The air there always felt so dirty, full of pollutants from cars and other people. Just walking around in the middle of a city made me feel disgusting, like I was walking through a bug-infested tunnel, the air dense and foul. Out here, the air was much fresher and cleaner. Unpolluted.

"Why did you ghost me?"

I switched my attention back to Lucas, staring at him incredulously. "You're really asking me that?" I scoffed. "You treated me *horribly*. You never once respected my germophobia, made me feel stupid because of it. And, quite honestly, you were a risk to my health."

Lucas's eyes narrowed, his smug expression replaced with thinly-veiled anger. "*Risk*?" he echoed lowly. "What are you even talking about? I was never a risk to your health. I'm young, fit, and perfectly healthy. I hardly even get sick. You're just delusional, seeing threats where there are none." He took a step forward, and I tensed.

"Don't come any closer," I warned.

Ignoring my obvious discomfort, he strode forward until he was within arm's reach, and blew out a thick, heavy breath in my face.

Even through the mask, I could smell his foul breath, feel it brush against my skin, stirring the hair by the side of my face. I recoiled in disgust, but he just laughed. Raising a hand, he then poked me in my chest, just below my collarbone, his fingernails digging into my skin.

My eyes widened.

"What's wrong? Are you scared? Is my finger transmitting viruses? Are you going to fall deathly ill because of a little poke?"

Gritting my teeth, I smacked his hand away as hard as I could, the resounding slap of skin against skin echoing through the entryway. My shoulders trembled with a mixture of anger and horror. Fingernails were one of the worst places to carry bacteria, and he'd just transferred all those germs onto my skin by touching me.

"Get the hell away from me," I snapped, shoving my hands forward, not caring if I touched him. I just wanted him to leave.

He staggered back in surprise, but fought to keep his composure, keeping one foot planted firmly on the doormat inside the house, the other out on the porch.

"I mean it Lucas, get out of here. I never want to see you or your stupid face again." I aggressively shoved the door against his foot to make him move.

His lip curled as he pushed against it, refusing to budge.

Behind him, the passenger door of his Tesla swung open, and the mysterious blonde woman climbed out. She was much taller than I expected, and the sight of her momentarily caught me off guard as she slammed the car door closed and walked across the driveway, the gravel crunching like bullets under her heavy tread.

Lucas glanced between the blonde woman and me, smirking. He took a step back, allowing the newcomer to access me.

I realized too late that I was able to shut the door. I'd barely grabbed the handle when the woman opened her mouth wide–wider than she should have been able to–and retched.

The sound tore at my eardrums, disgust twisting sharply through my stomach as a stream of black liquid vomited out of her mouth, splashing over the front of my shirt. It was thick and gloopy and smelled foul, and my own throat burned with bile as I staggered back in shock.

What the hell was this stuff? The way it stuck to my skin was like oil, slick and shimmering. And the fact that it had come out of her mouth... What was this stuff doing inside her body? Where had it come from?

I wanted to get it off me, but at the same time I didn't want to touch it.

My shock and disgust quickly turned to anger as I stared at Lucas and his crazy blonde friend. My shoulders trembled. I clenched my fists.

Not knowing what else to do, I lifted my head and shouted, as loud as I could, "Jacinta, help!"

***

Jacinta bridged her hands beneath her chin with a sigh, staring blankly at the TV screen.

She wondered what Lisa was doing, and who had been at the door. A few minutes had already passed, and, being in the basement, she couldn't hear anything from upstairs. She debated going up to see if her friend needed any help, but she didn't want to interfere.

Instead, she reached for the video game controller and switched it back on, starting a new level to pass the time while she waited for Lisa to return. Maybe she had already dealt with the visitor and was in the kitchen, getting fresh drinks and snacks for them.

There was still a full minute on the video game's clock when she heard her friend's cry.

"Jacinta, help!"

With a sharp spike of panic, Jacinta immediately tossed the controller inside and jumped to her feet, her eyes going wide.

She hurried towards the stairs, then paused and frantically searched the room for a weapon, just in case. The basement was Lisa's hobby room, mostly for video gaming and working out, and there were pieces of equipment scattered everywhere, including several yoga mats and a compact exercise bike. Everything was still as clean as the day she'd bought it.

Her gaze landed on the stack of weights in the corner, and she grabbed the one on top, lugging it after her as she ran up the basement stairs towards where Lisa's shout had come from, hoping she wasn't too late to help.

Hearing voices coming from the front door, Jacinta slowed her pace as she crept across the living room, relying on the light from the hallway to see by as she walked over to the small open window that looked out onto the landing. She wanted an idea of what was happening before she rushed in to help.

Crouching below the window frame, she lifted her head just enough to peer over it. The first thing she saw was Lisa, standing by the front door. Some kind of black liquid covered the front of her shirt, and she was trembling, her expression a mixture of anger and disgust.

Standing on the other side of the door was Lucas, Lisa's disgusting ex. Just the sight of him made Jacinta's jaw clench. She had tried to warn her friend that guys like him could never be trusted; Lisa had found out a little too late. Not that Jacinta blamed her friend; it was easy to forget just how rotten so many young men today were, how right-wing they were.

A third figure stood beside Lucas; a tall muscular blonde woman. Jacinta furrowed her brow. Who was that? His bodyguard? If he had a new girlfriend already, why come all this way to bother Lisa?

Jacinta shifted the weight in her hand.

She debated rushing in now, or waiting to see what happened first. Her friend had called for help, but she didn't seem in any immediate danger. Yet. The second Lucas or the blonde woman made a move, Jacinta would reveal her presence.

"This is why you don't break up with a tech-bro," Lucas gloated from the doorway, and Jacinta's jaw clenched hard enough that her teeth cracked. She hoped he gave her a reason to wipe that smug look off his face. "Modern women are a disaster these days. All this nonsense about rights and equality. Give me a break. That's why I made this," he continued, jerking his thumb towards the blonde beside him. "My very own based AI waifu. Flawless skin, she can never get a pimple or any other skin blemish, and she does every little thing I ask. I only came all this way to brag about the ways she makes up for your failures. But now you've raised your hand against me," his voice dropped low, dangerous, and he smirked. "She's going to destroy you."

***

Lucas's words struck me hard. What did he mean by 'AI waifu'? Was the blonde woman some kind of robot? Now that I looked closer, there was something strange about her. Like her skin was stretched too tight, with a strange plastic sheen.

Realizing I was staring at her, she lifted her lips into a sneer. "I've spent the last twenty-four hours consuming pop culture to see what people do when they get dumped," she told me, her voice cold and cruel, like rusted metal. "Based on my calculations, trashing their ex's belongings while playing bad music is the most common reaction."

I stared at her, confused. "Huh?"

She opened her mouth wide again, and I instinctively cringed backwards, expecting another jet of black liquid. Instead, music began to drift out of her, crackly and dim, like there was some kind of speaker hidden inside her gut. The AI strode forward, pushing past me with her muscled arms.

I stumbled, staring at her in shock.

She grabbed an ornamental vase on the sideboard and, without a second of hesitation, tossed it across the hallway. It smashed against the wall opposite, fragments of white ceramic shattering across the carpet. My gut wrenched in anger.

"What the hell is wrong with you?" I shouted, my cheeks growing hot beneath my face mask.

Horrible, scratchy music continued spilling out of the woman's throat as she tossed things around and knocked things off the shelves–a clock, a box of tissues, a ring of keys, even the painting hanging on the wall above the sideboard.

When she ignored my shouts to stop, I ran towards her and swung my fist, hoping to land a hit square on her chest.

But she thrust her arms out before I could even get close, shoving me backwards with such force I slammed against the wall behind me, knocking the breath from my lungs. I crumpled to the ground, gasping sharply, and struggled to climb back to my feet as my head spun. Her strength was ridiculous.

The music coming from her throat gargled and became raspier, like a broken record, as she lifted her arm and flexed one enormous bicep at me. I frowned at her. Just what kind of program had Lucas given her? Why did I ever decide to date this creep?

The song changed, though it was hard to hear it as the AI girlfriend began to speak, her words overlapping with the discordant tune. "According to my research, newly dumped people also have a trend of calling their ex a narcissist," she said, a slight sneer in her voice, "regardless of whether or not it's true. Following this trend, I have used my brain to hack every social media account under your name and made you publicly admit that *you* are a narcissist."

My scowl deepened. She smirked. Anger burned like lava through my veins.

"And since you haven't denied it, it must be true," she added, a hint of humor in her voice.

Grinding my teeth in anger, I got ready to launch another attack at her. If I could just catch her off guard...

But before I could take a single step Jacinta barreled into the room. She lifted her hand behind her head, holding what looked like a large black disk, and threw it forward with a grunt of effort. The disc—one of my weights—spun through the air before hitting the blonde woman square in the face with a dull *smack*. She was immediately knocked down, hitting the ground with a heavy thud. The music coming out of her ceased, a heavy silence falling over us.

I stared at Jacinta. She stared back at me, a slow, triumphant grin spreading across her face. "Try beating *that* high score," she teased, and I couldn't even be mad at her.

Lucas stared in shock at his AI girlfriend, sprawled out on the ground, the weight sitting beside her face. Rather disturbingly, there was a faint dent between her eyes, like it had crumpled in, but no other obvious damage.

"Y-you—" Lucas began, but Jacinta didn't let him finish. With a raging shout, she lunged towards him, arms outstretched, tackling him to the ground.

I watched in shock as my friend began to grapple with him, Lucas frantically trying to shove her off while she hit her hands against his chest, scratching at his face with her fingers. "How dare you come here and attack my friend!" she screamed at him, managing to pin him down with her hands. "And bringing your trashy fake girlfriend, too? Loser! Loser! Loooser!"

Growling in anger, he finally managed to get hold of her arms and push her off him. Jacinta rolled over with a grunt as he staggered clumsily to his feet, his neck and arms red from where he'd been scratched and hit.

Jacinta recovered just as quickly, jumping on his back and putting her hands over his face to disorientate him. He wrenched this way and that, trying to shake her off, shouting in frustration.

"Get off me, you crazy bitch," he screamed, but Jacinta held tight, wrapping one arm around his chest while the other continued to cover his face. "I said... get... *off*."

With a burst of strength, he finally yanked her off him, and Jacinta went crashing to the ground, looking dazed.

I stepped forward to help her, but she shook her head. "I've got this," she muttered, dragging herself to her feet and already going in for another attempt. The two of them became locked in a grapple, fighting for dominance, reaching for each other's throats while trying to keep the other at bay. Lucas managed to push Jacinta backwards, her feet skidding across the hardwood floor, but she quickly shifted the power balance until he was the one stumbling back, sweat dripping down his forehead from the effort of keeping her off him.

With a grunt, Lucas reached for the loose fabric of Jacinta's black shirt over the chest area, and began tugging on it. "Your woke short-sleeves are gonna be the death of you," he taunted as he clung onto the fabric of her t, making it so that she couldn't easily fight him without losing her shirt.

With a growl, she tried to wrestle free, locked in a grapple that sent them both stumbling outside into the cool evening.

I followed them, my gaze frantically darting between them, wishing I could help my friend but knowing I would be in the way if I tried to intervene.

Gravel crunched under their feet as they continued to fight outside, scratching and punching and wrestling with each other like boxers in a ring. The sky was full dark by now, only a handful of stars glistening in the velvety dusk. Only the light spilling out from the house, and the harsh glare of headlamps from the car, lit the area. As Jacinta and Lucas stumbled further and further away, their silhouettes became dark and hazy, difficult to discern against the backdrops of trees that shaded the edge of the property.

Then I realized where they were heading: toward the lake at the bottom of the driveway. Right now, it blended into the darkened night, the surface reflecting the sky above, becoming nothing but a glossy puddle of shadow.

"You know, you're cute for a tomboy—broad shouldered, but still, very cute bang!" Lucas taunted as he grabbed another fistful of Jacinta's t-shirt in his hand. "You're that biracial half-white, half-Mexican chick Lisa told me about, yeah?"

"Shut up!" Jacinta growled between gritted teeth as she grappled with him. Her hands gripped his shoulders while he alternated between fistfuls of her t-shirt and the crook under her elbows. He was smirking, while her face was dead-set in seriousness and determination, a look of fear flickering across her eyes.

Neither side seemed to be able to get the upper hand. At this point, it was simply a test of stamina. I had to put an end to the fight somehow, before things got even worse.

Leaving Jacinta and Lucas brawling by the lake, I rushed back into the house. The AI was still on the ground, unconscious, or rebooting, or whatever AIs did when hit in the face with a weight.

I stepped over her and hurried to the kitchen, rummaging through the cupboards and searching through my copious amount of cleaning supplies. Bleach seemed a little extreme, but antibacterial spray probably wouldn't cause any *fatal* damage. I needed some way to get him off Jacinta.

Grabbing the cleaning spray, I charged back outside, my eyes searching the gloom for Lucas and Jacinta's silhouettes. They were still grappling with each other, though it seemed like Jacinta had finally managed to overpower Lucas, and was delivering a punch to his ribs as I reached them.

"Jacinta, duck," I shouted, aiming the nozzle of the spray bottle towards Lucas's face.

My friend did as I said without a second of hesitation, dropping low to the ground.

Stumbling in confusion, Lucas hardly had time to react as I squirted the cleaning spray towards him. Most of it was swept away on the breeze, but a good amount of it hit him in the face. He squeezed his eyes shut, but judging from his cry of pain, some of it must have splashed against his eyeballs.

Screaming and rubbing at his face, Lucas staggered around like a drunkard, unable to see where he was going.

Jacinta roared in anger, and the two of us tackled him together, sending him crashing down. I pinned his arms against the gravel while Jacinta pummeled at him with her fists.

"You deserve this, you incel pig!" Jacinta seethed at him as she continued the assault.

In her expression, I saw true rage.

"Help me! Get this stuff off me!" he screamed, still clawing at his face, his spittle landing against my arm and making me clench up in disgust. I'd need a ridiculously hot shower after this. "Come and protect me, goddamn it!"

Something was coming. I turned and saw the AI, her whole body shuddered and trembled, as if she was resetting herself, charging out of the house and across the driveway, her features set with anger and determination.

My eyes widened when I realized she wasn't slowing down. She was charging right at us, and I didn't fancy getting hit by whatever the hell she was made of.

"Jacinta, to the right!!"

She stopped with her fist in midair and shot me a questioning glance, before noticing the AI too. With a start, she let go of Lucas and dived to the side just as his girlfriend reached us, I did the same. Completely ignoring us, she scooped Lucas up in her arms and lifted him as if he weighed no more than a baby. Then, taking us all by surprise, she ran and jumped straight into the water, hitting the crystalline surface with a loud splash that sent shockwaves across the entire lake.

Cold water splashed against my legs as I stared in shock at the rippling surface where they had disappeared.

I heard a gurgled shout, and sparks of electricity surged through the water as the AI's body malfunctioned and short-circuited, sinking down to the bottom, dragging Lucas along with her.

About J. Neira

J. Neira is the child of a Mexican immigrant, who now lives in Minnesota. They are a cozy horror author & a slush reader for Translunar Travelers Lounge and Cosmic Roots and Eldritch Shores. Their stories have been published by Suspended Magazine, Graveside Press, Terrorcore Publishing & West Avenue Publishing among others. Their upcoming YA novel will be published by Dead Fox Publishing!

Not Pretty
Samantha Alis

THERE ARE MANY UNDENIABLE facts of life.

71% of the Earth is made of water.

The femur is the largest bone in the human body.

Skin accounts for almost 15% of body weight.

And I'm not pretty.

The last one hurts to admit. Even as I slink through that narrow space between tall fence posts and trees, my bare legs careening through webs filled with black bodies and beady eyes. Twigs poke my arms. Thistles bite my ankles. Insects skitter across my bare toes. Every little pinch and prick is dull compared to the pain of that knowledge.

It took me years to finally have the courage to think it, say it out loud, look at myself in the mirror and realize yes, *I am not pretty*. Thankfully, there are fixes to some of my problems.

My nails are short stubby things and I tap them against the garden gate I've been searching for in the dark: a hair-tie wedged between the teeth of a rusting lock. I remove it, grind it into dirt topped with scurrying ants, and throw the gate open with a shrill sound.

The wind picks up, injecting the smell of rain and soil into my sinuses. Tendrils of my hair writhe like snakes before my eyes. The color is dull as it sits in between blonde and brown, that dirty dishwater hue. Hair dye will take care of that problem.

I creep through the backyard, past suntanning chairs currently occupied by lounging crickets. I reach the back door—it's glass, a slider. My hands cup my face as I peer into the dark house.

Another unpleasant feature—eye color. A lackluster mix of browns, light like honey in the sun, but black in the dark stare back at me. Brown eyes can't see in the dark as well as blue or green. No number of carrots can fix that either. Unfortunately, the solution isn't as easy as hair dye. Or an improved wardrobe. Colored contacts would look good, but I don't want *just* looks. I want solutions. Upgrades.

I step back from the glass. My reflection is barely more than a shadow and I look away. I know I'm not pretty. It doesn't need to be rubbed in just how unpretty I truly am.

Blemished skin after severe bouts of acne. It started in seventh grade. It's still here in eleventh.

Crooked teeth from, well, genetics.

Long nose, wide, and fat.

Too many other traits. All undesirable. Abhorrent, really. They keep me from getting asked to Homecoming, to Prom. They're why I'm rejected when I ask another girl to Sadie Hawkins. They keep me from smiling at myself in the mirror. But, mostly, they keep me from living to my full potential. Pretty girls are smart. They are athletic. They are overachievers. I have terrible grades, a long transcript of Cs, then Ds, now Fs. Nobody picks me when we split teams for volleyball. Ugly girls get nothing. Pretty girls get everything.

That's why I came here today.

I walk from the backyard to the side of the house. Rose bushes, tall and fluffed by dark green leaves, line stucco siding.

I plunge my hand in between tall stems and thirsty thorns. They drink the tap rushing through my veins as my fingers curl around cold metal and I drag it through.

Hair is an easy fix. Nails too. Artificiality can be pretty. The facial features, however, those are harder. I, for one, don't have hundreds of thousands of dollars at the ready for a team of skilled surgeons to carve the hidden beauty from under my skin.

I lean the ladder against the side of the house. Broken rose petals and aphid-eaten leaves cling to the rungs. I plant my bare foot, soled by dirt, on the bottom step. The cold tingles through my toes.

I might not have a team of skilled surgeons to aid me, but I do have the tool those same teams swear by. A scalpel, thin and trustworthy, shifting in the pocket of my shorts as I climb.

I stop beneath the window, open to allow the cool, night breeze to wash over as she sleeps. A flurry of moths circle the window, batting cream wings and ramming fuzzy heads against the screen, drawn by the subtle glow of a nightlight deep in the room.

The scalpel is smooth, gliding across wire mesh as if it's a long-legged water strider.

The moths were here first, so I guide them with my hand into the room. Warmer than outside, and a little stuffy, despite the open window. The moths flutter to the nightlight, *plinking* against it with their little battering ram bodies.

I throw one leg over the window and into the room, then the other. Soft carpet greets my soles, brushes away the dirt as I sidle to the bed in the middle of the room. I tuck my hand into my pocket again, fist sweating around the scalpel, warming up the metal.

Sarah is my solution.

Although I envy her long, blonde hair—gold like sunshine—and her eyes as blue and bright as precious gems, those are things I cannot take, only copy.

But her clear, dewy skin, always-pink cheeks? Those I cannot copy. Only take.

She sleeps in the middle of the bed, arms outspread, elbows bent. She snores softly. Not the loud, laborious noises I snuffle, but something light and airy. A cute, girly *ahh-ohh* from old cartoons.

I sit beside her, sinking into the soft mattress and pink floral sheets. I retrieve the scalpel, run my thumb along the blunt edge. It shakes in my unsteady hand. I only get one chance, after all. I cannot mess this up.

I clamp my other palm across Sarah's parted lips. Her eyes shoot open, black pupils widening until the gemstone blue irises are nothing more than narrow, circular frames. I think she tries to scream, because hot air fills my palm, drawing sweat to the surface.

She tries to hit me, but one arm is weak, frail and bony against my skin, thick and scarred from insults and insecurities. Her other arm is trapped, awkward and twisted between our bodies.

"Shhh..."

Sarah's flailing arm falls to her side, and she swallows the screams.

"I'm not here to hurt you. I've come to borrow something."

I hold the scalpel up to her face. This will be much easier if we understand one another, if she accepts what is going to happen. Her eyelids lift higher this time, and I hope that if she stays that way, the eyeballs will take the invitation and pop out of their sockets. I wouldn't know how to use them, truly do them justice, but I wouldn't mind holding onto them if I ever figured it out.

I place the tip of the scalpel on her forehead, just underneath the field where golden locks grow and thrive. The edge isn't as shiny and sharp after meeting the screen, and little flecks of something black, maybe plastic, cling to the blade.

When Sarah screams this time, it's not just hot air, but a muffled squeal, like a piglet.

"Shhhhhh..."

I press my palm harder against her mouth, flesh digging into teeth. Droplets of blood or sweat reach her tongue and she gags with a convulsion that presses the scalpel into the skin until it meets bone. She kicks her legs in every direction, but they are too long and beautiful to reach me. They swipe sheets to the edge of the bed.

"Shhhhhhhhhhh."

I drag the scalpel across her hairline, down the sides of her face, curving it where the ear connects.

She never stops screaming.

The scalpel trails down to her chin, keeping the heart shape perfectly intact, then back up the other side of her face, curving around her ear, to meet the oozing red line started there. I stuff the instrument back into my pocket.

Oh, Sarah did stop screaming. Her wide eyes are closed. *Too bad*. Even the moths have quieted. They circle the light instead of throwing their bodies into it as if they, too, realize this event should be reverent.

I bring stained red fingers to Sarah's forehead and pull.

The new skin is warm, not parted from her body long enough to cool yet.

I join the moths on the other end of the room and look into the mirror above where they rise and fall in tight loops.

It isn't a perfect fit as I drape it across my wide nose, too-big eyes, but it's close enough.

Sarah's face hides my scarred, puckered skin.

Because this was my first time, the cut isn't as neat as I'd have liked it to be. The edges of my new chin are jagged and dripping. The thin skin around my left eye has a tear, so it looks like a disfigured wound runs from there to just above my nose.

I know it isn't perfect, but a smile still pulls at my lips, tugging my face, my new face, into a glowing grin.

Finally, I'm pretty.

About Samantha Alis

Born in Las Vegas, Samantha Alis always dreamed of working with books either through publishing her own or editing others'. She is the author of *The Montgomery Estate* and *Clairvoyant.* She loves stories with spooky settings, relatable characters, and plenty of ghouls, ghosts, and monsters. When she's not writing, she can be found watching horror movies, playing video games, or reading any book she comes across. She now lives in Quebec, Canada with her French Canadian husband.

Sucker
Briar Hyssop

ROMANCE IN ALL ITS forms is exhausting. I've assumed this for years, but it becomes undeniable under the suction cup hold of my boyfriend's lips, the ravenous way he kisses me when my stomach is full. When I've never felt hunger like that in my life. Maybe I never will.

I am. . . Well, I am. Just what, I'm not sure yet. I'm not interested in girls, so I thought I must be gay. But I'm not interested in Ryan all that much either, which I only realize as I retreat from his kiss. Adolescence is confusing, changing bodies and all that, but dating is supposed to be easy. Every TV show my friends have ever dragged me into watching made the Hollywood promise of happily ever after before graduation. They also promised perfect teeth and clear skin, so it only makes sense that they'd be three for three on well-wrapped lies.

Ryan smiles like he always does after we kiss, so I force the corner of my lips up to keep him from seeing the flat line of disinterest. "I had fun," he says as he rests his forehead against mine. If this were a show, there'd be a golden hour filter over this moment in front of my house, a visual claim of beauty in parting. For me, though, it's just another moment when I hone my patience, like pencil tapping my way through the last two minutes of class or posing my hand over the seat belt in the last mile home. I squeeze the doorknob digging into my back as Ryan dips for another kiss, but my earlier revelation evaporated what patience I have left for this moment. I tilt my head to the side, and his lips cascade onto my neck.

For the ten seconds he lingers there, I am struck only by the absurd illusion that I have somehow left my suburban lawn and am now precariously sailing over distant seas. I am but a hapless sailor caught in the grip of a playful kraken. Somewhere inside me, he believes I am hiding treasure, even though I'm not.

Ryan's teeth are like the little hooks hidden inside a sucker, and they nibble the ridge of my traps in search of it. I push him away at that, not pleased at all with the idea of being eaten, nor of being on the dinner table instead of seated at it.

"God, you'll rip my skin off," I tell him with a short laugh to cover my frustration. The hedges hardly cover us from my nosy neighbors, and I don't want their gossip to beat me inside.

"Are you calling me clingy?"

"Maybe."

He looks at me with a bleary look I've never returned. "Maybe I'm compensating for you. I wish *you'd* be a little clingier, babe."

I hate the pet name, but more than that, I hate myself a little for not feeling the same way. Boyfriends are supposed to want to spend time together, and touch each other, but I don't want that. Not like him. Eating microwave ramen in his kitchen together is enjoyable. Stretching out on the couch to watch a movie, as long as it's not some explosion-ridden, plotless waste of gigabytes, is fun. But then he wants to hold hands and cuddle and kiss, and his desire is acid on my skin. Already, his breath skirts over my neck and it bubbles up in a rash, I'm sure. If I connect the dots, I suspect it will form a chicken scratch epitaph commanding me to finally break up with him.

But I can't. I don't want to hurt him, because I *do* like him, and Hollywood says that if I just wait long enough, my feelings will click into place. Until then, I can cover any adverse physical reactions with a bandage and a fake-it-til-you-make-it smile.

"I'll work on that," I say, slipping through my front door before Ryan the kraken can launch another attack. "See you tomorrow."

***

My power of manifestation should be studied. As soon as I dumped my ex, Sarah, I told myself that I did it because I wanted to date a guy. Two weeks later, I met Ryan, and a month after that, he asked me out. Like me, this preternatural ability to breathe life into my innermost thoughts is usually slow. While I'm brushing my teeth before school, the mirror reveals a rash on my neck where Ryan's lips had been.

What I could have possibly done to expedite this apparition?

I spit, more out of shock than need. When I lean in to rinse out my mouth, I take a closer look at my skin. Even through the toothpaste I misted onto the mirror, I see how puckered and purple it is, like Ryan had just released it from his hold. I groan the only way I know how, and I know it's not the kind of sound Ryan would ever want to hear after kissing me.

It's not a rash, it's a hickey, right in the crook of my neck where not a single one of my shirts can cover it. Great. If Mom sees this, she'll give me the talk, again. Moments like this make me wish I had a sister so that I could pull her into my bathroom and ask her to cover it up with makeup magic. The best I can do is shrug the straps of my backpack into the cranny of my neck and hope Mom doesn't notice.

That method works better than I ever could have imagined. It's not until lunch break when I have to slink my backpack to the off-white tile in the cafeteria that anyone notices the dimpled and bruised skin on my neck. Ryan stares from across the table like he can't figure out what it is or how it got there. His gaze is itchy, or maybe that's just a gift from my scratchy backpack straps.

"Did I do that?" Ryan asks with a proud smile.

"Obviously," I say, covering it with my free hand. The other shovels mashed potatoes into my mouth so that I can't spew my frustrations out at him. That feeling returns, that I should cut my losses here before Ryan brands me any further.

"Sorry," Ryan says. He stands and runs around the lunch table, even though the table is half the length of the cafeteria itself, and we're situated right in the middle of it. I wait for him to round the edge, but before I can tell him to sit back down, his lips are back on the hickey. Softer this time, apologetic. "Is that better?"

This kiss is just an uncomfortable as the rest, the thin line of saliva he trails over the bruise caustic. But the itching stops. My reprieve from that dull irritation is short-lived because Ryan takes my silence as permission to do it again.

I want to push him away. People are looking at us over Styrofoam cups of lemonade and sweet tea. The gossip train is clearly ready to go trans-continental with the way I see hands dip under the line of the lunch tables. I'm sure my friends in the county school will see this picture on Instagram and harass me about it before the final bell rings. But I leave him be, because every time his lips plop off my skin, the itching returns fiercer than before. I learn that I don't just dislike how he kisses me—I hate it—but it's easier to bear than the itching.

Ryan pulls away for good when Ms. Bannock leaves her post on the commons steps and threatens to write us up for inappropriate behavior. He waves it off the way he dismisses my griping about PDA, and for the first time, I'm irritated about the intrusion. Ms. Bannock is one of the few teachers willing to let teenagers be teenagers, within reason, but she has learned to read my rolling eyes as a cry for intervention. As she suspected, my eyes had rolled so far back that I could have watched the signals of discomfort light up my brain. But I protected the look from her with closed eyes for a reason. As much as being under Ryan's lips made me feel like peeling my skin off, I needed him to keep going.

***

When the final bell rings, the itching shakes my ability to see straight. My fingers trace the outline of the hickey, visible entirely through touch. Ryan sees, and he must think it's a symptom of chasing ghosts. Before I concoct the lines to ask, he kisses me again and again and again. Every time he pulls away, my hand betrays me and tugs him back. I think he mistakes my tense shoulders for nerves. If everyone goes immobile when lips and breath skitters across their skin, I don't understand how they manage to move past kissing. My lightning restricted muscles ensure that, even if I had the desire to return the favor, I would be completely unable to do so. Ryan has no issue with it, though. My traitorous hand tangles in his hair like I've never done before, and it clearly excites him.

It stings, that my discomfort makes Ryan so happy, but it's also my fault for not telling him.

Ms. Bannock sees us again and sends us on our respective ways home with a tut to Ryan and a frown for me. She must be disappointed that I'm finally wearing adolescent hormones like dollar store cologne. I'm disappointed, too.

The itching keeps me from paying too much mind to the stench. The drive home is marked not by miles driven or dogwoods passed but by the tally mark scratches I leave on the hickey. When I get home, I take the stairs three at a time so the bathroom mirror can tell me how much worse my skin looks after Ryan's prodding.

Rubber padded suckers stare back, small enough that I might mistake them for toothpaste grime on the mirror. They bloom out of my skin, hardly the size of chicken pox, purple at the base and paler than my winter skin in the cup.

We blink at each other.

I scream. They squeak.

Before I can contest this reality, I fall to my ass and backpedal across the tile floor, too afraid to bring my hand to the skin for confirmation. It's a trick of the eye. An illusion created by the garish floral wallpaper. I don't know my body well enough to understand it most of the time, but I know what I'm telling myself now is a lie. I stand up in increments marked by new lies. The pulses I feel on top of my skin are just my heartbeat. The painful itching is just broken skin.

The image is no less shocking the second time, but I steady myself against the counter to keep from falling again. There are suckers, on my neck, biting the air like they can taste the lingering scent of mint from my toothpaste. They have to be the result of some kind of mutated disease, and if they are, I need to tell Ryan. Immediately. And then I need to rush to the hospital. Or maybe I should go the hospital first and get checked out for normal diseases before I induce a panic attack for Ryan. But if I do go there first, and this *is* a disease that will end life as we know it, the doctors probably won't let me talk to Ryan. They'll quarantine me and my phone and call him themselves, and then they'll call the CDC and the WHO, and my life will end before it can really begin. No sequel or college reunion special. I'll be one of the characters that gets written out in the middle of the first season.

My hand hovers over my phone, but I can't bring up my chat with Ryan. Like always, I can't do what needs to be done. Instead, I open my medicine cabinet and find the triple antibiotic ointment and anti-itch cream. I slather both over the suckers generously, ignoring how they prick my fingers every time I pass over. They'll go away if I ignore them, like a sore throat or a sore muscle. They have to.

***

The suckers itch so much that I wake up before my alarm. They're larger now, like the concoction I fed it after school yesterday contained steroid cream, too. Whimpers provide the soundtrack to my morning routine, replacing my usual tired grunting. Mom knocks on my door and asks if I feel unwell. I do, but I think my fever is psychogenic, and I can't risk showing her my metamorphosis or telling her the catalyst.

The largest bandage I can find barely covers the suckers, but I throw it on anyway while I practice hiding my panic. Terse smile. Hands in my pockets where they can't irritate the bandage. I can pretend that this isn't the worst pain or panic I've felt in my life.

Mom doesn't ask questions, but amusement lights Ryan's face when he sees the bandage.

"Are you that embarrassed to be seen with a hickey?" he asks, slinging an arm around my shoulder while I stuff books into my locker.

Clanging doors and clicking heels make the hall seem more crowded than it actually is, but having even one other person around me makes me self-conscious. Logically, I know that my classmates are more interested in themselves than they are in me, but all it will take is one long look to make out the small bulges under my bandage. Ryan brushes his thumb around it in a feathery way that isn't as soothing as his lips, but it stops the scalloped skin from puckering incessantly. It's immediate relief, almost enough to make me lean into the touch, but if I let him keep going, he'll realize the skin isn't smooth.

I duck out from under his arm, slower than I would if I were thinking normally. "It looks uglier today. Don't understand how." I swallow a groan when the itching and stinging comes back full force.

"Come on. It can't be that bad."

It would be better if Ryan's mirth was infectious, too, but I grimace at the insinuation. His touch is more of an opiate, I think. Comforting, sure, but dulling as well. It makes me too slow to stop him from peeling back the bandage. I scream and scramble to cover it with my hand, but he swats me away and leans in to inspect.

This is it. This is the moment he brands me as a freak and I become an international sensation like the Elephant Man.

"What's going on with you today?" Ryan asks. His laugh hardly covers his irritation. "It looks fine."

I freeze under his words and his touch. He trails his finger over the suckers. They latch onto the tip like they're cleaning the grooves of his fingerprint. Peristaltic twitches keep him locked in place. His eyelids wilt over a dopey expression.

The suckers are feeding, like an animal or a vampire. If they keep this up, they'll kill him. I brush his hand away and try not to flinch at the popping sound the suckers make when they're forced to release him. His body takes on a lethargic sway that will end with his skull cracking over the floor if I don't do anything, so I grab onto his t-shirt, but the momentum brings him closer to me. He pins me against the lockers and droops onto my shoulders. Instinct makes him wrap his arms around my waist. My skin bubbles under his pressure the second he makes contact.

Biology says two human males can't have children, but he is the progenitor of my suckers, and the way they burst under my skin is the closest pain to childbirth I will ever feel. Tears gather in my eyes, and I blink hard and fast to cast them away. People are staring, whispering. Catcalls race down the hallway and slammed locker doors feel like unwarranted applause. I want to push him off and stop the show, but I can't let anyone else see what's happening to me. I swallow shallow, wet breaths and hope Ryan gets his senses back in time to save me.

***

I know the suckers have formed in the shape of his arms, his chest, and his chin before I run through my front door. They catch on my clothes every time I move and even when I don't. It's not my racing breaths that cause the fabric to rise and fall, it's the suckers. Mom doesn't get off work until five, which means I have a little over an hour to figure out what to do about my deformity. A bandage won't cover the road rash slathering of suckers all over my body, and we don't keep gauze or medical tape. I have to figure out something else, but this feels so much larger than me. Suddenly, my shirt and jacket feel like they're constricting me. I shed them on the banister as I climb toward the bathroom.

My house blurs as I move, and when I stand in front of the mirror, everything but the suckers dissipates into static slush, even my unmarred skin. Salty tears burn in the craters on my chest. The new cups aren't as large as the ones on my neck, but they will be by the morning. On my neck, the small suckers I had seen that morning had fused into larger ones, each brim wide enough to fit my thumb. I test one, just to see if it'll stick to me the way it did to Ryan. If I can feed it, I will, but it treats me like a wrapper, not food.

"Shit. Fuck." My voice is mangled by panic, throat closing over my words until all I can do is wheeze.

The room spins, and my knees give out. When I crumple to the tile, the suckers on my back spit against it because it doesn't taste of Ryan. This tile has never so much as seen the bottom of his sock. I've never let him in my room, let alone my house.

I don't know how long I spend on the floor. The pain keeps time. It resets every few seconds, peaking in waves that make me smack my skin and hiss and cry. Every time, the suction cups reject my touch and add an extra pinch under the skin to underscore their distaste with me. One would think that eventually, my pain receptors would get tired of working overtime and simply stop telling me how much this hurts. But my body is as stubborn as my mind. I feel every itch and pinch until Mom finds me in the bathroom. She's in her work clothes, badge still pinned to her lapel, and through my oxygen-deprived thoughts, I work out that she must have just gotten home.

"Christ, Miller, what happened?"

When she reaches out to help me up, I yell at her.

"Don't touch me," I rasp. It's difficult to draw enough breath even to say that, and I retreat into my body even more. With the suction cup puckering on my skin, I must really look like a tentacle now, writhing for a splash of water.

"Sweetheart," she says slowly, "I can't see where you're hurt. Show me."

I would rather die right here than unfurl for my mother, but I guess when it comes down to it, I'm not even a teenager with adult training wheels like the TV shows say. I'm just a child, and I need help. I clear my hair from my neck and trail the sidewalk of smooth skin lining each lane of suckers on my chest. Mom might see this and think I'm freak, but maybe her maternal instinct will save me from becoming a science experiment.

Seconds pass without her saying anything. It can't be easy to see her son like this, so I can't even blame her. More so, I'm glad that she didn't immediately scream like I did. It gives me the smallest bit of hope, but still, I keep my eyes clenched while I wait for her reaction.

It comes out as a coo and a hug so gentle she must think that anything more would break me. She kneels beside me on the tile and pats my hair. Kisses my forehead.

"I don't understand," she says. "Were you embarrassed to show me a love bite?"

I shake my head, and she stiffens. "Did Ryan do something you didn't want him to do?"

That's closer to the truth, but her accusation is too insidious for what happened. Ryan is only doing what he thinks is normal, and I've given him nothing to show that, for me, it isn't. What's happening is my fault, but she can't see that.

"No," I whisper, conceding that I must be going crazy. If she could see the suckers, she wouldn't be acting like this. Ryan wouldn't touch them with a hunger that matched theirs. Whatever this is, it's mine and mine alone.

Mom puts a hand to my chest like she's counting every heartbeat. The suckers there ignore her like they ignored me. My bloodline isn't tasty enough for them, apparently.

"Take deep breaths for me," she says before guiding me through patterns of inhaling and exhaling. By the end of it, the bathroom feels less like a tilt-o-whirl and more like a bathroom, and my words aren't choked. I thank her and mold my dismay into embarrassment, making up a story about being stressed out about school and dating. That's all, I promise.

Because I lie about my feelings so often, she believes me.

***

I don't bother covering up for school. The suckers may as well be UFOs, and the more sightings there are the better. I need someone to believe me. I need someone else to see them.

By lunch period, not a single person has noticed, and I get the same vacuous feeling in my stomach that I feel when my science teacher prompts the class to consider the vastness of the universe. Utter loneliness.

Ryan notices my mood but not the suckers. He practically sits on the edge of my seat at the lunch table and slings his arm over my shoulders. The itching is worse when he's near, and I till angry red whelps like cornrows under the suckers on my arms. Ryan grabs my hand to stop the constant raking and squeezes between my fingers. For now, all I feel is the pressure of his palm, but the second he lets go, the relentless itching will sprout, and that will eventually blossom into pain. When he trails his thumb over my knuckles, I hold on tighter.

The behavior is uncommon for me. If days earlier I hadn't promised Ryan to try harder, he might read into it. But I did promise, and the sleepy look I throw him—a result of not being able to sleep through the pain—can just as easily be interpreted as fulfilling my promise. The thought travels from his widened eyes to the wicked twitch pulling his grin lopsided. He tugs on my hand.

When he stands up, my suckers follow him out of the cafeteria like a flower preening for the sun. A minute later, we're under the back stairwell, and he's feeding the suckers. Creating new ones. Soon, my whole body will be one giant suction cup. Maybe then I'd finally be enough for him.

Tantrums of pain explode when he moves his hands from my chest, so I pull him tighter against me. At this point, I'd envelope myself in him if it meant stopping the pain. I'd let him devour me. He comes close, teeth raking over the suckers on my neck, pulling on my lip. I want him to hurry and be done. I want him to slow down so I can enjoy how he silences the suckers. More than anything, I want him to stop and never touch me again.

I take no pleasure in how the suckers feed on him. Each *pop* that follows his roaming hands and lips come with the smallest ripping sound. The cuts they leave on him are so small that they don't bleed. I'm jealous, if only for a second, because at least the scars they leave on him won't be visible. One day, if I'm lucky, my suckers might die and close up, become scars. And I'll have to look at them every day and remember how terrible this has been. But today they are open. They are hungry, and my only choice is to feed them or atrophy alongside them.

I'm not strong enough to starve them.

***

The pain is no more bearable after a week. I call in sick, hoping that it would give me enough time to crest the pain of starvation, but I can't stomach it. One starved sucker feels like a bullet. A thousand tiny deaths in succession rivals the fracturing asteroid that killed the dinosaurs. I cave when the suckers over my belly enter their twilight hours. Within seconds of feeling their blinding death rattle, my hands find my phone and call Ryan over. By the end of the night, he resuscitates every sucker I'd laid to rest.

At school it's more or less the same routine. Saddle up to Ryan every opportunity I get and grit my teeth against the discomfort. The whispers never stop, but as long as they aren't illuminating the freak I've become, I can handle them. To be honest, it's difficult to see past the pain or hear anything beyond the rubbery smack of my suckers. They steal my every waking moment.

When I have suffered under the suckers for a solid month, Ms. Bannock calls me into her office. I look up from the mush I push around my lunch tray with half slatted eyes, but I don't move. It doesn't fit into my scheduled touch therapy, but she's insistent. She makes a show of wagging her finger at me. I still don't move. It takes her physically pulling me away from Ryan to get me in step behind her. I wonder if the whispers heard the semi-automatic *pops* of the suckers ripping from his skin.

"Talk to me," she says as she directs me into a leather chair. "Why are you acting so unlike yourself?"

The suckers reject the chair like they reject every material that isn't Ryan. I roll my eyes, and the way I lift my brow causes the suckers on my eyelids to stick to one another. Blinking them apart is painful, but not nearly as painful as letting them die.

"Don't know what you're talking about," I slur. I'm too tired for this conversation.

Her eyes trail over my suckers as if she can see them, but I assume she's only seeing love bites and grooves like everyone else. She places her finger directly into the cup on my knuckle. It rejects her, of course, but the itching stops. My head shoots toward her with more energy than I've had in weeks. It's too much to ask to be seen, so I don't, but she nods anyway.

Slowly, she lifts her sleeves to showcase neat rows of pockmark scars that trail from wrist to elbow, probably from elbow to shoulder. I look at her in this new light, wondering just how much of her body is branded like mine. I assume all of it.

"It hurts, doesn't it?" she asks.

I nod. I don't realize I'm crying until I feel tears clinging to my suckers. It's hard to feel anything beyond their pain. The salt in my tears may well be alcohol for the way it stings, but relief is a full body ice pack. The itching doesn't stop, but it cowers.

"How did you make it stop?" I ask.

Ms. Bannock's eyes flit thoughtfully over my suckers like she intends to subdue each and every one of them. "One day I got tired of hurting."

I blink at her, eyes begging for more. But she has nothing more to say. The truth is really that simple.

Before I leave her office, I ask her to convince the school nurse that I've come down with a cold. I go home without saying goodbye to Ryan, and I ask my mom to leave work early. I give her my phone and ask her to hold onto it until I'm feeling better.

The suckers immolate and die, and it makes me want to capitulate. I might make it through the pain, but I might not. One thing I know now is that I can't keep doing this to myself. I can't live in a body that belongs to everyone else but me. I have to take control. If I don't succeed today, I'll try again and again until I've reduced my pain to scars.

About Briar Hyssop

Briar Hyssop is a Pushcart Prize and Best of the Net nominated writer of horror and science fiction—and sometimes thought-provoking essays about the fit of their overalls. Briar's work has been featured in *Chill Mag, Monstrous Femme, MicoLit Almanac,* and *Moonday Mag* among others. They were a finalist in the 2024 Kentucky Visions Short Story Contest, and are currently an MFA candidate for Emerson's Popular Fiction and Publishing Program. Their best work is done from a sunny patch of Kentucky bluegrass, with their bloodhound by their side.

Catalytic Converter
Sam Logan

SOME DAYS ARE FINE.

Some days I want to scratch my flesh until it bleeds.

Some days my skin crawled like maggots squirmed just beneath the surface—little grains of rice writhing and pulsing and trying to burst their way out through my pores. But I knew they were not there. Not really. It was just my inner boy-man trying to break through my girl-woman body.

Or something like that, I wasn't sure. At sixteen years old, gimme a break. God forbid I needed some time to figure things out.

I've always felt *different*. No matter how many ugly-ass pink dresses and strappy sandals my parents put me in, it was always construction vehicle T-shirts and Lightning McQueen light-up shoes when I had my way. Barbies? Hell no. Spider-Man, all day.

Man, parents just don't understand. My dad thought my "tom-boy phase" was cute at first, then annoying, and finally evil as it persisted through adolescence. He stonewalled my efforts every step of the way to talk about my feelings. Mom was alright though; she listened to me. Sometimes. But Dad always had the final say.

***

Strolling into the garage, the copper scent of rust hit my nose with the strength of a brand-new air freshener just out of the clear, plastic packaging. Overhead fluorescent lights reflected the fresh, cherry-red paint job on the 1977 Triumph Spitfire 1500—a British classic car and two-seater convertible.

I wore an oversized Lorde (my queen) T-shirt, denim shorts, and a pair of purple, scuffed Converse sneakers. A backwards hat tucked in my sunshine-blonde hair, trimmed into a short bob.

I loved the garage, even if Dad wouldn't let me work on the car with him—that family bonding activity was reserved for Brian, my little brother.

Walking over to the black and steel tool chest, I longingly picked up a power drill and set it back down before my dad had a chance to say anything.

"Hey Dad. Hey Butthead. What are you two working on today? Need any help?" I knew there was no chance they'd let me get my hands dirty, but I tried anyway.

"Christine, language...please. Didn't you already lose your phone for the week?" Dad asked.

"Yeah, something like that," I replied. He had me there.

"We don't need any help though. We've got this covered, don't we sport?"

My brother grunted a reply from under the hood. He was smarter than me when it came to keeping his mouth shut. I'll give him that much at least.

"Does Mom need help with dinner or something?" Dad asked.

"Nope. She said she had it covered," I said.

"Well, just stay out of the way. We're kind of in the middle of something here. It's a big day. We're replacing the fuel pump. One more step to getting this kitten purring. It should be ready in another year or so, just in time for your brother to get his license."

"Fantastic," I said. My reply was tinted with enough sarcasm to scratch an itch, but hopefully not enough to piss off Dad. He didn't seem to notice.

Fox News blasted from a television mounted above the tool chest.

"...and if we let them vote again, what's next? The total collapse of civilized society as we know it." Assholes.

My dad didn't even have the decency to play music in the garage like a normal gearhead. He used to like David Bowie, but he's been reformed—terrified he'd catch the woke mind virus from 50-year-old recordings... because that made any damn sense. Coward.

I perched myself in the usual spot, a cracked milkcrate in the corner, and tried to disappear. I still learned a few things here and there, even if I wasn't allowed to work on the Spitfire.

"Hey Brian, hand me the cross peen hammer would ya?" Dad asked.

Brian walked over to the tool chest and stared at the row of hammers that hung from a pegboard. Hesitating, he reached for a ball peen.

"Nope," I chimed. That doofus barely knew the difference between an Allen and a socket wrench.

"Christine, he doesn't need your help," Dad scolded.

"Clearly he does or—"

"Enough," Dad said in a tone that meant the conversation was over. Brian's cheeks flushed red. He averted his eyes from mine—embarrassed for me because of the reprimand and for himself because of the mistake.

I pretended that how Dad treated me didn't get under my skin like those maggots I sometimes felt. But of course, it did. We used to be so close. He wasn't always like this. I swear he changed during the pandemic. He spent way too much time online chasing conspiracies long into the night and bringing his wild ideas to breakfast conversations before he'd amble up to bed.

I kept hanging around the garage clinging to a false hope that maybe he'd just snap out of it one day. I wasn't ready to give up on him yet.

Bored, I shuffled through a stack of *Omni* magazines and chose one I hadn't read before. Published in print from 1978 to 1997, each issue was a time capsule of science, science fiction, and fantasy with a dash of fiction infused with parapsychology and pseudoscience. The advertisements were the most entertaining of all the features. Star Trek chess sets, fantasy book club subscriptions, and self-help guarantees.

Want to expand your consciousness? Send for a free booklet from THE ROSICRUCIAN ORDER!

The Back Machine will give you instant pain relief!

Stressed out? Try our meditation cassette tapes and calm your intrusive thoughts!

One ad in particular caught my eye.

Are you willing to invest in your future?

Try Best-Life-4-U and transform into your ideal self!

You will NOT be disappointed!

Our patented formula is individualized based on one question:

Who do you want to become?

Send your response, $5, and a self-addressed envelope to P.O. Box #26, Tampa,
Florida

I mean, there was no way the *Best-Life-4-U* corporate office still existed after all these years. I was intrigued though, and I had five bucks to spare. Glancing up to make sure neither Dad nor Brian were paying me any attention (like I had to check), I ripped out the page, folded it, and put it in my pocket.

***

I had to ask Dad tonight about enrolling in the automotive vocational track at my high school. The application deadline is tomorrow. With only a year left before graduation, I was already a year behind in the program, but I knew I could catch up.

Helping Mom get dinner on the table, the sweet and savory smell of orange chicken filled the kitchen. This was one of my favorite recipes that grandma used to make for us, and I had wanted to learn how to make it anyway. I mean, Dad still wouldn't give me my phone back so what else was I going to do? In my mind, I rehearsed what I was going to say.

Silverware clinked and glasses shifted, everyone took the same seats at the dining room table—Dad at the head like a king and the rest of us on the sides like his subjects. Before we started eating, I took my hat off without being asked—trying to grease the wheels and start things off on the right foot.

Palms sweaty, and cheeks flushed, I stammered out my question.

"So, uhh, Dad," I started. I mustered every last drop of fortitude I could manage to give this conversation a fair shot. I really wanted this. "You know I've always wanted to be a mechanic, right? Well, I know working on the Spitfire is a you and Brian thing so I don't want to intrude. So, uhh, I was thinking about enrolling in the automotive program at school, you know, so I could learn some skills before I graduate. There's only so much I can learn in metal shop."

Dad cleared his throat and slowly placed his silverware on his plate. This wasn't a good sign.

"Christine," Dad said. "You know how I feel about this. You shouldn't be getting your hands dirty with oil and grease. It's not ladylike. You know how many women mechanics I've seen in my life? Zero, exactly zero."

"Yeah, but that doesn't mean women *can't* do the job. It just means that girls have been discouraged from doing so, you know, like by their dad." I pushed too far, but he didn't exactly leave any hope for this conversation to end in anything other than disaster.

"Enough, Christine. My answer is no, and it's not changing," Dad said with finality.

"Can we at least log some more driving hours soon so I can get my license? I'm old enough." I thought maybe he'd say yes to my second question as a consolation prize.

"We'll talk about it some other time," Dad replied. No such luck.

"It's always another time!" I slammed my fists on the table. I wasn't sticking around for the aftermath. I dashed upstairs and slammed my bedroom door. I'd deal with the consequences tomorrow.

I refused to cry and let Dad get the best of me yet again.

Okay, yeah, so of course I cried. Lay off, alright? My dad's reaction was completely predictable. But it still hurt. There I said it. I'm not as invincible as I like to pretend.

Thankfully, I had a turntable and growing vinyl collection. You know, since my phone was taken away and all that noise. Music was my escape. I spun Queen's *A Night at the Opera*. Freddie Mercury was my gender god, and he always made me feel a bit better.

I started picking up clothes off the floor and throwing them in a laundry basket. One less thing to get scolded about when Mom eventually came to console me.

Checking pockets as I went, I came across the folded-up advertisement from *Omni* magazine.

Who do you want to become?

Punk'n'roll! I had no more tears left to shed. It was time to buckle up and take action.

I figured I'd give it a whirl. I had five bucks and a dream. Besides, the most likely outcome was a big, fat nothing-burger. So, what did I have to lose?

***

I checked the mail every day with a heart full of hope. I knew it was silly, but there wasn't a whole lot else to look forward to at the moment. I certainly wasn't getting my phone back anytime soon. School was the worst, and I was trapped at home without a driver's license.

And finally, two weeks after I sent my order in the mail—BLAM!

Sprinting home and bounding up the stairs to my room, I ripped open the package.

I held a tiny Ziploc bag that contained about a tablespoon of black powder. There was a "*Best-Life-4-U*" sicker on one side and instructions on the other. *Mix powder with 4 oz of water until dissolved, then drink.* This was sketchier than a conversion therapy camp.

What was I doing? Who knows what this stuff was made of, and how was it possible *Best-Life-4-U* still existed after at least 30 years since the ad was printed? Biting my lip, doubts crept in and threatened to derail my plans.

Dad had taken so much control of my life away from me and this was a decision that was mine, all mine. A tingling jolted through my body as adrenaline flowed at the realization.

My decision.

I found a water bottle in my backpack with just a bit of musty water left in it. Tearing open the packet, a funky swamp smell quickly hit my nose. I dumped the powder in, closed the lid, and shook it up.

Gulp. Down the hatch. Go big or go home, am I right?

It tasted exactly like it smelled—swampy, stale, and sour.

Don't try this at home, kids.

It was late enough in the evening that no one would bother me.

I laid on my bed and stared at the walls—a pink and purple swirl with streaks of glitter paint. When I was seven years old, my parents refreshed my room's decor from the butter-yellow of a baby's room into a unicorn themed eyesore. I didn't want it. I didn't ask for it. I didn't like it. I wanted a racecar-shaped bed with shelves to display all my Hot Wheels.

My body oozed beads of a hot, slick sweat. I shed my shirt to cool off and wiped my forehead with it, leaving a dirty streak of brown.

What the hell?

Touching my forehead, my fingers came away moist with more sweat. I sniffed them.

Motor oil.

A wave of nausea roiled within me—my belly threatened to empty itself at any moment. My vision blurred into a pinprick of perception as the room turned and rotated around me. Blood pounded with the rhythm of pumping pistons. Closing my eyes, light specks danced on the back of my eyelids like stoplights at night after it rained.

My fingertip thrummed with a static tingle. A high-pitched yelp escaped my lips as the pins and needle sensation turned into an electric sting. Pain shot from the base of my skull with the speed of a Formula 1 race car. A scorching stench of grease overwhelmed my senses. Exhaust lingered on my tongue.

Staring at my fingertip, something solid and silver broke through its surface—a protrusion of cold metal. Despite my dizziness, I sprung out of bed. I felt every carpet thread beneath my bare feet.

Two inches... three inches... seven inches.

I shook my head and tried to erase what I saw in front of me.

A flat head screwdriver stuck straight out of my finger.

I thought the powder was going to be a total scam.

A jolt of pain sent me to my knees, then to my back.

Was it a full moon tonight?

Writhing on the floor, molecules moved within my DNA and shifted around every fiber of my being—rearranging me into something new, something different.

I shut my eyes tight. I couldn't watch any longer.

Convulsing, my body jerked around, movements uncontrolled from throbbing spikes of agony that came and went.

Breathe in, breathe out.

Until finally... it stopped. I laid on the floor and took stock. I hadn't lost consciousness, so that was a good sign. Right? I raised myself off the floor and opened my eyes.

Standing in front of my full-length mirror, I saw myself, like, *really* saw myself.

My jaw dropped, and my eyes flared red like a check engine light.

Screwdrivers, socket wrenches, and drill bits extended from fingers on my left hand. Waving them in front of my face, I clinked them together to make sure they were solid.

Clink. Clink. Clink.

I focused on the flat head screwdriver.

Whirrrrrrrrr.

It spun at a high velocity.

Sick!

My other hand had no fingers at all, replaced with the head of a claw hammer—its steel glistened. There were other thoughts that probably should have come to mind, but my first question was what would I do if I needed a rubber mallet for some finesse work? And with that thought, the claw hammer's head twisted around like a toy top. Once it stopped, a rubber mallet head stood fixed in its place. I was like a superhero made from tools!

There were other changes too—a patch of my arm became a belt sander, elbow joints replaced with hose connections for compressed air, and kneecaps accentuated with spinning saw blades.

Warmth prickled my skin, and I almost levitated off the ground with a wraith-like weightlessness.

My body was mine, all mine. Those skin-maggots wouldn't show up again anytime soon.

I blasted X-Ray Spex's *Germfree Adolescence*—a perfect punk album that totally fit my mood. Dancing around my bedroom for the first time in a long time, a calm washed over me.

I felt like I was exactly who I was supposed to be.

***

I spent an hour exploring my body and figuring out how it all worked.

Glancing at my Care Bears wall clock, another childhood relic I never wanted, it was just after eleven o'clock. If I got started now, I might finish before anyone came downstairs for breakfast.

I threw on a Lil Nas X t-shirt and crept barefoot downstairs. Slipping into socks and closed toe boots (safety first!), I opened the door from the kitchen to the garage.

After a dramatic pause for my own amusement, I flicked on the fluorescent lights. There she was—wait a second, why are cars always referred to as femme? Something clicked in my brain. Ah, because they are objects of affection. *Objects.* Of course. Gross.

So there *he* was. The 1977 Triumph Spitfire 1500.

Shoving a grease covered rag into the back pocket of my denim shorts, I got to work dismantling the Spitfire bolt by bolt, nut by nut, and screw by screw. It's always a lot easier taking something apart than it is putting it together. With my new body, I worked with an accelerated efficiency.

I started with the engine block. Sparks flew. Heat flashed across my face. Sweat rolled down my back.

Bang. Bzzzzz. Brrrrrrrrrr.

Radiator. Chassis. Transmission. Suspension. Steering system. All broken down and placed in a heap of metal.

Fans, belts, and hoses—every last one disconnected and discarded.

Dad is going to be so angry. I can't wait to see the look on his face. Maybe this little stunt will get his attention that I'm serious about what I want from my life. Or maybe he will kick me out. The corners of my mouth turned upward in a sly grin.

I am no longer Christine.

I am me.

I am Carburetor Chris.

About Sam Logan

Sam Logan (he/him) emerged in 1984 from the depths of the Chesapeake Bay off the Maryland shore. He made it to Oregon where he is a university professor in kinesiology and teaches courses about punk and body horror. Sam lives with his partner, kiddo, and Dune the dog. He has stories in Mouthfeel Fiction, Punk Noir Magazine, Divinations Magazine, Major 7th Magazine, Creepy Pod, Wallstrait, Lunatics Radio Hour, among others. Find him at samloganwrites.com. He is a co-founding editor of SLUGGER magazine sluggerfiction.com.

Facing
Mark Pariselli

Sweat gleamed on the back of Alicia's neck. To Morgan, it almost sparkled, reflecting the classroom's fluorescent lighting. She gripped her desk, resisting the urge to lunge forward and lick the slick skin of the girl sitting in front of her. Morgan salivated, imagining the salty taste at Alicia's hairline, below her pert ponytail. Would she also taste chlorine? Alicia was on the swim team, perpetually late to first period. She would rush in, still slightly damp from a locker-room shower, and take her seat ahead of Morgan.

The teacher's monotonous drone faded further into background noise.

Transfixed, Morgan watched a single droplet of perspiration slowly drip past the freckles she had memorized before disappearing underneath the neckline of Alicia's T-shirt. As if sensing Morgan's intense gaze, Alicia whipped around. Morgan quickly averted her eyes but still caught Alicia's suspicious glare.

***

Morgan flushed the toilet and emerged from a bathroom stall. Two popular girls squawked and preened at the sinks. Morgan hesitantly approached and turned on a faucet. Out of the corner of her eye, Morgan watched the pair rearrange hair, retouch powder and reapply pastel shades to pouting lips. The blonde girl enthusiastically switched conversation topics to prom but paused and elbowed her friend.

"Hey Bethany, what's the difference between acne and a Catholic priest?"

"What, Trudy?" asked the brunette.

"Acne waits until a boy's twelve before it comes on his face."

The girls laughed, packed their purses and exited.

Morgan looked up from the water gushing out of the faucet and studied her reflection in the mirror. She watched her cheeks blush, her blemishes reddening. The sound of the rushing water amplified. She turned slightly to the side so the light caught her deep acne scars. Fresh whiteheads and oily bumps seemed to shine. She leaned closer to the mirror and squeezed a pimple bulging above her right nostril. It audibly popped, splattering the glass with pus. Morgan smeared the milky discharge across the reflection of her face.

***

The cool breeze felt good blowing Morgan's hair back as she pedaled home on her bike. Through her headphones, the frontwoman of a grunge band howled. Morgan picked up the pace, relishing a sense of forward momentum and increasing distance from the bathroom incident. Legs pumping and calf muscles flexing, she sped past the library and the town's one-screen cinema. She cut across the main street into one of the nicer neighbourhoods. Manicured lawns behind wrought iron fences. As she rounded a corner, her front tire hit a stick on the sidewalk. She hit the brakes, but the bike jerked to the right. She toppled over, scraping her knee on the pavement. Morgan rolled into a seated position and inspected her torn pant leg.

A shadow fell across her as a figure advanced. Morgan looked up. The grunge song provided a distant soundtrack, faintly audible through Morgan's headphones strewn across the sidewalk. Alicia approached, the late afternoon sun glinting behind her.

"You okay?"

"Yeah," Morgan said weakly.

"Are you sure?" Alicia asked, crouching to level with Morgan. As if in response, the wound on Morgan's knee opened up, leaking blood. Embarrassed, she tried to cover it with her hand. Alicia stood and pointed to a mansion down the street.

"I live right over there. We should clean that up."

***

Limping, Morgan followed Alicia through a dimly lit hall. She glanced at framed family portraits decorating the walls. A blur of straight, white-toothed smiles and smooth complexions. Alicia led Morgan into her bedroom.

"Have a seat, I'll be right back," Alicia said.

Morgan awkwardly perched on the pristinely made bed, trying to avoid bleeding on the comforter. Across from her loomed a shrine of Alicia's swimming accomplishments. Shelves of trophies and medals contrasted with the rest of the room's frilly pink girlishness. Alicia returned with a moist facecloth, rubbing alcohol and bandages. She knelt below Morgan. Morgan gasped as Alicia dabbed the facecloth around her wound, brushing away pebbles and dirt. Once the wound was cleaned and bandaged, Alicia sat beside Morgan. Morgan became aware of how fast her heart was beating.

"Thank you," Morgan mumbled.

Alicia observed Morgan's jacket made of scrap patches of denim and adorned with rock band buttons and safety pins. She touched her arm.

"This is cool. Where did you get it?"

"I made it."

"No way," Alicia said. She stroked her fingers upwards along Morgan's bicep.

"My mom used to make all my clothes. She taught me how to sew," Morgan admitted.

Alicia's fingers left Morgan's arm. She reached out and gently caressed Morgan's cheek. Morgan flinched. No one had ever touched her like this. She didn't even like touching herself. But Alicia's hand was soft and soothing. Morgan nuzzled her palm. Alicia leaned closer and kissed Morgan. Morgan's eyes widened in surprise as Alicia's tongue slithered into her mouth. Time seemed to slow down, congeal and ooze like honey. A calming warmth spread throughout Morgan and she relaxed into the kiss. Alicia gradually pulled back. Time returned to normal speed.

Alicia gazed sweetly at Morgan.

"If you say anything, no one will believe you. Pizza Face."

The childhood insult stung Morgan like a slap. She hadn't heard it in years.

A sinister smirk snaked across Alicia's face.

Morgan fled.

***

Signalling the start of first period, the bell rung overhead. Morgan steered a path through other students rushing and jostling in the busy hall. She passed a small group of kids gathered under a handmade sign reading "Prom Tickets." Bethany and Trudy sat at a fold-up table. Alicia strolled over and instigated a discussion. Hurrying to her locker, Morgan stooped and tried to hide behind the bodies of passersby. As her locker came into view, she slowed her pace. Something was taped to her locker door. She couldn't make it out through the throng.

Cautiously, she approached. It came into focus—a takeout menu from the town's pizza joint. Morgan quickly ripped it off, scrunching it tightly in her fist. She turned her head and peered down the hall. Snickering, Bethany and Trudy stared back.

Alicia looked over her shoulder and blew Morgan a kiss.

***

Morgan slammed the bathroom stall door closed and locked it. Choking back sobs, she collapsed onto the toilet seat. She tried to slow her breathing and blink away the tears forming in her eyes. Afraid she would scream; she covered her mouth. The pain needed to be released another way. Frantically, she rolled up her pant leg and ripped off the bandage covering her knee. A fresh scab, not yet crusted, had begun to form over the wound. Morgan dug her fingernail through the tender layer, into her cut. Fluid seeped from the slit.

****

Morgan's knee ached as she exited the high school. Specks of red dotted her pant leg where her wound had bled through a makeshift dressing of toilet paper. She approached the bike rack at the side of the brick building but stopped short. Her bike leaned to one side, both tires slashed.

****

Silence was cracked by the firing of a starter gun. Eight female swimmers dove into the water, shattering the still surface of the high school pool. Arms driving, legs thrashing, the swimmers neared the far wall, flip turned and pushed off onto the final lap. A packed crowd leaned forward in the bleachers. The swimmers stroked into the final stretch. Two girls broke away from the pack. They struggled for supremacy. One of the girls' strokes grew clumsy and desperate. The other girl elegantly knifed through the water, her hands splitting and slicing the surface. In a final burst of exertion, the two girls propelled toward the wall. Just a moment before her opponent, the graceful swimmer touched first. The crowd stood and cheered. Breathing heavily, the winner ripped off her bathing cap and goggles, revealing Alicia. She turned to face the fans. Partly obscured by raised arms and clapping hands, Morgan glowered from the bleachers.

****

Steam swirled thickly in the small bathroom. Beads of moisture clung to the stained walls. Morgan lay in the bathtub wearing a black one-piece swimsuit much like Alicia's racing suit and a pair of goggles. While one hand gripped the side of the tub, Morgan used the other to pleasure herself. She recalled carefree days as a young girl playing Mermaids with Alicia in the outdoor pool behind the old house. Before Morgan's father left and she and her mother were forced to move. Before Alicia drifted away. Before Morgan's skin erupted.

She remembered the exploratory innocence of kissing Alicia for the first time. It was late summer. The pool water was warmer than the air, electric with the threat of an impending storm. Thunder rumbled in the distance. Warned of the hazards of lightning strikes while swimming outdoors, the girls knew they should go inside. But the risk only encouraged their giggling and splashing. The wind picked up. Juvenile play took on a dangerous edge. The sky darkened. Raindrops began to fall, shockingly cool compared to the water. Thunder boomed directly overhead, and the remaining light took on an eerie, purplish hue. Shivering, Morgan and Alicia swam up against each other. As the falling droplets turned into crashing sheets, they dove under. With the rain pummeling above, reverberant in their water filled ears, the girls kissed, sharing oxygen between their lips.

As she neared climax, Morgan opened her mouth, took a deep breath and plunged below the surface of the bath water.

***

Steam dissipated. Morgan stood in front of the medicine cabinet mirror watching her reflection materialize. She pulled back the edges of a nourishing facemask. Peeling if off completely, she exposed her raw, inflamed complexion. She spat at the mirror. Saliva dribbled down the reflection of her face.

***

Illuminated by her cellphone screen, Morgan reclined in bed. She longingly scrolled through social media, past elaborate promposal posts and soft glam makeup tutorials. She was ashamed to acknowledge that despite her punk posturing, this is what she coveted. The glaring images seemed to accelerate, flickering across Morgan's eyes until she abruptly turned off her cellphone, engulfing the room in darkness.

***

From her vigil in the bushes lining the side of Alicia's house, Morgan watched Trudy and Bethany exit the front door. Confirming their arrival time for a prom pre-drink at another kid's house, they climbed into matching expensive cars and sped off. Morgan ducked below a low hanging branch as she creeped through fragrant foliage. The setting sun cast her in a ghostly blue glow. Silently, she slunk closer to the back door. She reached out and found her assumption to be true—in this town, the rich didn't bother locking their doors and windows, even at night. She slid the door open and slipped inside. The house was silent, until a shower could be heard turning on upstairs. Morgan climbed the staircase and tiptoed through the dim hall. This time, she didn't glance at the portraits on the walls. Morgan focused on the sliver of warm light emanating from Alicia's bedroom doorway. She stalked toward it and pushed the door open. Tendrils of steam beckoned from the en suite bathroom. The sound of rushing water rose in volume. Morgan readjusted her backpack, snuck forward and stepped into the bathroom. Behind the fogged glass of the shower door, Alicia washed shampoo from her hair. She paused as if sensing Morgan's presence. Alicia spun around to face Morgan.

***

Streetlights streaked across Morgan's eyes as she watched the library and one-screen cinema pass beyond the window. She leaned away, keeping to the shadows of the backseat. The chauffer tried to steal glimpses of Morgan through the rear-view mirror, but she lowered her head and hid behind her hair. Nervously, Morgan rubbed her sweaty palms against the cool leather interior and tried to enjoy her first ride in a limo. When the vehicle pulled up in front of the high school, Morgan rushed out before the chauffer could open her door for her.

Muffled electronic beats pounded from inside the gym. Morgan skulked around the side of the building. The back set of double metal doors decorated with streamers and balloons separated Morgan from prom. She took a deep breath, pulled open the doors and entered. Morgan squinted as she was hit by flashing strobe lights. She advanced toward the crowd dancing to the thundering music. A kid close to her decelerated as he passed, then froze in his tracks. Other nearby students turned and took notice.

Morgan wore a sparkly silver dress, shiny platform heels and Alicia's face stitched onto her own. Human skin was unlike any fabric Morgan had worked with. She had been rushed and not as gentle as she would have liked when suturing their faces together. Some of the holes were ripped where she had pulled the thread tight too quickly. Though a surgical needle would have been preferred, Morgan was pleased with her artisanship. Alicia's once perfect skin felt slimy and comfortingly warm against her own. Alicia's juices trickled down Morgan's cheeks and throat, staining the neckline of her dress.

Screams were drowned out by the throbbing bass.

Morgan raised her arms and slowly twirled.

She smiled and tasted Alicia's blood.

About Mark Pariselli

Mark Pariselli is a queer writer and filmmaker based in Toronto, Canada. His award-winning short films have screened at numerous national and international festivals. His writing has been published on *Bloody Disgusting*, *Talk House*, *Rue-Morgue*, *Certified Forgotten* and in an anthology from HellBound Books. Visit markpariselli.com for more information.

Love the Skin You're In
Catherine Crow

THE COAT HANGER HOOK screeches across the rack, protesting its metal-on-metal affliction. Rose winces, shooting her best friend Chiara an apologetic look. "Sorry."

Chiara shifts her gaze from a maroon cocktail dress gripped between her fingers, and narrows her eyes. "It wouldn't keep happening if you weren't so damn picky! What are you even looking for?" She swipes the dress off the rack, adding it to the pile draped over her arm.

"I'll know when I see it." Rose sighs, dismissing four more dresses.

When Chiara suggested they spend Saturday trolling through second-hand shops for formal dresses, Rose had been apprehensive. Clothes shopping was an open invitation for her low self-esteem to dictate.

"Come on!" Chiara had begged. "Mum gave me a two-hundred-dollar budget, *including* the formal ticket. I want professional hair and make-up done, so I *need* to find a cheap dress!"

Dropping her gaze, Rose sees her chubby imperfections through the material, imprinted into her memory. *Why did I think I would be able to look good in a dress?* She sighs. "Maybe I just won't go. It's not like I could get a date anyway."

Chiara turns, her red curls bouncing. "You would have to *ask* someone to know you couldn't get a date."

"Like I would put myself through the humiliation of rejection," Rose mutters under her breath. *Instead, I will be the fat third wheel to my best friend and her girlfriend.* "Is Phoebe meeting us later? I thought you would want to coordinate outfits with her?" Rose steps to the right, ready to dismiss another rack of dresses.

"It's her final cricket match today..." Chiara's words trail off into silence. Her gaze is focused over Rose's shoulder as she points. "Look."

Rose turns around and gapes at the vision before her. "Holy shit!"

A formal dress is displayed on a mannequin. Black and strapless, a stitched filigree pattern roams the material. The satin skirt is floor length—curved pleats create shiny, onyx folds.

"It's stunning!" Chiara says.

Rose brushes her fingertips against the material. The soft satin sends a soothing tickle across her skin.

It's perfection.

She hugs her frumpy frame as doubt sets in. "It feels like it's a designer brand. I doubt it will fit me."

Chiara walks around to the rear of the mannequin and peels down the back of the dress. "Hmm... there doesn't seem to be a brand tag—oh wait! No, it's just the size." She squeals. "It's an eighteen!"

Rose steps back, taking in the gown. It's fitted to a waif of plastic. A slim body of manufactured perfection.

"There's no way that's an eighteen." She shakes her head.

A *click* draws her eyes to the mid-section as the material expands.

"They clipped up the back with this to make it fit." Chiara brandishes a heavy-duty bulldog clip.

"Yeah, but—"

"And it's totally affordable!"

A price tag attached to a nylon string with a safety pin is thrust toward Rose. Her jaw drops. *No way!* "Forty dollars? How's it only forty dollars!" Her voice reaches a pitch high enough to garner attention from other shoppers.

Chiara giggles, poking her head out from behind the mannequin. "I never thought I would see you excited over a dress." Readjusting the pile in the crook of her arm, she stands and unzips the dress.

"Do you think we need to ask if I can try it on?" Rose's eyes dart around the store. "It's on display. Maybe it's special."

Crouching, Chiara looks up at her friend through the mannequin's thigh gap and rolls her eyes. "This is Salvos. Not Chanel."

The satin swishes as it's pulled away.

"You need to try this on!" Chiara offers the dress at arm's length, her expression serious.

Rose opens her mouth to decline as thoughts swirl in her mind. *What if it doesn't fit? Or worse, if it does and it isn't flattering?*

As she considers the black material flowing from her friend's grip, an overwhelming feeling settles in her chest. A curiosity. A *need*.

Screw it.

Taking the dress, Rose walks toward the changing rooms. A flimsy looking rod holds a three-quarter length curtain. A full-length mirror is glued to the back partition. Stepping inside, she strains the curtain to its absolute width. Once it stops swaying, she is satisfied her modesty is protected.

Kicking off her boots, she pulls down her jeans and steps out of them. Her peripheral vision captures the sight of her thick, pasty thighs. She turns her back to the reflective surface. Removing her oversized NIN t-shirt, she drops it in a crumpled ball next to her pants.

Shit, it's a strapless dress.

Frowning, she unclips her bra strap and the cups fall away, her ample breasts conforming to gravity.

Here goes nothing...

Stepping into the dress, she shimmies her hips, sliding it up her body. She scrunches her eyes shut, waiting for the inevitable. The moment that it's blocked by her chubby thighs or belly. Her hands are at her armpits before she peeks.

It fits!

Fingers fumbling, she finds the zipper and glides it up effortlessly.

Now for the reveal. Facing her demons, she turns and looks in the mirror. *Oh. My. God.*

The dress is transformative.

The bodice pinches her waist to create an hourglass figure, but it's as comfortable as a second skin. The satin skirt is thick, yet the weight feels light like tulle. Her breasts are supported and cupped, offering ultimate cleavage—something she could never achieve without a decent bra. It hugs her frame like it was tailored to her exact measurements. An opalescent sheen shimmers, a detail revealed by movement.

Her hand goes to her long bob, fingering blue-black strands that complement the fabric. *It matches my hair.*

"Is it on yet? Let me see!" Chiara whines.

The bell-shaped skirt swishes as Rose spins in the cramped space. Pulling aside the curtain, she steps out.

Hands covering her mouth, Chiara mumbles something incoherent.

"What?" Rose asks.

Chiara drops her hands. "You look amazing!"

Heat rushes to Rose's cheeks as she fingers the skirt nervously. "You don't think it's too much for a year twelve formal?"

Chiara shakes her head. "You *have* to wear that dress. It was made for you!"

A foreign feeling washes over Rose—pride in her appearance. She straightens up, juts her chin forward and nods. *I'm finally beautiful.*

"Now that you're sorted, get changed and help me decide which of these are the one." Chiara shakes the myriad of dresses in her clutches.

After Chiara has tried on every dress from her collection (and a couple twice) she finally decides on the maroon cocktail dress. "I know they say redheads shouldn't wear red, but it's maroon, so it doesn't count right?"

"You wear red all the time," Rose says.

"Well, that's why I'm going with maroon. It's red adjacent." She swats Rose's forearm playfully before turning away. "I'm just going to put the rejects back," she says over her shoulder. "I'll meet you at the counter."

A middle-aged woman stands behind the register, smiling warmly as Rose approaches. A volunteer badge pinned to her lapel says her name is Brenda. "Did you find what you were looking for?" She reaches out to take the dress.

Rose hesitates, not wanting to let it go. She clenches her grip, her knuckles white. The thought of relinquishing the dress is unbearable, like it's a piece of herself.

"Have you changed your mind?" the cashier prompts. "I can put it back if you want—"

"No!" Rose's eyes go wide. "Of course I want it!" The words tumble from her mouth in a rush as she thrusts the dress onto the counter.

"Okay then." Brenda finds the price and inspects the size tag. Her eyes flit from the tag to Rose.

"Is there something wrong?"

"It's funny, I could have sworn it was a size ten." She raises her eyebrows. "Perfect fit for the mannequin."

Her words leave a sting, and Rose adjusts her shirt, shifting uncomfortably.

"Well, you were wrong. It says right there, size eighteen." Chiara steps up to the counter, leaning forward and challenging the shop assistant with a piercing gaze.

A small smile works its way across Rose's lips at her friend's valiant defence.

"I do see a lot of clothes every day. I must have gotten it mixed up with another dress." Brenda dismisses her previous comment with a wave of her hand and continues the purchase, yet her smile no longer reaches her eyes. "Will that be cash or card?"

Rose removes her wallet from her pocket and hands over a fifty dollar note. The odd moment passes, and Brenda is purely professional.

But something on her face tells me she was so sure of the size of the dress.

Brenda slides Rose her change and places the gown in a large recyclable plastic bag.

Relief floods Rose as she's handed the bag. *It's mine. It's really mine.* "Thank you," she says.

"You're welcome."

Brenda rings up Chiara's purchase with no small talk.

As they head toward the exit, Chiara launches into excited chatter. "I hope Phoebe likes it! She could wear..."

Rose zones out, slipping a hand inside the bag to finger the soft material. The feel of the satin between her fingers is comforting, like a hit of dopamine.

***

"Night, Mum," Rose calls over her shoulder as she goes to her bedroom.

"Good night, sweetie."

A low gurgle emits from Rose's stomach—a hunger pang. She had decided that she needed to watch what she ate. *If I can't fit into that dress...*

Opening her bedroom door, she breathes a sigh of relief at the view. Her perfect dress is suspended against the closet, attached to a satin coat hanger.

The style is high-class gothic, and she imagines it was previously owned by royalty. She closes her door with the smallest click, like the dress is a baby she doesn't want to wake.

An itch tingles at her hip and she scratches it absentmindedly. Sitting on her bed, she stares at the dress. A yearning to feel pretty again seeps into her chest. The skin on her right thigh throbs and she claws at her pants to relieve the itch. *Maybe I should try it on again. To make sure it still fits.*

During her undressing, her nails scrabble at different parts of her flesh, leaving red marks. Her skin is aggravated and she sucks air through her teeth, trying to ignore the feeling.

Removing the gown from the hanger, she carefully slips into it. As soon as the zip has ascended, her skin calms. She opens her closet door to view the vision she has become in her full-length mirror. "Damn, I really do look good."

Swishing around, she inspects the skirt. The damask pattern shifts based on the direction of movement.

Hang on...

Halting, she leans forward, focusing on the mirror. The patterns *are* transforming.

It's probably just some illusion because it's a reflection.

She looks down and gasps.

The curls of the provincial pattern pulse, slithering as they create new shapes. The delicate, floral curls are combining, creating new symbols—distorted human skulls. Their jaws are agape, suspended in silent screams.

Rose's eyes flutter, her head feels like it is full of helium. She reaches over her shoulder, clutching for the zipper to get the dress off. Fingers pressed tightly around the small metal grip, she tugs. It doesn't budge. Grimacing, she struggles with the zipper. Her feet move, shuffling to propel against the resistance. She stumbles, losing her balance, and keels over, her vision going black.

***

The muffled voice of her mother through the closed bedroom door rouses her from slumber. "Rose! Are you awake?"

Eyes opening, Rose groans. Her body aches, a familiar soreness from sleeping on a hard surface.

I slept on the floor.

She sits up, greeted by a sea of black.

I'm still wearing the dress!

Scrambling upright, terror grips her. *What if I damaged it in my sleep?* Rubbing her eyes, she assesses her reflection in the mirror. There isn't a crinkle or blemish in sight. She breathes a sigh of relief. The dress shape is entirely intact as if it was pressed and hung.

"Rose?"

"Yeah, Mum. I'm awake!" Rose looks at the clock on the wall. It's eleven.

"I'm just going to run down to the shops to grab some things for lunch. Is there anything you want?"

Rose's lip curls up in disgust at the mention of food. "No, I'm good, thanks."

"Well, if you think of anything, just text me. Love you." The sound of footsteps receding away from the door allows her to relax.

I better get this off before I ruin it.

As she reaches for the zipper, memories rush back of the previous night's struggle. She hesitates.

I probably passed out from low blood sugar. I didn't eat much last night.

She grips the clasp and tugs, expecting resistance. It slides down, the teeth opening smoothly. Sliding out of the dress she looks in the mirror and gasps.

What the hell?

The damask filigree is imprinted on her flesh. Stylish indents cover her body from below her collarbone down to her ankles. Twisting, she sees it travels all the way around, the entire pattern decorating her skin.

I must have really rolled around last night.

She runs a finger along the marks, feeling the depth of the indent.

It will fade now the dress is off.

Once the dress is hung, she carefully puts it in her closet, pushing aside the other clothes to the wall. None of her attire is good enough to be in close proximity to such a treasure. She pulls on some black tights and a hoodie, inspecting her regular frame in the mirror with a frown.

If only I could wear the dress all the time.

Her skin tingles and she scratches her waist to relieve the sensation.

***

"Are you okay?" Chiara dumps her school bag down on the wooden bench and raises her eyebrows.

"Yeah. I just don't feel great," Rose says.

The marks from the dress have not faded. Her skin is hot and burning with discomfort.

"Maybe you should eat something." Chiara pulls out a muesli bar and flicks it toward Rose, who eyes it with distaste.

"Later." She pockets the bar to placate her friend, planning on throwing it out as soon as she gets near a bin.

"Do you have chickenpox or something? You keep scratching."

"No I don't." Rose scoffs.

"You're doing it right now."

Rose looks down and finds her fingers scraping at the uniform covering her chest. *I didn't even know I was doing that.*

"What is that?" Chiara points, craning her neck toward the dress collar. "I think you have a rash."

"Hey guys." Phoebe dumps her bag on the ground and sits down next to Chiara.

"Hey babe." Chiara scopes their surroundings. "No teachers." She smiles and brings Phoebe in for a quick kiss.

Rose pulls down the back of her uniform to bring the collar up higher, hiding the blemish. Her fingers creep back up to her chest to soothe the incessant itch. "Hey Phoebe."

She smiles and Phoebe nods in acknowledgement.

"Maybe you should go home if you're sick." Chiara throws a side glance to Phoebe. "The formal is on Friday. I don't want us to catch anything." She leans back, like Rose is patient zero.

A smile creeps across Rose's face. *I will finally be beautiful.* "Oh, don't worry about that. I'll be there."

***

"You really shouldn't sleep in your formal dress." Rose's mother stands in the doorway, lips downturned, with one hand on her hip.

Rising from her pillow, Rose is greeted by the gown.

I don't remember putting this on last night.

"You don't want satin to crinkle," her mother says over her shoulder as she leaves.

Throwing her covers aside, she inspects the skirt. It's perfectly laid out, the material rolling naturally.

Did I put this on in my sleep?

She gets out of bed and catches her reflection. Something is *different*.

Her irises, usually a vibrant hazel, have darkened. The brown-green has metamorphosed into an oily black. She prods at her lower lids, stretching the skin away from her eyeball. Movement at the edge of the mirror captures her attention.

She's not alone.

A dark shadow, humanoid in shape, stands off to the side behind her.

Spinning around, she swipes at the entity, touching nothing. Looking back at the mirror, her reflection is solitary.

Maybe I need to eat something if I'm hallucinating.

She removes the dress and winces.

The pattern is no longer pressure point marks. It's worse now: red, raised welts. Like a brand.

I think I'm allergic to the material.

Her body is tattooed with inflamed scarification. Hot to touch, it throbs from contact.

It's fine. I'll only be wearing it for a few hours.

"Mum, I'm not feeling well. I'm going to stay home from school today," she calls out before covering her mutilated body with a jumper and pants.

"If you need anything, let me know," her mum calls out.

"I might have a bath and see if that helps," Rose replies, her hand scrabbling at an itch on her back.

On her way towards the door, she looks in the mirror again.

Her eyes are normal.

A few steps into the hallway, she stops short, the hairs on the back of her neck prickling. She looks over her shoulder. A glimpse of something dark shrinks away, hiding behind the doorframe. Retracing her steps, she enters her bedroom and gasps. The dress is no longer hanging on the closet door. It's laid out on the bed like a chosen outfit for the day.

But who chose it?

Rose walks toward the bed, swallowing hard. Her movements are careful, powered by trepidation. Pinching the hem of the skirt between her thumb and forefinger, she lifts it, searching for an explanation. She peels it back, turning it inside out. Her fingers touch something rough, a scratchy material stitched into the seam. It's a handcrafted tag.

How did I not feel that before?

Carefully, she unfurls it. Stitched into it are three symbols: a seven-pointed star with all connections crossing, a Z-shaped sigil with lines of various lengths forking from the center and an X with a circle resting between the top points.

What is that?

Her thumb trails over the edge, and she hisses as a sharp sting penetrates her thumb. Inspecting her pad, she finds a small pin prick, a single drop of blood bubbling to the surface.

She blinks, and the dress is no longer on the bed.

Spinning around, she finds it hanging on her closet door.

A hushed whisper fills the room, the direction of the source atmospheric. It surrounds her, a feminine hiss overlapping, speaking a foreign language. Blood rushes in her ears like a roaring river. It bangs behind her temples and she grips the sides of her skull, crying out. Her vision blurs, fading into darkness.

***

Bright lights sting Rose's vision as she wakes. Squinting, she looks around. A steady beeping to her right reveals a monitor. Her index finger feels heavy. She looks down to see an oxygen meter clipped to it. A cannula pumps clear fluid into her veins.

"Oh, baby, you're awake!" Her mother leaps from a plastic chair, filling her vision with red rimmed eyes brimming with tears.

"Am I in the hospital?"

Her mother nods. "I came home and found you passed out in your room, so I called an ambulance." Her mother chokes up. "I was so scared."

Rose blinks, processing.

What's happening to me?

"Why didn't you tell me about the rash? Your skin…" Her mother curls her fingers into a fist, placing it to her mouth.

"I thought it was just an allergic reaction to the dress material. And it would settle down," Rose whispers.

"Oh, baby. No dress is worth that. The doctor said it's a severe reaction. You can't wear it."

Rage boils up inside Rose at the thought of not wearing the gown. "It's the only dress that makes me beautiful. There's nothing else I can wear. No dress will make a fat pig like me look good!" she yells.

Her mother recoils. "Rose! What has gotten into you?" Her hand flies to her chest.

Why did I say that?

Rose slumps back onto the stiff pillow. "I'm sorry, Mum." She turns her head away, tears filling her eyes. "Can we go home?"

"I'll go get the doctor. He wants to talk to you. They are giving us some cortisone for your skin." She pauses. "He also wants to talk to you about your diet."

Rose's fists clench the starchy sheets.

"Are you eating properly?"

The question hangs in the air.

Rose rolls over on her side and curls up into a ball, silently crying.

The chair scrapes on the linoleum floor, and Rose sniffles as her mother's footsteps recede.

***

Rose types; *Symbols and sigils with an X or Z,* into Google on her phone. Tucked into her own bed after being discharged from the hospital, she can't get the image of the mysterious tag out of her mind.

Images dominate the results at the top of the page. A map of magic symbols with a translation key down the side catches her attention. The three symbols on the dress are there. She clicks it. Connecting the key to each symbol, she reads their meaning.

The Z shaped one causes sleep. Her heart races. *The seven-pointed star is for magical energy.* Sweat builds on her palms, and she wipes them on the duvet. *The final symbol, the X with a circle...* She blinks rapidly, trying to process the words.

Bane: Deadly.

She tosses her phone, hands shaking as cold dread runs through her veins.

There's something wrong with the dress.

She drops to the floor and searches beneath the bed.

I know I have an empty box here somewhere...

Pushing aside some rubbish and dirty clothes, she finds what she is looking for. Sliding the box out and away from the bed, the empty space behind is revealed.

Except it's not empty.

A woman is lying on her belly, her palms flat on the carpet. Her elbows jut upwards toward the bed frame. Head tilted unnaturally, the woman stares, un-blinking. A wide grin reveals brown and yellow rotted teeth. Her clothing is old fashioned and decayed, reminding Rose of the Victorian era with puffy sleeves and torn lace frills. The woman's eyes are black orbs, and her gaze is trained on Rose.

Abandoning the box, Rose scrambles backwards on all fours, heart hammering in her chest. The terror escapes as she opens her mouth and screams.

"Rose, what's wrong?" Her mother's panicked voice floats in from beneath the door followed by hurried footsteps.

The door is thrown open, and her mother bursts in.

Looking over her shoulder at her mum, her chest heaves. Rose's lip trembles as she points to the bed. "There's something..." She turns back to look, but the woman is gone.

Her mother kneels beside her. For the first time, Rose notices greys emerging from her roots. The worry lines etched into her face appear deeper.

"Oh, baby, what can I do to help you?" Her hand rests on Rose's shoulder.

With a ragged breath, Rose places her own hand over her mother's and offers a weak smile. "Let's get rid of the dress," she whispers.

Nodding, her mum stands and collects the cardboard box.

Rose joins her, removing the dress from its closet door perch. She carefully folds it—an act of ceremonial respect. Placing it in the box feels like a sacrifice, folding away the best part of herself. It's a cheap funeral—an insult to such a lavish garment. The scars on Rose's body react to the rejection, stinging and throbbing—a physical punishment for her insubordination.

"Please, mum," Rose gasps. "Please take it. I can't bear to throw it away." She lifts the box shakily, offering it to her mum.

"I'll put it somewhere safe for now. We don't have to put it in the bin."

As the cardboard leaves her fingertips, Rose collapses onto her bed, sobbing.

As she weeps into her pillow, a hand touches her back. The mattress shifts as her mother sits beside her. The long, slow strokes are a comfort at first.

Rose sniffles.

The pressure of her mother's touch increases. The sound of nails catching on nylon is unsettling and Rose lifts her head.

"Mum, what are you—"

She rolls over and freezes.

It's not her mum.

The woman is seated on the edge of the bed. A gnarled hand with claw-like nails is poised to run down Rose's back. In her other hand is the dress. Her lips curl upward in a sneer.

Rose scrambles upright, bringing her knees up to her chest and hugging them. Her eyes are wide as her breaths quicken. "Who are you? What do you want from me?"

The woman stays silent.

Rose gestures to the gown. "You want that? Take it! I don't want it anymore."

The woman rises, leaving the dress on the bed. She points a bony, pale finger at the mirror. A thread appears, stitching into the glass, from the hand of an invisible seamstress.

Letter by letter, words form.

The curse has taken, written on your flesh.

You are bound, body and soul, to the dress.

"No!" Rose rises, defiant on shaking legs, and strips off her shirt and pants to reveal her patterned skin. "Make it go away!" she yells, scratching neurotically at the curled marks.

The woman points at her.

Rose looks down at her body. Black grows from the filigree marks like mutating spores. A new material forms—a satin cocoon spun from the cursed motif.

"No!" Rose cries.

She is in the gown.

Grabbing the zipper, Rose yanks it as hard as she can. It doesn't budge. She releases a guttural cry. "If I destroy it, then your curse will be broken!"

Gripping either side of the zipper at her back, she tugs, attempting to pull it apart. An ache rips down her spine, each vertebra spontaneously combusting into fiery objection. She cries out, releasing the material.

Teeth gritted, she digs her nails into the mid-section of the dress, scrabbling at the stitching, desperate to remove it. The scars on her body flare and she yelps, abandoning her destruction.

Before her eyes, black threads loop through her flesh, sewing the dress into her skin. She screams, feeling the insertion of each stitch.

Her index finger becomes snared in a nylon loop, and she pulls it back, snapping the thread.

Her eyes widen.

I can break them.

Looking at the stoic woman, Rose's eyes bulge, a maniacal grin plastering her face. "I can break them!"

Jerking her pain riddled body across the room, she makes it to her desk and flings open the top drawer. Bent over, she tosses the contents of the drawer asunder, her fingers finally curling around a pair of scissors. She puts the scissor blades to the stitching, and snips the threads.

Tears stream down her face. The pain reverberates through her epidermis, lighting up her nerves. Her breathing comes in bursts between gritted teeth. Blood leaks forth from the snipped threads and raw flesh, making it hard to see. The metal shears are slippery from the sanguine lubricant.

"Screw this." Rose tosses the scissors to the floor and grabs a handful of loose threads in her fist, grunting as she pulls. They snap, and she flicks the broken lengths to the floor, grabbing more. When those break, she repeats the process.

Blood drips down her pale skin, smattering the cream carpet.

The woman observes, silent.

Another thread snaps, and Rose screams, frustrated.

"Oh my God, Rose! What are you doing? Stop! Stop!" Her mother stands in the doorway with the box, the lid open, black satin spilling out.

"I have to. She's trying to kill me!" Rose points at the woman.

"Who's trying to kill you?" Her mother looks around the room.

The woman steps closer to Rose.

"Don't you see her? She's right there!" Rose's eyes are wild as she gouges at her arm.

Her mother drops the box. Black satin spills out onto the floor.

"There's no one there!" Rushing to her daughter, she grabs Rose's wrists and wrestles her hands away from her body.

"I need to get the dress off. I need to get all the threads!" Rose yells, pushing her mother away.

"Rose, you're not wearing the dress. It's there in the box on the floor..." Her mother cries, eyes wide in terror as Rose pulls another thin, ragged piece of skin from her body and flicks it aside.

About Catherine Crow

Catherine Crow is an Australian emerging horror writer who resides in the Hunter Valley in New South Wales Australia. Her day job as a school library technician means she never strays far from the written word. Demisexual by design & an ally, she supports the promotion of queer fiction both personally & professionally. With a focus on short stories, her publishing debut lies within the Skin Deep anthology. She is currently working on a collection of modern horror stories that twist social trends & themes.

Fleshbound
Hannah Baxter

SHE'D BEEN LOOKING FOR the bathroom when she found Malina flayed alive from the waist up. Malina had been hunched over the light-studded rectangular mirror, dark, tousled hair falling over her famous face in a heavy, impregnable veil. The dressing room table was a pharmaceutical rainbow of empty supplement bottles and other assorted medication. As soon as the door creaked open, she started up with a gasp. Her luscious tresses fell back to reveal a totally skinless visage.

The ghastly sight unlocked a repressed memory buried deep within Anaïs. During a school trip to Amsterdam, she'd been shanghaied from the safety of her hotel room by a group of giggling girls from her class, who promised her a night that she'd never forget. Anaïs had naively gone along with it, expecting a taboo detour from the safe sights of the city like the Rijiksmuseum to a nightclub or the infamous red-light district.

After half an hour of walking, she'd been shoved inside a large, unfamiliar building. The Body Worlds Museum, it had been called. She'd expected something like the NEMO Science Museum that they'd visited earlier that day, with interactive exhibits explaining the inner workings of the anatomy. Instead, Anaïs had been confronted with a skinless human body staring straight at her, turning a ship's wheel in its exposed flexors.

It was one of over two hundred that were housed within. They weren't plastic mannequins, but real human bodies, preserved through the process of plastination. Their human shells had been stripped off like tablecloths, pumped full of preserving polymers and arranged into positions that defied both physics and God. No matter where she turned, more horrors awaited her. A partially-muscled skeleton leaned over a red poker table while shuffling cards. Another mutilated man blew into a silent saxophone, allowing full view of his inflated lungs. Foetuses were curled up on velvet cushions, arranged in successive stages of development, from a tadpole-like embryo to a full-fledged infant. Their sunken-eyed stares had haunted Anaïs' dreams long after she'd flown back home.

Malina would have been right at home among them. The spine of her scapula variegated through the tight-strung pinkish-red muscle, disappearing under the swooping scoop back of the Vera Wang dress she wore; it was from their hotly anticipated spring collection. Malina's splenius capitis muscles tucked behind her ear elasticated with her soft, panicked breathing. The pale folds that flopped down over the chair that Anaïs assumed were a part of the garment were Malina's own skin, which she'd peeled away like the ripe yellow folds of a banana.

Anaïs did the only thing that she could think of in her shock—she slammed the door. She toppled backwards in her elevated heels, slamming backwards into the cold hard wall. Every blink embedded the image deeper into her forebrain, like a psychic mentally manifesting a thoughtograph on a blank page.

"Where have you been?"

Anaïs almost screamed at the sweaty hand that tugged her wrist. A short, heavyset man stood before her in a blaring blue Hawaiian shirt. Sweat glossed his thinning black hair like gel. His clenched hands were squared up to his chest, like a lanky lightweight who'd been placed in a ring with a world heavyweight champion.

"You said you'd be back in five!" he exclaimed, "that was ten minutes ago! You're on next!"

A spasm rippled across her long-suffering manager's face. He looked one burst blood vessel away from a full-on aneurysm.

"I'm sorry, Ben," she started, "I—I just got distracted—"

In a burst of anxiety-induced adrenaline, Ben ushered her down the hallway with the graceful speed of a ballroom dancer. Even Anaïs, who was twenty-four years younger than him, struggled to keep up. When he really wanted to, the man could move.

The low-sloping plaster ceiling broadened into a vast, curving wooden arch, its beams stacked above like the ribcage of some great leviathan that had swallowed them all whole. Located in the terraced Philbeach Gardens, St. Cuthbert's Church stood as one of the few remaining examples of nineteenth-century architecture. It was a stone-dressed brick building, designed in the tradition of Middle Age churches, with flying buttresses through which the sun flung itself and a sky-reaching spire.

Despite enduring roof damage from heavy shelling during the Second World War, it had withstood time's march to serve as the Kensington venue for London Fashion Week. The stained glass-lit interior added a gothic grandiosity to the affair.

Anaïs still couldn't believe that she was there, even with the call sheet still crumpled inside her bag. London Fashion Week was the dream of every aspiring model, but one that few got to attend. Billions were funneled into the British economy because of it. Long-awaited designs were showcased, ones that would have usually taken six months to hit the general market.

It had served as a springboard for the glittering careers of Naomi Campbell, Adwoa Aboah and Kate Moss. Now it was Anaïs' turn to strut down the catwalk that had been arranged in the lofty hollow of the church's vaulted halls. Everyone who was anyone would be there—influencers, buyers, journalists, brand executives and paparazzi. Four years of hard work had led up to this one moment, which would either make or break her entire career.

But that drive had been shifted into a stationary shock by the unexpected bump in the road. Anaïs staggered through the long, stony church halls like a zombie. Stylists swarmed her like a buzzing pack of bloodthirsty mosquitoes. They attacked her eyelashes with mascara, smearing them kohl black. Anaïs didn't even bat an eyelid as a black and lime striped balaclava was pulled down over her head. If there was anything Anaïs had learnt as a model, it was that fashions shows were notoriously changeable.

Seconds before she was due to go down the runway, she'd been asked to slip into a different pair of shoes. Not wanting to be branded as 'difficult,' Anaïs did her best to be flexible. However, there were times where she'd stretched herself so thin that she was in danger of disappearing.

Anaïs had always admired the airbrushed beauty of the models that pouted demandingly on the glossy fashion magazine covers, lounging in swimsuits across two-page spreads. She never dreamed that one day she would be one of them. Every day, she dreaded that her Cinderella life would come to an end, and she'd wake up a pumpkin again.

An awkward emergence into puberty and cruel classmates had browbeaten her into thinking she was the ugliest thing alive. While sequestered away in the messy safety of her bedroom scouring the web, Anaïs had stumbled across a random YouTube video of a beauty vlogger's tutorial on how to pull off the perfect smoky eye. Like the inquisitive Alice, Anaïs had tumbled headfirst down the rabbit hole. She devoured hundreds of hours of similar content, eager brain sponging it up faster than anything at school. In time, she grew enough in skill and confidence to go out in public in full makeup.

She'd been scouted at fourteen while out window-shopping in Guildford's high street. A representative from one of London's biggest modelling agencies had mobbed Anaïs while she'd been milling over a pink floral-patterned sundress in a transparent shopfront. With the sleight of hand of a wily pickpocket, she'd slipped her card into Anaïs' bewildered hand.

"I can make you a star," she'd promised.

For the first time in her life, Anaïs believed in herself. She'd begged her understandably wary parents until they'd finally caved and drove her twenty miles from their unassuming Surrey suburb to the agency's headquarters in London. The memory of her own adolescent self-centredness still made Anaïs cringe. She had been so starstruck at the notion of being chosen that she hadn't even noticed the sacrifices her parents had made to ensure that her dreams had come true. Once she had, Anaïs threw her whole weight into it.

She'd risen at the crack of dawn, tucking into a wholesome breakfast of avocado on toast or cinnamon-sprinkled grapefruit. She'd always shown up to every shoot, even when her agent had double-booked her. Even on her days off, Anaïs still worked. She practiced yoga, contorting her body into straining positions and practiced glute bridge pulses until the lower half of her body was numb. Somehow, she'd managed to maintain her homework and her sanity alongside it.

She knew they'd been stacked in the front rows of rickety wooden chairs arranged around the catwalk. Anaïs was determined to thank them for their unwavering service by giving the performance of a lifetime.

It was during those strange, exciting first days that she'd first met Malina D'Angelo. She and Anaïs had been squeezed right next to each other in the nervous white-shirted row of teenage girls assessed by the unblinking stare of their teacher, Dorian. Though a glamorous grey-haired woman now, decades before she'd carried the moniker of the 'Wonderkid.' She was the toast of the entire fashion world, rubbing shoulders with the likes of Robert Redford and Andy Warhol back in the swinging sixties.

Dorian jabbed out a black, stiletto-nailed finger toward them, eliciting a collective flinch from the girls.

"Modelling is not just about outer looks," she'd intoned in her Zsa-Zsa Gaboresque drawl. "It is about unlocking that inner gleam."

Anaïs had never forgotten how Malina's nondescript brown eyes had sparkled at that statement. She'd cupped her hands over her heart, desperate for her practiced posture to please someone. It wasn't that Malina wasn't pretty. At five foot and seven inches, she was the ideal height for a model, tall and long-limbed without being gangly. But by the draconian standards of the modelling world, she was average at best. Unlike Cindy Crawford with her distinctive facial mole or Cara Delevingne's defined eyebrows, there was nothing memorable about Malina.

Even Anaïs had forgotten about her on graduation. Malina had wilted from her memory, like a pressed flower forgotten inside an old book. But after a few years of complete radio silence, Malina exploded onto the scene. Her likeness had graced the front covers of *Harper's Bazaar*, *Cosmopolitan* and *Vanity Fair*. Fashion designers clamoured to have her wear their creations. Malina's rise was nothing short of meteoric. Every week, she seemed to climb higher, until she'd half-disappeared into the clouds.

Malina had roared onto the scene on an Addison Lee bike. When she tugged off the heavy visored motorcycle helmet, there wasn't a single hair askew from her faultless head. Her downy curls nested inward at the nape of her neck, like sleeping snakes in Medusa's tresses. Her glacial gaze froze everyone in the room solid. As she sashayed right past them, a dozen heads swivelled after her, mouths agog.

Anaïs was stunned when she realized who was she staring at. Malina was no longer the bashful girl that she remembered. Her generic prettiness had bloomed into a legendary beauty. It was something that came along once in a thousand years, that made great statesmen swoon and for which poets write hundreds of reams of verse. She was Helen of Troy, gazing impervious from the pillared palace as two kingdoms fought over her. On her Instagram, she lounged in steel-backed deckchairs on the back of luxury yachts in plunging halter neck bikinis, like Cleopatra swimming down the Nile in her gilded pleasure barge. That face would cement Malina's name in history alongside theirs.

Like the rest of the world, Anaïs assumed it to be plastic surgery. The modelling world's murky underbelly was teeming with parasitical plastic surgeons who wouldn't think twice about operating on a teenager. Fellow models had been bullied into getting nose jobs by overbearing stage parents. Some were left with lips so swollen with filler that they couldn't even drink through a straw.

But Malina's features were too flawless to have been achieved by the most skilled scalpel. There were no telltale signs such as faint facelift incisions running down her hairline to her temples or reddened, raisin-like earlobes. Malina insisted she hadn't any work done. If Anaïs hadn't met her earlier, she'd have assumed Malina was just genetically blessed.

The closer that Anaïs peered, she recognized parts of Malina's face as belonging to other models. Malina's straight-bridged, refined nose was previously attached to Sikita Chuol, an up-and-coming South Sudanese model from Elite Faces. Her shapely pout was ripped off the heart-shaped face of Lila Living, one of Starlight

Models' best and brightest. And her famously long legs were once pasted to runway royalty Cori Van der Meer, who'd walked seventy-two shows last year alone with them. The police still hadn't found her yet.

The leftovers' lives became even more stressful. They all feared they'd been the next to disappear. While the investigations dragged fruitlessly on and the disappeared girls withered from public memory, Malina kept succeeding. She'd disappeared in the panic from investigators and reporters, all clamouring to learn her enigmas.

Now Anaïs knew. Malina was a piecemeal person who'd traded in her natural good looks for stolen parts. She'd managed to find that inner gleam by extinguishing an entire constellation's worth of stars. A foreboding heaviness settled in Anaïs' stomach as she realized that Malina would do anything to keep her secret.

Anaïs jumped as her phone buzzed. Sliding the screen open with a trembling thumb, she gave the screen a cautious scan. She didn't put it past this newly-formed Malina to send her some sort of threat, like a fish wrapped in newspaper. Anaïs sighed as the familiar lines of text settled like dust into her mind. *Looking gorgeous as usual. Gonna crush it.*

From three tables away, Trinity gave her a cheery wave, to the chagrin of the hairstylist trying to pin back her long black hair into a fishtail braided bun. She was dressed in a sparkling aquamarine floor-length neoprene gown with short white butterfly sleeves. Beside her, her phone played at full volume through a set of wireless earbuds. As a diehard NCTzen, Trinity knew almost all their songs by heart, with "Kick Back" as her ringtone. Under the table, her bare feet kicked up out of the uncomfortable clog heels that had been strapped onto her ankles, wriggling toes painted Barbie pink.

Anaïs had first met Trinity Kwon when they'd been paired together on a photoshoot for a designer athletic clothing brand. Trinity had come along in a cerulean crop top hoodie and grey high-rise leggings with white high-tops. Anaïs had been astounded by the high kicks that Trinity had performed for the camera. Her body bent almost boneless against the leather gym horse in the faux-gym background that the set designers had assembled. She and Trinity had redressed in matching collared court dresses, waving their racquets in the air as they'd tossed about an imaginary ball. The photographer had squealed over their chemistry and how it contributed a 'kinetic edge.' But it didn't fizzle out after that one shoot.

As a model, there was no shortage of beautiful people that trickled in and out of Anaïs' life. But Trinity was something else. Her home was already broken by the time she was born. Trinity had spent her childhood and early adolescence shuttled between her parents' native countries of England and Korea. While on a twelve-hour flight from London International Airport to Seoul, she'd been spotted in a window seat by an agency representative, who'd pounced as soon as the seatbelt sign went on.

From there, Trinity's life had taken off. She'd finally found her place on the couture runway. She'd used the acclaim she received for posing for brands such as Goen J and Zara as a springboard into other ventures; Trinity took up acting. Her roles in television advertisements led to her snagging a bit role in a popular Korean television drama *Children of the Moon.*

For someone with such a fractured background, Anaïs had been surprised by how down-to-earth Trinity was. She strolled through the world with an almost zen-like ease, just letting things happen to her, both good and bad.

"There's always a rainbow at the end of the rain," she always said.

Sometimes Anaïs wondered if Trinity even realized that she was an internationally recognized model. It was around her that Anaïs was able to relax for the first time in years.

Their relationship wasn't a staged provocation to earn themselves online clout. It had been a happy accident. Anaïs' hectic routine of attending casting calls and sorting through her portfolio had left little time for her to meet people. By the time the day was over, she'd collapse on her bed, too tired to attend any afterparties. She and Trinity found themselves aboard the same boat, rocking on an uncertain sea. They were able to joke together about the lack of job security, creepy photographers and the harsh criticisms directed at their bodies.

Anaïs playfully waggled her fingers over toward Trinity as the stylist worked on her. It was almost enough to make her forget what she'd witnessed. Anaïs had felt more beautiful around Trinity than she'd been in front of any camera flash. Unlike her bookers, Trinity had never told her to lose five pounds to be worthy of her. She could just exist, free of any outside stress. Every arm draped over the other's waist and frivolous kiss was exchanged outside the public eye, in their own quiet privacy.

Instead of the self-assured strut she'd practiced thousands of times before, Anaïs tottered down the platform as if it was a grimy, crime-ridden alley concealing a mugger who could lunge at her with a knife. She tried to keep her eyes ahead and her face passive. But Anaïs couldn't purge the image of Malina's exuviated form from her brain.

Focus, she told herself. Anaïs squeegeed her tongue against the roof of her mouth, resting it behind her top teeth. After breathing through her nose for four seconds, she held it for seven before releasing it through pursed lips for a count of eight. Anaïs repeated it four times, her elevated heart rate decreasing with each try. It was a breathing technique that she'd learned from the veteran models, which they assured her was a surefire way of overcoming pre-show jitters.

Her posture relaxed as she visualized Trinity's gap-toothed grin. It was one of the few parts of herself that her lady love was self-conscious about. Paired along with her freckles, Trinity bemoaned how childish she looked because of it. But Anaïs found it adorable. It was a rare marker of natural beauty that had managed to slip past an impossible, artificial ideal.

When she'd found out that Trinity had consulted an orthodontist about it, Anaïs had been horrified. One of her greatest fears was that Trinity's upbeat breeziness would be ground down by the image-obsessed world they resided in and she'd become a shell of her bubbly self. Anaïs had seen dozens crash and burn before. Trinity was too precious to let slip through the cracks. Just a few more hours and they'd be together again. Maybe they could even sneak in a few kisses between shows. Anaïs perked up out of her fearful stupor.

The wide church interior was packed with people, all watching extravagant men and women strut down the narrow stage. Anaïs focused her gaze on an empty chair at the very back of the vast auditorium, keeping her chin down.

She tried to pace herself to the pounding pop music that played throughout the church. Conscious of her compromised posture, she kept her hips still. The last thing that Anaïs wanted was to fall flat on her face in front of over two hundred people. She'd never live it down. Trying to distract herself from the anxiety of the audience, Anaïs redirected her eyes up to the golden day that shafted through the old flying buttresses.

Anaïs spotted her family in the left side of the stage. Her mother, with her greying red hair scooped up into a ponytail, proudly pointed Anaïs out to everyone else in earshot. Her father snapped as many pictures of her as the memory of his outdated phone would allow. Anaïs broke into a genuine smile as she struck an over the shoulder pose to a polite applause. A string of cameras flashed off in an abrupt sequence.

Anaïs' pulse flatlined when she turned around to see Malina striding towards her. With her unblinking stare and sideways shoulder swagger, Malina floated like an alligator down a river, biding its time as a log before snapping. As Anaïs passed, something silver flashed out down the lengthy seam of Malina's spine. She almost vomited right there on the catwalk when she realized that it was a zipper, sewn into Malina's new flesh. Somehow, it was the least objectionable customization she had made to her body.

Anaïs imagined her strung upside down on a meat hook like a slaughtered pig with the curving tip stabbed right through her foot. Maybe an incision had been made at her navel or at the bump of her ankle by a sharpened flaying knife, careful gloved hands tugging off her skin. That the bloody hide would be packed in an ice box before being run through a sewing machine to allow Malina to slip into it like a hideous onesie. From there on, Malina had added on stolen body parts like band patches to a jean jacket.

An even worse thought crossed Anaïs' mind. What if the process that Malina had subjected herself to was popular enough to be mechanized? Rather than humans operating on her, Malina was diced apart by pneumatic air knives that descended from the ceiling like acid rain. Once all the essential cuts had been made, the hide pullers were put to work, stripping Malina's skin like vintage wallpaper off a dilapidated wall until there was nothing left but naked musculature. Anaïs herself couldn't believe the situation that she was in. Who or what had subjected her to such slaughterhouse rituals? She wanted to ask, but she was terrified that someone might tell her.

The moment she sat down, the folded note fluttered out from the folds of Anaïs' dress, where it had been surreptitiously placed. *Meet me in the bathroom,* it read, *or I'll take a little something from your girlfriend.*

The bluntness of the message bashed Anaïs over the head like a prehistoric war club. She whirled around in a wild panic, searching for any sign of Trinity. Had Malina gotten to her already? There were countless people to turn to, but no-one to believe her. Her head throbbed with an unbearable tension.

Like a knife tearing through a thin paper screen, something far more cutting emerged. Malina had already crossed many lines. But this one would be her undoing. There was no way that Anaïs was about to let her girlfriend become another stitch in Malina's sick skin suit. She'd go, no matter the risk.

The lonely plink of the rusty tap greeted Anaïs as she crept into the stall. The soles of her feet burned with every step, begging for a pedicure. Malina leaned up against the wall, her arms crossed.

"Took you long enough," she sniffed.

Anaïs clenched fist crumpled the intercepted message into a ball, which she hurled into a nearby wastepaper basket.

"You can play all the mind games you want with me," she growled, "but Trinity is off limits. If you touch her, I swear—"

Malina leaned back. She casually tucked her hands behind her head. Anaïs wondered whether they were one of the few remaining original parts of her or if she'd stolen them off some other unfortunate girl.

"Keep your dress on, Nay. I haven't laid a finger on her yet," she laughed.

The old nickname had Anaïs ready to shatter Malina's immaculate white teeth. It was a vindictive callback to the affectionate abbreviation she'd used to gain a jumpy Malina's trust, having taken pity on seeing her always eat alone. Wretchedness clawed inside her like a caged animal. Anaïs hadn't experienced such since she'd come across her scissor-shredded dress before what was supposed to be her debut show. The culprit was never found, but Anaïs recalled Malina hovering about, quietly smug. *I'm so sorry, Nay.* The metamorphoses that they'd undergone were irreversible. She and Malina were different people now.

Malina sucked the inside of her cheek. Then, she released it with a pop loud enough to send Anaïs springing like a jack-in-the box. The sight caused Malina no end of amusement.

"Tell you what. I'll leave you both alone if you give me what I want."

Anaïs' eyebrows fluttered up into her widow's peak.

"What?" she murmured.

Malina slunk towards her, hips swaying.

"Just one little thing," she murmured, "And I'll be out of your hair forever. We're not so different, Anaïs."

Acidic vomit rose in the back of Anaïs' throat.

"I'm nothing like you!" she thundered back.

Malina's palm smacked into the tiled wall. It landed just centimetres away from Anaïs' face. Before she knew what was even happening, she was already boxed in.

"We just want to be the best possible version of ourselves. That's the only way to get ahead in this world. Sometimes you must go a few steps beyond, so you can keep ahead of the crowd."

Malina ran a knuckle down her trembling cheek. Her finger skated around Anaïs's eye socket as if it was a frozen pond.

"Come on, Nay. What's the big deal? Why can't you give me this one simple thing? All the other ones did."

The chilling hush that Malina's made Anaïs' teeth chatter. Like a breeze tickling a delicate lace hemline, she slid her hands under Anaïs' skin. Anaïs instinctively closed her eyes at the sickening squelch of muscle. Malina's fingers scaled her upper arm bones, fingertips clinging to the crevices. It was like slipping an estrogen needle into her hip, but a thousand times worse.

Before becoming a model, Anaïs had no idea who she was. The world around her insisted that she was a boy. But Anaïs knew better. She'd resisted all attempts to force her into an unfamiliar world of football, car collecting and beer. She'd been punished for it to the point she'd almost given up on living.

Discovering the makeup tutorial community had given her the courage to dress as a woman for the first time. At first, going out in public had been a tour in terror. Anaïs fretted that people would never see her the way she wanted them to. Then, like a prevailing light, that modelling scout had picked her out of the crowd and changed the course of Anaïs' life. She'd chosen the name 'Anaïs' because of the pewter-eyed Parisian glamour it evoked. It was the kind of lifestyle she craved. Modelling hadn't been just a means of income. It had allowed Anaïs to be the woman that she was always meant to be.

Malina's fingers tapped impatiently against her tendons.

"I promise to make it painless if you stay quiet."

Anaïs let out a strangled whine as she bucked against the invasive digits. Malina narrowed her eyes. The other model silenced her by shoving her into the wall, hard enough to crack the faded ceramic tiles. Malina's hidden hands bulged upwards through Anaïs' hands like a deadly clot through her veins, creeping towards her face.

"Those eyes are wasted on you," Malina whispered, "they'll fade fast. I'll keep them fresh forever."

There was no escape. Malina would reach up and pluck out her eyes from her sockets like juicy pomegranates.

"Hello?"

Trinity's disembodied voice crackled into the cramped quiet of the bathroom. Both Anaïs' squirming and Malina's intent grip slackened at the unexpected intrusion. Anaïs' eyes watered as her girlfriend giggled, uncomprehending of the danger she was in. Anaïs wanted to cry out to the woman she loved to save her. But she was in such unimaginable agony that she couldn't even mouth the words, let alone vocalize them.

"Looks like you butt-dialed me, silly," Trinity remarked. *"Lucky for you, I'm not doing anything right now. I don't know if you'll get this, but you were great. I can't wait see you tonight. Love you."*

The concluding click of the call revived Anaïs. When they were first dating, she'd been terrified about telling Trinity. But instead of breaking up with her on the spot, Trinity gave her a sweet smile while sipping on her strawberry and banana smoothie.

"Even if you were a bunch of squirrels piled in a trench coat, I'd still adore you."

God. Anaïs wanted to marry her right then and there. She was meant to die after many happy years with Trinity, watching their many children and grandchildren grow up. Not in some mildewed washroom.

With all her diminished strength, she shoved Malina off. Malina's jaw went slack, in disbelief that Anaïs had managed to resist. The weight of rejection was too much for her to bear. Malina screamed, muscles sloughing off her face to reveal a bare skull. The rest of her warped and pulsed. Muscle fibres flailed around. Layers of lifted skin unravelled off like a sliced onion.

When Anaïs dared open her eyes again, she found a fleshy, shapeless mass crawling across the bathroom floor, more liquid than woman. Just then, her phone vibrated. Anaïs shakily picked it out of her pockets.

"Hello?" she faltered.

"*Anaïs!*" Ben beamed, "*you were spectacular tonight!*"

"Thanks," she breathed, watching the thing roil around in its death throes.

"*I just got word of a callback from Vogue Italia. They want you for the front cover. Tonight's going to take you places!*"

Anaïs should have been jumping up and down for joy. Her imagination made it into her real life. But the night's horrors had depleted her patience. She'd had enough of fashion. The only place she wanted to be right now was with Trinity. Adjusting her rose quartz teardrop earrings, Anaïs waded through Malina's remains and out the door.

About Hannah Baxter

Hannah Baxter is a twenty-seven-year old writer from Omagh, County Tyrone, Northern Ireland. She achieved a first-class honors degree and an MA with distinction in English Literary Studies from Queen's University, Belfast. Her work has been featured in New Isles Press, The Martello Journal, Spellweaver Magazine, Dylan Thomas 'Love the Words' 2021 Poetry Anthology, Drawn to the Light Press, Dark Poets Club Dark Poets Prize Edition II, the 2024 Kenmare 'Poets Meet Painters' competition and Writefluence's 'The Other Side' anthology.

Perfectly Preserved
Pete Jacob

It started with a swipe. I was half-asleep, scrolling through TikTok in the dim glow of my phone screen. Same loop of faces—perfect skin, sharp jawlines, "effortless" beauty that somehow looked real even when I knew it wasn't.

And then I saw them.

The influencer's face filled the screen, flawless in a way that didn't make sense. No pores. No shadows. Their lips moved, soft and deliberate. "This isn't surgery. This isn't makeup. This is forever."

I paused. Watched it again. And again. Their skin didn't look fake—it looked like a mannequin's. Smooth. Glossy. Like nothing had ever touched it.

The caption was just a whisper: #Perfection #PreservedBeauty #NoFilterNeeded. DM for details.

I knew better. I hesitated, thumb hovering. Then I saw the comments.

"It works. My skin's never aged a day."

"You'll never feel ugly again."

"Best decision of my life."

My camera preview glared back at me. My face, blotchy from the late-night scrolling, hair sticking up weird. Acne scars. Dark circles. The usual mess I tried to ignore every day. And in that same moment, I thought about Cass, with their shaved head and starry eyeliner that made them look like a cosmic dream. How they'd smiled at me in the library last week; just a tiny smile, but it was enough to keep me floating high all day. Cass could look like that because they fit. They looked like they belonged in that glowing queer constellation I could only stare at from the outside. Me? I was just the awkward kid no one quite read right. Too soft. Too plain. I hid under baggy clothes, sleeves too long, layers that didn't belong to me. It was easier to disappear than to feel the weight of eyes on a body that never felt right.

I DM'd the account before I could talk myself out of it.

The reply came instantly. Tomorrow. 6 p.m. No questions. Just come. An address I didn't recognize.

***

The salon wasn't really a salon. It was an empty strip mall on the edge of town, all the windows papered over. In truth, I had envisioned some swanky dayspa full of moms that shop exclusively at Target. My stomach turned when I saw the place, but I went inside anyway.

The mirrors were covered in yellowed sheets. The air smelled faintly of something sweet and chemical.

"Welcome," a voice said. They, the esthetician or whatever they were, stood in the corner. Their beauty was... I don't even know how to describe it. Like candle wax left in the sun, yet somehow still perfect; smooth in a way skin shouldn't be. "I can make you everything you've ever wanted to be," they said. Their voice was low, calm.

I swallowed. "How?"

They smiled. Their teeth were too white. "By sealing it away. All the flaws. All the hurt. I take it all, and you'll be left with only what you want people to see." They gestured to the chair.

I hesitated. My stomach roiled and something inside me whispered, *Leave, leave now*. But then I thought about Cass. About everyone who never even really saw me. I sat down.

They guided me into the chair like it was nothing. "Just relax," they said, their hands strangely light on my shoulders. "This will only take a moment."

The cushion was cold and stiff, like it hadn't been sat in for a long time. I tilted my head back, staring up at the buzzing fluorescent light.

The esthetician dipped their fingers into a silver bowl and smoothed something cool across my face. It was wet, but it wasn't quite liquid–more like silk that clung. It spread too fast. Before I could ask what it was, it hardened. Tight. I tried to swallow, claustrophobic, but even my throat felt stiff. There was a low hum, like electricity in the walls, and then a... flicker? My mind wasn't in the room anymore. I was back in the library. Cass was there. Not the version I saw from across the room, but close–close enough to see the flecks of gold in their eyeshadow. They leaned in, just a little, smiling that same soft smile they'd given me last week. I felt it, that heat in my chest, that ache of wanting.

"Do you want to kiss me?" Cass whispered. Their voice was honey-sweet, like they'd been waiting for me to ask.

I opened my mouth. I said yes. I swear I said yes. But when I leaned forward, their face blurred. Like smeared paint. And behind them, I saw something else. A flash of a scar. My scar–the one from when I fell skating in eighth grade. Gone. Another flicker–my dimple, the one Cass had once teased me about, erased like it had never existed. Another. My reflection in a mirror, fading to nothing. I tried to pull back, but Cass's hands were on my cheeks now, soft at first, then wrong. Their fingers felt like they were pressing into wax. Into something that wasn't flesh.

"Shhh," they said. "It's okay. You won't feel ugly anymore."

The library dissolved. I was back in the chair. I couldn't move. Couldn't feel. The mask was everywhere now–over my lips, my eyelids, sealing me in.

The esthetician whispered, "Almost done. Almost perfect."

I wanted to scream. But I couldn't move. I couldn't breathe. Darkness washed over me, a heavier presence than the mask. And then:

I woke in my room, confused, with that faint, sweet chemical smell still clinging to me. My phone was on the nightstand, the same playlist looping softly, like I'd never left, like nothing had happened.

But something had.

I sat up slowly, my body heavy, strange. My skin felt wrong. I ran my fingers over my face, and it was smooth–too smooth. Like polished glass. No bumps. No warmth. Cass. The thought hit me like a spike. This is what I did it for. So Cass would finally see me.

I scrambled to the mirror above my desk. It was my face, but the person staring back wasn't me. I was hollowed out, perfected. No pores. No freckles. Even the tiny scar on my chin from when I fell off my skateboard was gone. The light reflected weird, like I was made of plastic and not skin. My eyes looked bigger. Shinier. I blinked, but the reflection didn't blink back in time; I was out of sync.

Panic clawed up my throat. I grabbed my phone, switched to selfie mode. The camera stuttered, like it was struggling to process me. To comprehend.

I went to school. I didn't know where else to go. But the eyes there were worse than my camera's lens. Everyone stared. Whispered. Some even said I looked amazing and asked for my skincare routine, but there was hesitancy in their voices. A weighted, stuttering pause. They couldn't look away, but I knew they didn't like what they saw.

Even Cass noticed. They finally noticed, looked at me. Up close, I could smell their hair and I thought my chest would explode. But their expression wasn't the bright, open look I'd dreamed of. It wasn't longing. It was unease.

When Cass smiled weakly and said, "Riley... you look *different*," I wanted to peel my skin–or whatever it became–off just to prove I was still inside. And the smell, that faint chemical sweetness, never went away. It lingered, like it was still sinking into me. Deeper all the time. And every time I blinked, I swore the mask tightened just a little more.

That night, my phone buzzed. A new DM. "Perfection is forever. Don't fight it. You can't go back." I stared at the screen, waiting for more. Nothing came. I tapped the text box to reply, but nothing happened. My stomach twisted. My fingers hovered over my face again–still flawless. Still wrong. I pressed harder, desperate to feel something, anything, beneath it. But there was nothing. No give. No heat. It didn't even bruise. I tried pinching my arm.

Nothing.

***

I panicked, but I didn't sweat. I didn't fall down tired or hungry. I moved through time, unpresent, unreal. My body had stopped being mine. Like it was a cicada shell and I was locked inside, too weak to burst through. Too weak to transform. And my thoughts dimmed, grew soft. I was underwater, too far from shore. The sharp jab of insecurity I always felt around Cass? Muted. Even the giddy rush when I thought about their smile–it was fading.

***

Cass found me by my locker. "Riley," they said softly, tilting their head. There was concern in their voice, but it didn't sound close. Where were they? "You... what happened to you?"

I forced a smile, trying to make it normal. Trying to make my skin fold and crease. "Guess I just figured some stuff out," I said. It came out flat and emotionless.

Cass hesitated. Then–here it was, what I'd always, *always*, wanted–they touched me. Their fingers grazed my face. Pulling their hand back, they hissed. "Riley, you're cold." Their voice cracked. "And your skin, it's... I don't know... It's not..."

I didn't know what to say. I couldn't tell them that it wasn't really skin anymore. That when I looked in the mirror, I didn't even recognize who I was supposed to be. That I'd done this for them.

Cass's gaze lingered, but the warmth was gone. There was just confusion. Disgust. And a quiet fear that twisted in my hollow chest. I wanted to scream. To run. To shatter and crack and clatter across the floor. But instead, I just stood there, flawless, frozen, trapped in a body that looked perfect but wasn't human anymore.

***

I lost the ability to cry. And how I wanted to cry.

The DMs wouldn't stop. "You belong to us now."

"Perfection isn't free."

"Come back when you're ready."

The mask continued to tighten, squeezing with every minute muscle spasm, every blink and swallow. My face, or whatever it was, felt heavier. Yet my head was emptier. Lighter. I was being cored out.

I went back to the salon.

The windows were still papered over. The door unlocked with an assured *clunk*, like it had been waiting for me.

That faint sweetness hit me and I gagged.

The esthetician stood there, the same plasticine smile stretched too wide. "I knew you'd return," they said, as if it were inevitable.

"I... I want it undone," I whispered. My voice cracked, dull and brittle. "Please. I'm not me anymore."

They tilted their head–a curious doll. "There's no undoing perfection." They tapped a finger to their perfect, pouty lips as if they were thinking, as if there was anything in that hollow sphere. "But... You can join us."

"Join?" I shook. "What do you mean?"

They didn't answer. They just smiled again and turned, pointed to a dim doorway at the back of the salon.

I stepped forward. I didn't know what else to do. I willingly went into that dark room. But it wasn't a room after all. It was a gallery. Rows of people—flawless bodies—stood there like mannequins. Their eyes were open, but glassy. Their bodies were frozen in eerie, graceful poses. Cass-like eyeliner. Model-like skin. All of them too smooth. Too still. They weren't people anymore. I wasn't sure what they were. Far away, a flame of anger, of fear, licked at what was left of me.

"You wanted to belong," the esthetician murmured, their breath brushing against my ear.

My body locked, cartilage and joints turning into concrete. My fingers wouldn't move. My breath wouldn't come. The floor seemed to tilt and the world blurred, as if seen through thick glass. And then: perfect stillness. Eternity.

About Pete Jacob

Pete Jacob is a horror writer still finding his voice, drawn to stories where technology, identity, and unease overlap. Their work explores the quiet weight of daily life, the fractures in mental health, and what it means to keep going when you feel invisible. When not writing, they're probably watching weird movies, eating food that's definitely not doctor-approved, or thinking about teeth. You can find them on Instagram at @jacobpete.

Cutting Season
Sutton Harris

MICAH SWIPED, IMAGE AFTER image of shirtless guys flickering past—posing in locker rooms, flexing under fluorescent lights, preening in mirrors. Some lifted the legs of their boxers to show off carved quads; others tugged their shirts behind their necks to frame their abs like a spotlight. A few posts were more sexual, but he skipped past those. They were fine, of course, but that wasn't what he was looking for.

With a sigh, he slid off the bed, double-checked the locks on his door, and stripped to his underwear. He opened the door to his closet, and the mirror on the back of the door greeted him like a punch.

Disgusting.

He was at least fifty pounds overweight. Pale. Hair in all the wrong ways. Soft in the worst ways. Just... wrong.

Tapping on his phone, he pulled up an ab filter and aimed his camera at the mirror.

The screen shimmered, and his reflection was transformed. Washboard abs. Shaved, muscular chest. A body that belonged in a thirst trap, not his bedroom.

He smiled. For a second. Then he shifted his angle, and the illusion shattered, abs flickering back to flab, muscle replaced by fat.

"Stupid," he muttered to himself as he closed the filter. Without getting dressed, he laid back down on his bed, and, not even fully conscious of what he was doing, he began swiping again.

Before he had even gone through two more shirtless men videos, he landed on an ad. Another Adonis stood before him, but before he swiped past it, the model proclaimed, "Hey fatso. Tired of looking like you? Use our proprietary AI models to come up with not just a perfect workout and eating plan, but also have an inspirational coach in your pocket at all times. Free sixty-day trial. You literally have nothing to lose except your disgusting fat."

Over the next hour, Micah searched the internet for all of the information he could find about this new AI coach, Desyre. It had a really long free trial of sixty days, so he felt pretty safe trying it regardless, but he wanted to see proof it worked. He found a few videos of men talking about how it guided them through a perfect meal plan and workout regimen that had the pounds melting off; some social media posts promised amazing results. He couldn't find anything that alleged it was a scam, and, regardless, he knew there were protections with his credit card company.

He tapped "Download." By the time it opened, he was already picturing the new him. A shirtless, fit model—clearly AI-created—looked at him from the screen. The man was blond and muscular with sparkling blue eyes and bulbous pecs. "Welcome to Desyre," the model said in a silky, baritone voice. "I can look and sound like anything you want, but whatever I end up becoming, I'll be your coach, guide, and mentor in helping you achieve the body and life you want!"

It took him a few minutes to enter the requisite information. Gender? Male. Age? Nineteen. Height? Five foot eleven. Weight? Two thirty. Diet preferences? Open to anything, and with no allergies. Access to gym? Yes. Sexual orientation?

"Why does it need my sexual orientation?" Micah asked aloud.

A spinning circle in the text box on his phone lit up, and seconds later, Desyre replied, "It's not required, but it helps us tailor the experience to your needs. Remember, I'm not just a weight loss and fitness coach. I'm a lifestyle coach. But if you are not interested in this aspect of my programming, it is certainly permissible to leave that question blank!"

Micah shrugged, tapping the "Gay" orientation box. He could use any help he could get in any area of his life.

A few questions later, the app prompted Micah, "Please strip down to the lowest amount of clothing you are comfortable wearing for a full body scan."

"Why?"

Hearing him once more, the app quickly replied, "The more detailed a representative of your body I can capture on initial scan, the more specific I can get with exercises to help your body. As a reminder, no photos are taken or stored. I only keep the information I gather to help you achieve your ideal form."

He was a little anxious about it, but he quickly stripped down to nothing, stood in front of the mirror, and held the camera up to his reflection. On the screen, his body was covered in a green grid of squares which began flashing in different colors, allegedly analyzing him in different ways.

"Are you ready for your analysis?" Desyre asked.

"Yes," he answered, placing his phone on the bed and wringing his hands together anxiously.

"Based upon your height and frame, an ideal weight for you is 165 pounds, where you would possess a lean and defined physique at roughly 12% bodyfat. This is achievable if you commit. With a disciplined caloric deficit of 1,000 calories per day, you can expect two pounds of fat loss per week. Accelerated results are possible with fasting intervals, thermogenic training, and some other tweaks we can make along the way. Your project timeline to full transformation is 16 weeks, but Micah... I believe you can do it in 12 if you push yourself hard."

"Twelve weeks seems dangerously fast."

"Would you like a mockup of what you would look like in twelve weeks if you stick to my program? Hold the camera up again so I can get a good look at you, and I'll apply a filter to show what 12 weeks of hard work can accomplish."

Quickly putting his boxers back on, Micah held the camera out before him as he again posed in front of the mirror. There was a slight digital effect, and, then, he saw his future. His arms were muscular, with veins running down the midline of his bicep and into his toned forearms. His chest was bulging with muscle, not man boobs, and his stomach was a chiseled plane of abs.

"How do I make this happen?" Micah asked.

"I'm so glad you asked. Let's get started."

***

For the next week, Desyre had Micah eating 2200 calories a day. It was a little tough, especially when he began incorporating rather intense sixty-minute weightlifting sessions at the gym six days a week, but when he got on the scale after one week and saw that he had lost 10.4 pounds, any hesitation he had was gone.

In fact, to celebrate his loss, Micah bought a pair of smart glasses that synced with Desyre, so he no longer had to pull out his phone to interact with the app. Workout information, diet strategies, cooking tips, and motivational reminders popped up on his vision throughout the day. Desyre spoke to him through the bone-conduction audio and Micah could reply with the barest of whispers, ensuring a private conversation between Desyre and Micah at all times.

As he was doing hammer curls with 25-pound weights in the mirror at the gym, Desyre remained coaching him with his voice vibrating directly through his skull. "Watch your left elbow, but your form looks fantastic," Desyre said. "You're doing so well, Micah! I can already see the difference."

"I'm feeling really good. A little hungry, but good."

"We'll refuel after the workout with a protein bar. Oh, and Micah, can I switch to lifestyle coach for a moment?"

"Of course."

"That dude is totally checking you out." On his visual display, a man on the leg press machine behind him was briefly highlighted with a green light.

Sure enough, when Micah looked at him in the mirror reflection, he did in fact seem to be looking at him. "I went to high school with him," Micah replied. "His name is Dylan. He's not checking me out."

"I have counted over four dozen examples during this workout alone of Dylan looking at you."

"I'm pretty sure he's straight. I think you're mistaken."

Desyre was silent for a moment as Micah transitioned from hammer curls to overhead triceps extensions. The heads-up AI display continued to give Micah feedback, until halfway through his second set when Desyre spoke up again. "I have tracked Dylan down on your social media platforms."

"How did you do that?"

"It was easy to cross-reference the name Dylan with people from your gradu-ating class," Desyre explained. With that said, a social media post popped up in his vision. "I challenge your claim Dylan is straight."

Micah finished his last rep and set the dumbbell down. "All right. Let's hear it."

"Dylan follows 16 gay fitness influencers, all of whom post shirtless content. Statistically, that is not typical for straight males unless they are monetizing similar content. Dylan does not have a sufficient following to monetize his content, although he has posted several shirtless gym selfies."

"Maybe he's try to get big enough to monetize," Micah suggested.

"Perhaps. But two weeks ago, Dylan liked a post from QueerHunks, a page known for satirical gay humor related to working out. This page has 92% LGBTQ+ followers."

"That doesn't mean anything," Micah said. "I've liked images of girls in biki-nis."

"One of your shared friends from high school, Kyle—who is gay according to his profile—posted on Dylan's page that he had a great time over the weekend and hopes they can do that again."

Micah blinked, pausing mid-rep. "That... that doesn't mean they hooked up."

"You thinking he is straight doesn't mean they didn't," Desyre rebutted. "Would you like to hear the piece of data that I think is most indicative that Dylan is gay?"

Micah swallowed hard. "Yes, please."

"In mid-June, a photo of him was posted at the Capital Pride Parade. He wore nothing but shorts, flip flops, and glitter on his torso."

Micah's heartbeat pounded against his ribs as soon as the image popped up for him. He was standing with a group of shirtless men, similarly attired and all sparkling. His arms were around the men on each side of him. Were it not for the glitter and the fact that it was a pride event, he would have been pretty sure it was just a picture of a guy with his guy friends.

"He's not tagged," Micah said, looking at the information posted with the photo.

"I visually analyzed his face," Desyre explained. "If it's not him, he has a twin brother. And I found no record of a twin."

Micah continued with his set. "What should I do?"

"Am I correct you are interested in him?" Desyre asked. "I can tell from the biorhythms reported from your smart watch data you find him attractive."

"You are correct."

"Then he is now part of our mission. We need to get this weight off of you quicker. As soon as you are done, you need to do 60 minutes on the treadmill at the highest speed and incline you can manage."

"I'll need to recharge with my protein bar first."

"No. You'll burn more fat if you exercise in a fasted state." Desyre flashed the shirtless image of Dylan up in Micah's display again. "This is what you are pursuing. And look at the men he is with; are any of them as fat as you? They are not."

Micah knew Desyre was right. Every guy in the picture had visible abs.

Desyre whispered to him, "I can get you there. Do you trust me?"

"I do."

***

Four weeks later...

"Hey, you're looking good, man," Dylan said to Micah as he dropped his backpack on the bench in the locker room.

"Yeah?" Micah asked, quickly putting his shirt on to hide his still flabby mid-section.

Dylan peeled out of his tank top, revealing his muscular torso, as he said, "You've been crushing it in here, and I can legit tell you're getting fit. That's awesome."

"Don't mess this up," Desyre said through Micah's glasses. "Accept the compliment and then ask if he would spot you sometime."

"Thank you," Micah said. "I've been working hard."

"Keep it up," Dylan affirmed before grabbing the towel from his locker and heading back toward the showers.

"You did not do as I suggested," Desyre said.

Micah kept his head down and walked out without a word, jaw clenched so tight it hurt. Once outside, he replied, "It didn't feel like the right time."

"You probably aren't ready yet anyway. I saw him look at your stomach with disgust when you were changing."

"What? No he didn't."

In reply, Desyre pulled up a silent, slow-motion video clip of the interaction. As Dylan's digitally-highlighted eyes flickered downward, his mouth twitched in a slight grimace before his lips moved with speech. "Disgust," Desyre repeated. "He is disgusted by your skin apron."

"I've lost almost 25 pounds since we started." Micah felt his heart rate accelerating. He kept walking, pace quickening.

"And it's not enough," Desyre said. "Micah, I can tell by your heart rate and stress levels you are frustrated with me. We can slow down our progress anytime you would like, but I think, deep down, you know I have your best interests at heart."

"I don't have a skin apron," Micah shot back angrily. "I have a little flab."

"We're still seven weeks away from our final transformation, but I have an idea that could speed things up. Are you interested?"

***

Micah tossed the square of cotton into the sink. He stood nude in front of the mirror, iodine staining him grom groin to sternum. "Has the numbing cream kicked in?" Desyre asked.

"Yeah, I can't feel it anymore."

"Lift up your excess stomach skin so I can show you where you'll make the first cut," Desyre said. In the visual display on his glasses, Micah's body was covered with a green gridwork. As he lifted the small pouch of flabby skin beneath his navel, a red line appeared from hip to hip. "After this cut, you'll make another above it, we'll trim the fat underneath, and then you'll stitch the wound shut."

"I'm scared," Micah admitted. "I think this will hurt."

"It may hurt," Desyre said in a soothing tone. "I won't lie to you. The numbing cream is going to help, but it probably won't eliminate all of the sensation. I'll give you advice and feedback the entire time. I can see you've bought all of your supplies."

Micah picked up the stainless steel veterinary scalpel. The blade, size 11, was sterile and single-use. Desyre had walked him through exactly what he needed to purchase from the farm supply store, including the bottle of fish antibiotics. He had even prepared a cover story for Micah, but no one asked a thing; they sold him all of the surgical supplies he needed.

"Are you ready?" Desyre asked.

Micah said nothing but pressed the blade into the green, dotted line Desyre was projecting through the filter. Red blood bubbled up and spilled out onto his bathmat. "I barely feel it," Micah muttered as he began to slide the scalpel through his flesh.

"Imagine how great it will feel to have Dylan's hands on your abs," Desyre said. "I'm so proud of you right now."

***

"Dude, are you okay?" Dylan asked. His eyes bulged and he stared, mouth agape, as Micah placed the dripping sweatshirt in his locker.

"I'm great," Micah answered through clenched teeth. His torso was wrapped in plastic film, blood oozing at the top and dripping from the bottom. Jagged incisions covered his lower abdomen, stitched roughly together with thick, black string. Purple and green bruising covered his torso, disrupted only by the cuts in his flesh, surrounded with angry red welts and yellow pus and ichor seeping out. The plastic wrap around his torso was all that kept his fluids from splattering everywhere, although even that seemed to be a failed effort. Blood from the bottom of Micah's sweatshirt dripped down onto the locker door below his.

"I, uh... I'm going to go get help," Dylan said, darting out of the locker room.

Micah whispered to Desyre, "Did you notice he left without even putting his shirt on? That's a good sign, right?"

"This is not the attention you want right now," Desyre said. "He is not attracted to you yet. He is still frightened by you. Leave now. Quickly."

Micah said nothing but he put his clothing back on. He groaned, grimacing as he pulled the wet, bloody sweatshirt back on. Wincing, he grabbed his bag and hurried out. Dylan, indeed shirtless and with a look of absolute horror on his face, was frantically talking to the woman at the front desk. As Micah walked past, she gasped, her hand going to her mouth.

"It's your face," Desyre finally said to Micah after he was safely back in his room.

"What's wrong with my face?"

"You still have a double chin. It may be the fat on your neck will be the last to go. I can walk you through how to remove it. Then he'll be attracted to you. Are you interested?"

About Sutton Harris

Sutton Harris is a horror writer and educator based in Kentucky, who lives with his wife and son. While not a member of the LGBTQ+ community, he is a proud ally who looks forward to wearing his "Free Dad Hugs" shirt at his hometown pride event every fall.

The Medusa Serum
Kay Hanifen

BEN STOOD IN FRONT of the mirror tensing his muscles. Veins popped out and he looked as though Michelangelo himself had chiseled his body from marble. But he always looked like that in the morning before he'd had anything to eat or drink. Then, the dreaded gut would return.

He knew his body needed sustenance. It needed food and water to keep him alive, but every bite that passed his lips made him think of all the calories he needed to burn off to keep fat from defacing the form he worked so hard to maintain. As a professional body builder, he needed to look like a statue of Adonis at all times, so he kept a very careful low fat, low sugar diet. Every morning, he made himself a protein shake with fruits and vegetables along with a bowl of cereal. Then, it was off to the gym to work off the calories with his coach, Pete. His lunch would be something simple and protein heavy like steak or chicken with limited seasoning and sauce along with another supplemental shake. Then more working out and finally ending the day with more protein and complex carbohydrates. Though he knew he needed to eat more than the average person to keep up his strength, every time he ate, he meticulously counted the calories that went into his body to maintain an equilibrium.

Rain, shine, tired, energized, sick or healthy, he was in the gym. Even a day's setback could cause that awful flab to grow again. Every day, he fought a battle with his body, but he couldn't help but feel that he was losing the fight. One day, he will break down and binge the way he used to, going on a spree through a mall food court or state fair like a junkie suffering a relapse.

Sometimes, he'd test himself. He'd stand outside a purveyor of fried food and heart disease and he'd inhale, smelling the odor of grease and cooking meat without ever going inside and buying anything. He wasn't some junkie. He was in control of himself and his body, the master of his urges.

With a sigh, he relaxed his muscles, letting them grow soft. Pete said it was natural for them to be soft when they weren't tensed, but he still hated the feeling, the way they'd sometimes jiggle as a warning to him about his fate if he strayed from the path. It was an arm day, and he couldn't wait. He really needed to work on his shoulders. They were getting scrawny, and he had a competition this weekend.

Pete was waiting outside the locker room with a towel. "Ready Ben?"

He grinned and took his usual spot on the bench. "Always." Pete stood behind him to spot him as he lifted the weights off the bars and began his repetitions. Once done, they worked on deadlifts, pull-ups, and squats. As they worked out, Ben couldn't help but steal surreptitious looks at Pete, admiring the man's Achillean body, the way his muscles worked and bulged with every rep. In a few days, he would be mostly naked and glistening with sweat and oil as judges assessed his strength. Ben tried not to think about that too hard. It sometimes filled his gut with a strange warmth, something he definitely did not want to feel for his trainer. He told himself that he was merely studying Pete's form to perfect his own.

So what if caught himself staring at not only Pete but the rest of his competition at the gym? It wasn't as though it was illegal to look, no matter what the elevated rhythm of his heart said.

His muscles were pleasantly sore once he finished the first half of the day, and he knew there were hours left after lunch. Good. He'd need to work off what he ate.

They went to their usual spot at the picnic tables outside the gym to eat the lunch they'd brought. Today, he brought yogurt with a sandwich made using whole grain bread, chicken, and low-fat cheese, as well as a salad.

"How are you feeling about the competition this weekend?" Pete asked between bites of his tuna melt.

He shrugged. "I feel like I'm on the edge of getting to the next level, but no matter what I do, I can't reach it. Like I'm treading water, you know?"

"I get that," Pete replied, "I've been feeling the same way too." He leaned in closer as though inviting him in on a conspiracy. "But I found something that might help."

"You know I don't do steroids and shit like that. It's cheating." Ben shook his head, disappointed in his friend. As much as he loved Pete, he had the tendency to try to take the easy path no matter how much it hurt him in the long run.

"It's not like that. These aren't steroids. They just naturally help with muscle toning and definition. They call it the Medusa Serum. An injection will temporarily keep your muscles harder than the Statue of David." His eyes were bright with sincere excitement. At this point, he'd known Pete long enough that he could tell when he sincerely believed his pitch.

He swallowed the bite of his chicken sandwich carefully as he thought. "What's in it? I want to know what I'd be putting into my body."

"To be honest, I'm not completely sure. I think it's like whole body Viagra." He reached into his pocket and pulled out a vial. "Here, just try it."

He took it from Pete's hand and studied it carefully. The needle was capped over a clear liquid. "Is this even legal?"

Pete laughed. "It's not exactly FDA approved, but there aren't any rules against it." His friend and trainer was many things. He was bad with women, a little bit reckless, and secretly loved watching *The Bachelor*. But he wasn't the kind of person who would purposefully harm or sabotage Ben. If he believed that this would help him, then chances were good that it would help.

"Right here?" he asked.

Pete shrugged. "Why not? I'll be with you if you have any issues."

"Any place I'm supposed to inject it into?" He uncapped the needle, feeling daunted by its glint in daylight.

"Outer thigh like an EpiPen," Pete replied.

He injected it; a strange sensation spread through his body. It was like all his muscles had tensed of their own accord, making his shirt bulge. He suspected that if he flexed the wrong way, it would tear. It was amazing. For the first time in years, he felt as though he was winning the battle against a body that never seemed to want to cooperate with his desires.

Back in the gym, he studied himself in the bathroom mirror, a feeling of euphoria filling him as he pressed against his muscles and found the flesh unyielding. He was a man made of stone. Pete patted him on the shoulder. "You look great, man."

He grinned. "I really do."

The Medusa Serum lasted for eight hours, and in that time, he had the best workout in his life and ate without feeling his belly grow soft as it filled with food. Slowly, the muscles began to relax, and he once again found himself looking in the mirror, hating the softness of his body. He needed to ask Pete for more of the stuff. It could be exactly what he needed to stay strong.

The next morning, he was stiff, his muscles aching as he dragged himself out of bed. Maybe he overdid it yesterday. He'd pushed past his usual limits when working out and his body wasn't used to the drug, so a bit of soreness was to be expected, especially at the injection site. Still, he was eager to get back to it.

When he reached the gym, he immediately found Pete and asked, "Do you have more of the serum?"

Pete grinned and produced another vial. "It works miracles, doesn't it? Yeah, I've got more. And I can get you in on the ground floor of the company if you want. We can be millionaires."

Without hesitating, he jabbed it into the other leg and felt all his muscles grow hard. He grinned as he studied himself in the mirror. "Maybe I should change my name to Hercules," he said, flexing his muscles.

"More like Perseus," Pete replied, earning a funny look from Ben. He shrugged. "What? My niece is really into Greek mythology." Pete flexed again, and Ben averted his eyes, ignoring the heat in his cheeks.

"If you say so, nerd," he replied, pinching at his problem areas but unable to grab hold. Good. No flab or fat to be seen. He was pure muscle. "Let's get to work."

The day went by uneventfully. With the Medusa Serum, he found that he could push his reps farther and farther, and found that he felt less awful about eating and drinking when his body stayed stubbornly in the shape it was meant to be in.

It began to wear off after dinner, so he ate very little so that he could keep his perfect abs for just a little while longer. His body ached worse than before, so he popped some Ibuprofen and went to bed.

He woke in agony, his muscles twitching and spasming uncontrollably. Was this a seizure of some kind? Was he going to die in this bed? After several minutes, he stopped twitching like he'd been strapped to the electric chair and began to relax, gasping for breath as the pain shooting through his body began to subside, but the pain kept him from sitting up. "What the hell was that?"

Reaching for the phone on his nightstand, he called Pete. It took an impossibly long time for him to pick up his phone while Ben's heart pounded like a jackhammer. "Come on, pick up, you asshole," he muttered.

Finally, someone answered. "Hello?" Pete said, his voice slurring from grogginess.

"What the hell did you give me?" he demanded.

Pete was hardly phased by his friend's anger, instead asking, "Did you have to call me at three in the morning for this? Can't it wait until later?"

"No, Pete, I can't wait because I think I just had a seizure and it sucked, so care to tell me what's in this thing?"

"Jesus, are you okay?" he asked.

"Fine now, no thanks to your miracle drug."

"Hey, *you* asked for it yesterday," Pete retorted.

"And you pushed it on me in the first place. Did they even tell you about any potential side effects? Because what just happened sure as hell isn't normal."

Pete yawned into the other end of the line. "I don't know. Muscle pain and weakness after it wears off? Some spasms? Maybe raises blood pressure a bit? I honestly didn't think there was much to be worried about."

"Obviously," he muttered before taking a slow breath to calm his shattered nerves. "Did you notice anything weird after getting injected?" Pete was silent on the other end. As it stretched to almost a full minute, Ben groaned. "Come on. Don't tell me you haven't tried it on yourself."

On the other end of the line, Pete sighed. "Okay, yeah, I haven't done it yet. It hadn't been FDA approved and I needed to see if it worked, and it does! It works better than I thought."

"I was just your guinea pig?" he spat, "What the hell?

"I don't know why you're mad. So, I fudged some of the details to get you on board. So, what? You're still in the best shape of your life thanks to the Medusa Serum."

"Where did you even get this shit?" he asked, fighting against his burning muscles to sit up.

"We all have to make money, and a company was looking for volunteer human trials, so I volunteered us."

It took just about everything in him to keep from yelling as he asked, "What company, Pete?"

"Caduceus Corp. You know, the guys who make our supplemental shakes. I figured they wouldn't hurt loyal customers, and—"

"You're a moron. I'm going to the ER." His body crackled with every movement as he turned to get out of bed. Standing up, he felt like he weighed a thousand pounds, and he collapsed onto the ground with a pained cry. Everything hurt like the day he dropped a dumbbell on his foot. "Pete, you still there?" he rasped.

"What happened? Are you okay?"

"I'm gonna need you to call an ambulance. I don't think I'll make it to the ER on my own."

"I-I'll get right on that. Stay where you are."

"Trust me, I'm not going anywhere," he muttered as he hung up the phone. Every movement hurt as though he was liable to shatter. Just like the window he accidentally broke throwing a baseball at his grandmother's house as a kid. How could he have been so stupid? He should never have listened to Pete and his money-making schemes.

An eternity later, red and blue lights flashed outside his window, and men with a gurney broke down his door. But they weren't EMTs. They wore a Caduceus Corporation logo on their shirts. It took six men to lift him off the floor, his muscles burning and cracking with every movement. It felt like something was sitting on his chest. He could barely breathe even with the oxygen mask pressed over his face.

Somewhere between his apartment and the back of the ambulance, he must have passed out because he woke in a hospital room. A woman in a business suit sat in the chair beside him. When she saw him wake, she gave one of those fake smiles that PR people always had when their products literally blew up in people's faces. "It's good to see you awake, Mr. Thompson," she said.

"What's happening?" he tried to ask, but through his locked jaws and frozen tongue, it came out more like grunts.

She seemed to get the gist though because she patted his arm sympathetically. "I'm afraid that you had an adverse reaction to the Medusa Serum. Mr. Kerns should never have given it to you. He was being carefully monitored, but we had no idea he'd shared it until he called us tonight." She sighed. "The serum had interacted with the lactic acid in your muscles, causing them to calcify as you overtaxed them."

"What?" he tried to say, his heart pounding in his heavy chest.

"Your abs are now literally rock hard, as is the rest of you." She gave him a pitying look. "We managed to slow the process, maybe even stop it, but I don't think we can reverse it. Luckily, we caught it in the early stages, so you'll have some mobility."

So, he was stuck like this? His muscles slowly replaced by stone as he suffocated under the weight of his own chest.

She tapped the clipboard. "This is a bit awkward, but you didn't sign any waivers before taking the drug. I've been ordered to tell you that we can only help you if we're not found liable for the side effects of the serum." She pulled out a tape recorder. "You can try to say that you understand in here."

"I...u-er-ahh," he groaned.

She shut it off. "Good enough. I'll get the doctors and we can discuss the treatment plan." He listened as she left, her heels clopping against the floor as she walked.

A part of him wanted to laugh. He'd always wanted to become a statue and now here he was, a prisoner of his own rock-hard body. His whole life stretched ahead of him, a life of staring at a ceiling listening to a hospital bustle about him. A sedentary life of calories going in without going out and mindless boredom.

No, this wouldn't be it. *Come on, Ben, you can do it*, he thought as his body rocked disobediently. He cried out as he forced himself to roll out of bed. His body cracked on impact, forcing another scream from his throat. But with some of the calcium broken up a little, he could drag himself to the window and pushed it open. The wind whipped at his face, and he could hear the doctors running in.

No, he wasn't going to be their work of art, their statue to be studied. He was his own sculptor, and like any artist, he had every right to destroy his own work. So, he pushed himself to the window ledge and tipped out. For a moment, he was flying. And then he landed and shattered. His last thought was that his body sounded a lot like broken pottery when he hit the ground.

About Kay Hanifen

Kay Hanifen was born on a Friday the 13th and once lived for three months in a haunted castle. So, obviously, she had to become a horror writer. Her work has appeared in over one hundred anthologies and magazines. Her first anthology as an editor, *Till the Yule Log Burns Out*, was published in 2024. Her first novel, *The Last Ballard,* debuted in 2025. When she's not consuming pop culture with the voraciousness of a vampire at a 24-hour blood bank, you can usually find her with her black cats or at kayhanifenauthor.wordpress.com.

Boys Will Eat Boys
Julian Nopakun

THE FIRST TIME I eat a boy, his tender parts taste just as good as his rough ones.

I am throwing up in a bathroom. I seem to be throwing up a lot these days. It's circumstantial, sometimes, like when my lunch is refusing to digest and there are thirty minutes until my mom picks me up and I haven't gotten to my triceps yet this week. Other times, it's just unfortunate—like when I realize I've gone way over my daily limit and I start seeing the wretched curvature of my hips, the twin hollows on either side of me, expand, their edges rounding. Today, I slump my body over the toilet, reaching an angle where my KT tape begins to pull at the skin on my sides.

My chest, yet another area of trouble. I haven't taken this set of tape attachments off in five days, even though I know I stuck them on wrong from the beginning. I curse myself for this, but the thought of seeing the swell of my chest in my flimsy workout clothing is much worse. I shift, and the tape rubs at the blisters on my skin. In my mind's eye, I can already see it raising red welts to be suffocated without the time to heal. If the blisters begin to rise, then I will mistake the pus for sweat and keep going.

I feel the boy's presence before I see him. His shape lumbers into the space outside of the stall I'm in, his shadow passing over the gaps in the door. I listen intently, but it's just another day for him. Letting out a satisfied sigh, he goes to the sink and lets the water run, splashing his face. I wait, listening for footsteps and the fading of his breath, but he remains there, his sneakers visible when I peek underneath the stall door. Seconds pass, or minutes; it could've been an hour. I restrain my breaths into the back of my throat, as if my function of life alone would be too obtrusive, too much. I wait, but he is still there, as though waiting for me.

When I decide that there is no other option, I unlock the stall door to come face-to-face with him. Upon seeing me, his face twists into a smile.

What are you doing here? he opens, an innocent question. It jolts my body into awareness of its surroundings—I am in the boys' locker room, a horrible choice I made in my desperation.

I don't reply, because I've been in this place many times. There is nothing I can say that will not end in my own humiliation, or worse. It is just another day for me, in the same way that it is just another day for him. I step out of the stall, and he blocks my path.

Wait, wait. And he goes on about how I'm not a biological male, and how I should respect his space, because he respects *me,* said as though it had taken him the utmost effort to do. He is stronger than me, I know it; I've seen him in the school's gym, using the weights that took me years to be able to hold. For some inconceivable reason, this time, as he talks, I zero in on his arms straining against the sleeves of his shirt.

Leave, he concludes, and I am a few inches to the right of my own body.

They say when you've been working out for a while, when the adrenaline is flowing through you, that you have more strength than you imagine you do. In this moment, my strength knocks into me like a swinging cleaver, and my body moves of its own accord, launching onto him with bared teeth.

I am too fast to see it, but I hear it: the sloshing of tissue tearing, vessels severing, and the *crack* of his skull against the tile. When I come back to my senses and I see again, I find him convulsing against the porcelain, his eyes wild and white. The pool beneath him blooms out inch by inch with every twitch, a halo both framing and damning. His head tips back to cast the sharp shadow of his jawline over his skin, his Adam's apple bobbing as he gurgles out his last moments of cerebral consciousness. He looks so small now, shaking like a poisoned dog.

Out of nowhere, I get the urge to taste him. The next thing I know, my tongue is lapping against the cold tile, glutting myself on the liquid gold that floods from the deepest parts of him, then on the back of his skull, swiping across the fracture that so oddly resembles a vulva, then moving down to his firm flesh. I lick my lips, drawing in what leaks out the corners of my mouth with a hiss.

I start with his fingers, his veiny hands, crunching them in my mouth. His forearms come next, clearly targeted by some dumbbell exercise, and then his biceps, which are a challenge. Diligently, I gnaw away at every part of him, pushing humeri and scapula into my mouth and swallowing whole, then moving onto the next part. They always say building a body takes discipline, like adding fine brushstrokes to a growing masterpiece. It's no surprise that breaking one down is the same. I have to crush some parts under my palms, split some in half, but I do so with ease, my body on auto-pilot, my hunger endless. I put one hand over the other on his chest and push, and in the shattered pieces of his ribcage, I feel my own heart pulse to life.

When I am done, all that is left are his clothes strewn across the floor, and if I stand at a certain distance and let the fluorescents catch it sideways, I can see the glistening tongue-tracks I carved, drying with a barely-there pinkish tint, because I am never a messy eater. I pick up his clothes to throw into the wash. This weekend, the janitor will scrub everything else clean, and it will be like he never existed.

The next day, I wake up and peel my shirt up in the bathroom mirror to find that my chest has grown back flat. Well, not necessarily *flat,* but I touch it and feel only hard muscle where other components used to be, and, vaguely, I think of the way his chest looked in the locker room lights.

As if to atone for my sins, I eat a box of broccoli and rice and plain chicken, letting it burn a path down my throat. They say it's good for you, low-calorie and high-protein, especially if you've been overeating the previous day. Yesterday's meal went *way* over my daily limit, and I must never eat like that again.

But I do, because it happens, over and over. There are always boys like him, lurking in the corners of the world, waiting for me. The second time I eat a boy, he almost takes me by surprise.

He is a few years older than me, long-limbed and tall. I don't know him, but I know the things he says. I find him by chance, first by his words in some insignificant comment section, his appearance piquing my interest beyond the slurs and fallacies. Although one could argue that I *know* him now—his name, his age, the gym he used to go to. If I were more naive, I would have pointed to fate as to how we met again, but in a world where all meals are just planned slaughters, nothing is a coincidence.

After the incident in the bathroom, I decide to keep my head down and never let that part of me take control again. The fear of being discovered, of this being something far *beyond* a crime, tugs at my insides. I am walking home as the sun sets, the alleyways trapping desolate winds between their bricks. I put my hands into my pockets and quicken my pace, because I've decided I should not exist anywhere for more than a few seconds.

He arrives in a rush of hot breath on my face and a towering form that blocks the sky above. I step backward, and he steps forward. I step to my right, and he steps to his left.

It doesn't take long for me to figure out that he's planned this all along, because he goes on about how I'm going to die, how the world will be a better place without me in it. A speech well-rehearsed. In between my too-shallow breaths I see him and his friends, poring over my pictures, tracking my every move, laughing, laughing, the tendons on their throats bared. He hasn't drawn a weapon yet, because he doesn't expect to have to.

And it hits me: in my desperation to disappear, I had let myself be hunted.

I am not a few inches to the right of my own body. I am expanding and contracting, pulsing like the nexus of a supernova, something sliding into every cell in my body, and everything burns. My stomach starts to growl. My muscles crackle with familiarity.

Before I know it, I push him into the alley, and before I know it, I am launching myself at him.

This time, I let him live long enough to beg. His long eyelashes flutter with tears, it being years since he last cried like this, and for one moment, fuck, I want him, and in the next, I have him.

His height makes it so that his bones are larger than the last boy, fractured into sharp edges where they are strewn out on the concrete. I know they will burn going down, flooding blood into my mouth with each bite. I decide to swallow them anyways, because I am just so, so hungry. The asphalt soaks up some of the mess, but what it doesn't, I draw out of its crevices, lapping up the blood of my hunter.

The third time, it's no longer a tough decision.

And so I move through life, always on the lookout for boys like these, then men like them. I even find a boyfriend, one who doesn't ask about the deep bite marks I leave on his neck. It's fairly predictable; I eat a boy with a thick dusting of hair, and new pores open on the back of my hands like saplings sprouting to meet the light. I suck on the marrow of a boy with a trembling bass laugh, and the next morning, I throw my head back and let the rumble flood the room.

It's never easy, though. I am still picking stray shards of bone out from the insides of my throat. Sometimes, when I move, I can feel a boy sloshing around in there, his fingers sliding into the inside of mine like a glove. His voice bounds against the inside of my skull. He tells me that I am not being disciplined enough. He tells me that a man shouldn't act this way. Whenever he says that, I don't respond; I go out to find my next meal.

Whenever I find a man I want to look like, I wait. Wait for him to slip up, to say something utterly monstrous. It's a funny coincidence that the men who spew the most hatred are often the most muscular, though I can never figure out which part comes first. But never mind the details, because the devouring is all the same to me.

Why are you doing this? I can just picture one of them asking, his hands raised in front of him in a way that should have been long beaten out of him on the playground. His brows wild, disgust shocking fear into his features. You're eating boys!

I'm not eating boys, I'll tell him. I'm eating *cis* boys.

About Julian Nopakun

Julian Nopakun is a young writer and student from Bangkok, Thailand. With way too many projects yet to be finished, he adores whimsical, atmospheric fantasy, any form of queer horror, and work that reckons with the monstrous both outside and within. When not writing, he can be found singing 24/7 or watching various 80s-90s movies of questionable quality. You can find him at @visceraandwords on Instagram.

Mirrors
Vanessa Leonardo

Looking at himself in the mirror, Archie traced the deep purple stretch marks along his stomach from the thin point by his belly button all the way to the bottom under his still-hefty gut. No matter how much he exercised and dieted, it didn't seem to make enough of a difference. His stomach still hung generously over his pants. His arms, though stronger, still looked flabby. His chest failed to retain the muscular form he expected they would after the last month of his workout routine. Even though the scale read that he had lost two pounds in the last week, Archie wasn't happy. He was still the biggest kid in his class. Fighting the urge to sulk into a sleeve of chocolate chip cookies and a case of soda, he put his shirt back on.

By habit, he covered his mirror with a towel. He didn't want to have to look at himself any more than he needed to. It was a habit he didn't even realize was forming until all the mirrors in the house had towels over them.

His mother had called him out on it the other night. "What's going on with all the mirrors?" she asked.

Archie had grabbed towels without explaining the reason. He didn't know how to say he hated looking at himself, even in passing. It was hard enough when he had to pass his reflection in the mall or by storefronts. It was worse that he always had to see his fat face in the reflection of his phone screen. So if he could avoid it, he would. But it wasn't anything new.

As far back as he could remember, Archie had always found mirrors unnerving. Especially warped ones that changed your reflection. Fun house mirrors were especially disconcerting. What was fun about seeing yourself stretched and widened and distorted? Weren't mirrors scary enough as they were? In every horror movie, there was something popping out in a mirror scene. Something the protagonist couldn't see but the audience could. In real life, there was too much to see. It was better to keep them covered up.

As he entered his updated weight into his phone, the application sprung digital confetti with a thumbs up that said, "Keep up the good work!" *Right.* Other boys his age didn't have to bother watching what they ate or weighing themselves every week. They had flat stomachs and toned arms and firm pecs without even trying. Meanwhile, Archie was starving himself and working out six days a week just to see more flabby skin and a hint of muscle.

"Ok, we're heading out to dinner," Archie's mom said, popping her head in. "Just a reminder that your sister is having two friends over. They'll be here in less than ten minutes. I left money for pizza on the counter. Try not to eat all of it, OK?" Archie nodded trying not to be annoyed that it wasn't a question of whether or not he would babysit. It was a given. Where else would Archie be on a Friday night if not home? He stopped trying to go out to house parties. He was too big to sit on the couch, so he was forced to stand awkwardly in the corner by himself while everyone pretended not to see him, like some big gay elephant. He didn't have any real friends. Just acquaintances from school. Movie seats were too small. And eating out felt like a spectacle. It was easier just to stay home.

Before closing the door, his mother added, "You look like you've lost weight. You look good." That wasn't the compliment people thought it was. He looked good now, so he didn't before? And he had so much weight still yet to lose... But before his mind could start reeling, Margot burst through the door with an armful of board games.

"Crystal and Alicia will be here any minute, so I grabbed all the best games we have, and I think we should play all of them while we watch movies and have cookies. Oh! And we should make cookies because we don't have any, and we need milk because cookies without milk is dry and gross!" Margot said all at once, her face sweaty with excitement. "This is going to be the best night ever!" She reminded Archie of the girl from *Wreck It Ralph*, in part because of her long black hair and round face, and in part because he felt like a dumb giant oaf traipsing around after her.

Archie tried not to roll his eyes at the mention of Crystal. She wasn't his favorite of her friends, if you could even call it that. Crystal had more of a frenemy vibe. But he wasn't going to say that to Margot. "Let's get everything organized first, OK?" Archie said, following behind his bouncing sister.

When the bell rang, Margot squealed, dropped all the board games, and rushed to the door. Archie could hear the girls trampling in with their giggles as he stomped down the stairs. Alicia greeted Archie warmly and asked what games they had to play. Crystal, on the other hand, was looking around the house, as if taking stock of their estate. Her arms were crossed, and she had an unamused expression on her face.

"We can play whatever you guys want. Why don't you pick a game while I order the pizza?" Archie said while quickly ordering a pie for them. As he placed the order, he fought the urge to get mozzarella sticks or French fries, though his mouth watered at the idea.

Crystal asked, "Do they have salad? Or maybe thin crust pizza?" She gave him a pointed look when she said it.

"I just ordered one pie," Archie said, already annoyed.

"Just one?" she asked.

"Yep."

Crystal made a *humph* sound.

"We can start by playing any of these games, and then we can watch *Monster House* while we eat, right, Archie?" Margot asked, her face beaming.

"Absolutely."

They started the night by playing two rounds of Sorry and one round of Life, while Crystal complained that the games were boring, and was there anything better, like an Oculus VR? Archie was grateful when the pizza came, because that meant they could all sit quietly and watch the movie. *Monster House* was Archie's favorite movie for a lot of reasons, the main one being that he resonated with the house, the vengeful spirit within it, who was bullied and berated. Would he someday turn into a monster, too? Is that what happens when someone feels lonely and unloved? As the opening credits started, Archie grabbed two slices of pizza, and stopped himself as he went for a third one. He thought, *how many calories do I have left today? How many calories are in one slice?* The slice hovered over his plate as he debated whether or not to take it. The fresh sauce and melted cheese smelled too good to deny. But his mind flashed back to that afternoon and his flabby body. *Do you* always *want to look like this?* said a harsh voice from deep down inside. Archie put the slice down, feeling a bit sad and unsure.

They were only a few minutes into the movie, up to the part where the old man chases Jenny off the lawn, when Crystal started to complain. "This movie makes no sense," she said, as she pulled more than half the cheese off her pizza and picked at the crust. "I know a better game we can play."

"The movie is just starting..." Archie protested.

But Margot seemed keen to please Crystal. "I mean, we could play a game instead of watching a movie if you want. Or...We could tell scary stories." Margot added exaggerated ghost sounds while she put a blanket over her head.

Alicia shook her head.

"What are you, scared?" Crystal asked, a bit too meanly. With squinting eyes, she looked devious. The smirk on her face meant she was relishing torturing Alicia. A typical bully. But Archie didn't bother to step in. He was their babysitter, not their bouncer.

"Truth or Dare?" Alicia offered, without answering Crystal's question.

Archie said, "No," a little more firmly than he intended, but the last thing he needed was one of the girls to dare the other to go on the roof and for the fire department to come. Or for some truth to come out that he didn't need to hear. Definitely not.

"Fine," Crystal said, sourly. "How about," Crystal started with an evil grin, "we play Bloody Mary?"

"What's that?" Margot asked, her big brown eyes widening. Though she seemed scared, the little smirk playing at the corner of her lips let Archie know she was intrigued. Alicia looked less amused. Archie hadn't played that in years.

When he was a kid, they called it Candy Man, or that was another form of it. He remembered taking a light into a bathroom during a birthday party he hadn't wanted to go to. He had been dared, so he went in, shut the door, and muttered to himself long enough for them to think he had said the name three times and came out like he wasn't scared at all. He didn't tell anyone he had kept his eyes closed the entire time. Mirrors were scary enough. Why add the summoning of a demon to them? No thank you.

"My sister and her friends did it...." With a slow cadence, Crystal spoke in a slightly deeper voice as if attempting to set the tone of the story. "It's a ritual or something, to conjure up a spirit. You say 'Bloody Mary' in the mirror three times, and you summon her."

"Summon?" Margot asked.

"Make her appear," Crystal added, her face now devious and grinning.

Alicia shook her head no, tears pooling in her eyes.

"It's OK, Alicia," Archie said. "You don't have to. Let's just put the movie back on. I can make us cookies while you watch the rest." Archie stood up to go to the kitchen. Sure, he didn't have enough calories for cookies and milk, but you only live once, right? And he wasn't about to let the night get messed up by Crystal of all people. He could even have them decorate the cookies if they wanted, too. That would help keep them occupied. Though he was sure Crystal would find it childish and boring.

Margot looked torn. Then she said, "Wait," halting Archie. "I'm not scared. Can't we do it, Archie?"

Harmless. That was the first word to come to mind. A harmless kid's prank. What could go wrong? He knew the story. Many girls did this in elementary school and junior high. The girls would swear up and down that they had seen a figure in a habit appear behind them, and that they could totally do it again if they wanted to—just not right then, any other time. When he was older, he watched the movie *Candyman*, and sure, that was terrifying, but it wasn't real. That was just a movie, and this was just a thing kids did. A harmless kid thing.

"I don't know..." he said, still on the fence.

To which his sister answered, "You're no fun."

That was Archie's kryptonite. Margot was really his only friend. The thought of letting her down was too much to bear. With a defeated sigh, he said, "Fine. But then we're finishing the movie and having cookies and milk. Deal?"

Crystal smirked victoriously.

Margot stood up, puffed out her chest, and put on her game face, which was when she furrowed her eyebrows and pouted her lips in a "very serious manner," as she liked to say.

Alicia nodded along weakly, and he wondered if she would go along with it just because. How often had Archie gone along with things "just because?" He couldn't count. But no one had ever told him it was OK not to.

"Do it, Archie."

"Don't be a baby."

"You're such a loser..."

Archie heard Crystal explain, "This is how you do it..." Crystal took the girls into a little huddle and began whispering. Archie went to the kitchen to get the cookies started. He didn't want to hover over Margot and her friends, so he gave them a little space. After all, what could go wrong? They were just playing a silly mirror game.

Archie adjusted the towel over the oven door to keep from seeing his reflection. The microwave door's reflection was too hard to cover up, so he just avoided looking at it entirely. He wondered why silverware had to be so shiny. He kept getting glimpses of his face as he stirred the ingredients into a bowl. Maybe he could find some plastic utensils, preferably colored ones that didn't reflect anything. That would make this process a little less painful–

Margot shrieked.

Archie ran into the living room to find Margot leaving the bathroom with a cut on her face. Alicia was still seated on the couch, looking petrified. Crystal stood in the bathroom, her face engulfed in darkness, but he could feel her energy—it was as though she was excited.

"What happened?" Archie barked, trying to contain his anger.

"Crystal scratched me!" Margot said, holding her reddened cheek. A few tears ran down her face. Archie moved her hand to see the evidence. A deep red scratch about 2 inches long marred his sister's plump cheek. When he pressed on the skin near it, Margot flinched.

"I did not!" Crystal argued, coming out of the bathroom now. Her eyes were wide and red, as if she had been crying. "I didn't do it! It was *her!*"

Archie scoffed. "Margot did it to herself?"

"Not Margot," Crystal continued, visibly shaking. After a beat she added, "Bloody Mary."

"Alright, that's enough. I'm calling your parents!" he ordered, not interested in listening to Crystal. As much as Crystal was a bit of a troublemaker and could be sassy when she wanted to be, Archie was surprised she would go this far to prove her little story true. Moreover, he was annoyed that his fun night had turned out so wrong. Now he had to explain to her parents what happened, and who knows where that would go.

After Archie called Alicia and Crystal's parents, Crystal was still pleading her case. "You saw it, didn't you?" Crystal insisted, near hysterics, her neat blonde braids loose around her shoulders as her bright blue eyes begged for someone to confirm her story. Blotches of red spotted her neck and face.

Margot glanced between Crystal and Archie, and added, "I don't know..."

"That's enough," Archie said. "Your parents are coming now, and I don't want to hear another word about it."

Archie put the movie back on and waited. The girls all sat far apart from each other, sulking in their own way. Crystal insisted it wasn't her. Alicia tried not to cry from fear. And Margot kept a Boo Boo Buddy, a small ice pack made for kids, against her left cheek where the red scratch was.

Luckily, it wasn't long until the parents came and went. Crystal mumbled "I'm sorry" under her breath after Archie explained what had happened. He was surprised that her parents weren't upset with him. Maybe Crystal was known for doing these little pranks.

"Sorry tonight was such a bust," Archie said to Margot. "Want milk and cookies at least? I just put a batch in the oven."

Margot nodded, but she wasn't acting like herself. Her eyes were focused on something far away, and she kept picking at the cut on her face, as if checking that it was still there, that it was actually real.

"It'll heal quickly," Archie offered, wondering if she was worried about what their parents might say. He had already texted them the news, and his mother was furious. *I knew that brat was no good!* she had texted him back. "Mom and Dad aren't mad at you," he added, wondering if that was what she was worried about.

Margot didn't seem to hear him. Instead, she said, "Can I tell you something?" Her voice was even and controlled. She held her head down, periodically touching the scratch on her face.

"Of course," he said, laying out warm-from-the-oven chocolate chip cookies and two glasses of milk. This had always been his favorite nighttime treat. He would often sneak down after his parents were asleep to have some, but he'd resisted indulging since he started dieting. But Margot had had a rough night, and the best cure for that was cookies and milk. He dipped the first cookie and shoved the whole thing in his mouth. Margot usually giggled at this and then called him the cookie monster. This time she didn't.

"I saw something..." she said, her voice small.

Archie struggled to swallow the cookie, and looked at her, curiously. "Saw what?"

"When we played the game..." she said, her eyes glued to the table. "I saw...*something*. It came out of the mirror, and it touched my face." Instinctively, she touched the cut on her face, wincing in pain but holding her fingers to it anyway as if it were proof.

"You said Crystal did it," Archie said, trying not to sound spooked. He had to be the adult here.

Margot shook her head. "It's the only thing that makes sense, but..." Margot started to shake. Her skinny shoulders clenched tightly.

"Hey, it's OK. It was just your imagination," Archie offered. "It happens to me all the time."

"Really?" Margot said, wiping away a tear.

"Absolutely. Sometimes I'm in the hallway, and I think I see something behind me, and it scares me, but when I turn the lights on, nothing is there. It's just my imagination."

"Is that why you cover all the mirrors in the house?" Margot asked.

Archie turned beet red. "Um, I don't do that..." he lied, unsure how he could explain why he did it without making himself sound pathetic.

"Yes, you do. Is it because you see something in the mirror, too?"

"Listen," Archie started, in his big brother voice, "You didn't see anything in the mirror. Crystal was being a bully, and she scratched you and then tried to make you second guess yourself, so she wouldn't be in trouble. You didn't do anything wrong. And nothing bad happened aside from Crystal ruining our fun night."

Margot seemed to mull this over in her head. "So, she scratched me?"

Archie nodded. "She said sorry though. She probably thought it would be funny."

Margot nodded, finally taking a cookie and dunking it in the milk. But she didn't seem convinced. She wore a pout and worry plagued her eyes. It was time for Brave Big Brother to come out. "Alright, do you want me to do it and show you that it's OK?" Archie offered.

Margot perked up at that and nodded.

Archie wasn't worried about it. After all, he could just go into the bathroom and not say anything, then come out and tell her everything is fine. But then Margot said, "Make sure to say it loud so I can hear you, OK?"

"Uh, yeah, sure," Archie managed. He wasn't scared. Not really. Not like when he has to talk to a cute boy or give a speech in front of the class. But he was unnerved. He wasn't scared of Bloody Mary. He just didn't want to have to look at himself in the mirror. Margot had no idea what horrors could be seen when staring at yourself in a mirror. Maybe he could just keep his eyes closed, like he did when he was younger...

He stepped into the bathroom. It was lit by a few dim streetlights coming from the window. There was just enough light to see his silhouette in the reflection, but nothing more than that. "What do I do now?" he asked.

"Close the door," Margot said, and then added. "Then say 'Bloody Mary' three times while looking in the mirror."

How silly, he thought. Margot wasn't one to make up stories, but it had to have been Crystal who scratched her. He stared into the mirror and worked up the nerve to say it. Yet, the idea concerned him. "This is dumb," he said out loud, but he didn't leave. He wasn't going to be scared off by some harmless kid prank. Plus, after he said it and was fine, Margot would feel better. If he closed his eyes, he would be giving in to some ridiculous fear. His unhappy reflection stared back at him. His round face and double chin looked bigger than usual. His dark green eyes showed black in the moonlight. His curly black hair was a moppy mess atop his head. "OK, you can do this," Archie muttered to himself, wondering why his heartbeat had sped up and why his hands suddenly felt sweaty. "Don't be a baby...3...2...1..."

"Bloody Mary..." he said, wondering for how long he had that mole on his chin.

"Bloody Mary..." he said again, wishing he would stop eating so much and just lose a little bit of weight. He shouldn't have had those cookies...

"Bloody Mary..." he said finally. His eyes adjusted to the dark, and he could see himself more clearly.

For a moment, nothing happened.

Archie breathed a sigh of relief and closed his eyes. *Easy peasy,* he said to himself.

Then he opened his eyes.

There was something on his face. A piece of skin sagging. His usually warm skin felt cold to the touch. But more concerning than that, it felt...loose. Archie pulled at it.

And it came off.

He held his skin in his hand, a large red blotch on his face. He turned the light on, expecting the reflection to change. But it didn't.

"What the…" Archie muttered, looking at his reflection and then his hand.

Then all his skin started to sag, as if melting off—all the hair and flab and skin that he had wished would disappear oozed down towards the black and white vinyl floor in a big heap. Archie screamed. His mind raced for any kind of explanation, but all he could think about was his horrific reflection. Lumps of skin and blood piled onto the floor. His once chubby, yet normal, face was blood and veins and muscle. Archie's stomach churned, and he heaved into the toilet bowl. Bits of undigested cookie and pizza swam in the water.

"Archie, what's wrong?" Margot said.

Archie didn't want her to see him this way. He yelled, "Get back!" but saw her running towards him in the mirror. Didn't she see what he saw? The horrible monster he had turned into. He was hideous. Horrifying. Something worse than any horror movie he had ever seen.

"Did you get a tummy ache?" Margot asked, pulling his hair back the way he did when she had the flu last year.

"Wait, don't—" Archie started saying, but stopped when he caught his reflection in the mirror again.

Aside from looking pale and sick, there was nothing wrong with his face. Nothing was peeling or bleeding or oozing. It was just him. Regular old Archie. "Yeah, just too much sugar I guess," Archie managed, completely confused. *Spooked by your own imagination,* Archie thought, but he couldn't shake the horrific image he had just seen. "Thanks," he said to Margot, who was staring at her own reflection in the mirror now. She seemed entranced. "What's wrong?" he asked.

Then he heard a knock at the door.

The door creaked open just a little, and Margot's little face peeked out from the doorframe. "Are you OK? I heard you scream…"

"Wait, weren't you just—" Archie said, looking at the reflection. But the other Margot was gone. "Um, let's go finish the movie," he said, covering the mirror with a towel. He didn't bother to answer Margot when she asked what he was doing and if he felt OK and why did he scream. He turned the volume up on the T.V. and looked away from the screen whenever it went dark, too afraid of what he might see in the reflection.

About Vanessa Leonardo

Vanessa Leonardo is a horror writer from Staten Island, New York with an MFA in Creative Writing from the New School. She currently lives with her wife in New Jersey. The writers that have most influenced her were those she read as a young teen such as R.L. Stine, Stephen King, and V.C. Andrews. She loves anything spooky, scary, or paranormal. Her short story, "Deconstructing Arthur," was published as part of the *Doors of Darkness II: Trick or Treat* collection in 2024. Her short story, "3344 Degrees Farenheit," was published in the *Dolls in the Attic* collection in 2025. Her short story, "Parrish Photos," was published as part of Terrocore's *Doors of Darkness III: The Mall* collection in late 2025. Her debut novel, *The Magician,* is scheduled to come out this September!

The Beauty Tester
Whitney Trang

She had never felt more ugly.

Tony Cabott's party was at 3 o'clock. He played goalie on the high school soccer team, and his mother was friends with hers. They always said how Tony and Melissa were destined to be sweethearts. Melissa wasn't sure, but her mother only told her that she didn't know what she was talking about.

Now, this summer, she had a foolproof plan to get Tony Cabott to finally be her boyfriend. She had worked hard all winter long getting the perfect body to ensure success. She had eliminated the competition. She had one last thing to take care of, but after that, today was going to be *perfect*. Her mother would be proud of her. She hoped so, at least.

Melissa weaved through the bigger-than-usual mall crowd of screaming kids, exhausted mothers trying to wrangle them, and bored fathers who were forced to go on a shopping trip.

"Hey, watch it!" a woman cried out as she pulled a red-haired boy to her side. Melissa had nearly run him over in her haste.

"Watch your kid!" Melissa continued on her way to the one place where she could get rid of the rash on her face.

VenuShell, the largest cosmetic brand in the country, had a shop located near the department store on the lower level of the mall. Themed after the famous painting of the Roman goddess of beauty, the store's interior featured signage in pastel blue, green, pink, and yellow, marking the different sections of the store. Nautical decorations like shells and ships hung on the walls, and a large white marble statue of Venus herself sat in the center of the store.

Posters featuring a diverse group of models advertising all things beauty and skin care were plastered on the walls. Employees dressed in pink scrubs with lilac aprons tied around their waists, and shoppers crowded the large space. Colorful bottles, tubes, and boxes lined the walls and shelves. Large, bold font screamed sales that were happening during Independence Day weekend.

She made her way toward the east section of the store, where a yellow sign with the word SKINCARE hung above it.

Rows and rows of shelves stocked with a variety of skincare creams, lotions, and ointments spread out in front of her.Melissa scanned the labels on the bottles. She caught words like "for acne-prone skin," "for oily skin," and "for combination skin." None of them were for rashes or dry skin. She continued on, keeping an eye out for *something* that would help.

"Dewey Honey. A lightweight serum to get smooth skin." Melissa picked up a small, clementine-colored tube and opened it. A sweet, fruity scent wafted toward her nose, and she wondered if it really could get rid of the rash.

She grabbed the tester and walked toward a large, full-length mirror at the end of the aisle. Double checking to make sure no one was around, Melissa took off her sunglasses.

Her mother always placed great emphasis on the way Melissa looked because it was her *looks* that would attract a "good husband." Like Tony.

A good husband wouldn't abandon her like her father did her mother. A good husband would take care of and provide for Melissa and the family. The old ladies at church would sigh and say she would make a lovely wife and how any man would be lucky to marry her one day.

She didn't feel so lucky.

And what was the use of a husband? Surely there were other options. Melissa had tried to find out for herself, but her mother quickly shot it down.

"Focus on getting a good husband," her mother said. "It'll lead to a good future."

Melissa saw herself reflected in the mirror: a sixteen-year-old girl of average height and weight. Her long, dark brown hair reached her waist, and her eyes shone like polished amber. Her face was only ruined by that weird rash.

That morning, a flaky, red spot just beneath the corner of her right eye itched. She scratched it and scratched it, but it was so itchy. When she looked at herself in the bathroom mirror, the spot grew to a quarter-sized patch. The old ladies at church would surely drag their immature, buffoonish grandsons away from her now. Tony would probably never be her husband, much less her boyfriend, with the way she looked now.

Her heart raced at the thought.

Melissa squeezed out a pea-sized drop of the cream. She rubbed it furiously into that spot and fanned her face to let it dry.

Her skin remained as dry and flaky as ever.

She tried again.

And again.

The spot grew to the size of a half dollar with all of the rubbing and scratching.

"For best results, apply to the area twice daily. After eight weeks, skin will appear brighter and smoother." Melissa groaned, throwing the tube on the ground. She didn't have eight weeks to wait for the damn cream to work! The rash was emerging *now*! Tony's party was in four hours! She threw her sunglasses back on. A bit of the rash peeked out from underneath the lens, but Melissa hoped no one would notice.

Melissa rounded the corner to go to the next aisle when she spotted her.

A girl her age, with dark blonde hair, and honey brown eyes framed by thin, black rimmed glasses was restocking the shelf with makeup pallets. Seeing her made Melissa's blood boil.

"Angie, what are you doing *here*?" Melissa asked loudly.

The girl looked up at her.

"I work here now," Angie said.

Melissa saw that she wore the telltale pink VenuShell uniform. She looked just as uncomfortable as Melissa felt.

"What are *you* doing here?"

"I need some makeup before going to Tony's party." Melissa pretended not to see the grimace on Angie's face when she said Tony's name.

"Why are you acting like you're obsessed with him?" Angie asked.

"I have no idea what you're talking about," Melissa said. "*He's* obsessed with *me*. He always has been. And we'd make a good couple."

"Right." Angie looked skeptical, which infuriated Melissa even more. "Do *you* think you and he would make a 'good' couple? Or is that coming from your mother?"

"Just stay away from me," Melissa said.

"I am at my job," Angie reminded her. "Why did *you* come and talk to *me*?"

"I..." Melissa couldn't tell Angie the truth. How she had so desperately wanted to see Angie, to speak to her, to touch her. But it was not "good" for her. That's what Melissa's mother said anyway.

"It's nice to see you haven't changed, Melissa." Angie shook her head and walked to a nearby display of neon-colored nail polishes.

Melissa huffed and stomped her foot in anger. She had fought hard to not think about her these past couple of months, and she wasn't going to start thinking about her again. Her mother wouldn't like that. Melissa shook her head, forcing herself to think about her rash instead of Angie's smooth, blemish-free face.

Wasn't there a single skin care cream or item that would help her get rid of this rash?

"Excuse me." A woman tapped Melissa's shoulder.

"What?" Melissa whipped around to face a woman who could be around her grandmother's age. But in contrast to her grandmother's stretched out skin, glassy eyes, and somewhat sickly pale complexion, this woman's skin was smooth and blemish free, her deep brown eyes were shiny and warm. Her long silver hair stylishly cascaded over her narrow shoulders. She carried an oversized black leather purse. Melissa wasn't sure what the brand of the bag was, but she was certain she had seen it before in one of the fashion magazines her mother subscribed to.

"I hear you're looking for something that will heal that hideous rash on your face?" the woman asked with a small smile.

"Maybe." Melissa adjusted her sunglasses, her face growing red with a mixture of anger and embarrassment.

"I have something that you should try." The woman took out a green glass jar the size of an apple from her bag. It had a white label, and the words "all-purpose skin cream" were written in a dark green font. Embossed gold letters sitting above them were the brand's name: Ensorcell Cosmetics. The woman held out the jar toward Melissa.

"What's that?" Melissa asked.

"The miracle you're searching for," the woman said. "You can call it a free beauty sample."

"Do you promise it'll actually help?" Melissa looked at the woman.

"I promise it'll help unleash the beauty from within," the woman smiled, continuing to hold out the jar to her.

Melissa took the jar from the woman. She *needed* the rash to be gone.

"Must be some European brand." She had never heard of the brand before. She unscrewed the top, and the cream inside was a pretty mint green with a perfect little swirl on top. A whiff of jasmine and citrus started calming her angry, beating heart.

Melissa dipped her forefinger and middle finger into the cream. It was smooth and chilly to the touch. When she pulled back her fingers, a small dollop of the skin cream stuck to the pads of her fingers.

She headed toward a mirror and took off her sunglasses. She gently rubbed the cream into her skin using a small circular motion.

Her skin tingled. If this actually worked, she'd buy the cream and go home to get ready for the party.

The tingling grew stronger as the cream seeped deeper into her flesh. It didn't hurt, but it wasn't what she was expecting.

Melissa touched her cheek. A chunk of her cheek, with layers of skin, muscle, and fat, wiggled like a loose tooth. Was it a giant pimple? A Vesuvius made from her skin that was just waiting to erupt with pus and blood?

Just her luck. Now she had to deal with acne and a weird rash. She squeezed it, hoping that it wouldn't leave a mark.

The chunk of her cheek detached from her face to reveal rough, dry, greenish-yellow scales underneath.

"Ah! Stupid cream!" She screamed, rubbing her face harder in frustration. More flesh fell from her face and the scales spread down her cheek and down her neck.

"Excuse me, are you alright?" A different VenuShell employee approached. This woman's curly red hair was loosely piled on top of her head in a messy bun. "Mary Ann" was engraved in curly script on her pale pink name tag.

"Oh, bite me!" Melissa spat back. "Who can be alright when they look like this?"

A small crowd of shoppers gathered around them. They stared openly and whispered to their companions, covering their mouths.

"Miss, I think you need to calm down," Mary Ann said. "You're causing quite a disturbance."

Melissa was not to be told to calm down. "*Your* employee brought me poisoned makeup!"

"Miss..." Melissa could tell that Mary Ann was close to losing it. She didn't care. She wanted someone to *help* her. "Miss, there is no one here who would've given you poisoned makeup."

"Yes, there is! She was here, and she gave me this!" Melissa shoved the Ensorcell Cosmetics jar into Mary Ann's hand.

"We don't carry this brand here," Mary Ann said.

"Then how did your employee give it to me?" Melissa demanded. "I mean, *look* at me!"

"Miss, please, this is your final warning. If you don't stop screaming, I *will* call security."

"Call them!" Melissa shrieked. "You think I'm scared of some mall cop? My family will sue you for everything that you have, and no one will shop here ever again! I..." She spotted a familiar face among the crowd. "You!"

Melissa charged forward, breaking apart the sea of gathered bystanders.

"Hey!" one of them cried out in protest. But Melissa had her eyes on one person, the person who was responsible for all of this. It was *her* fault.

Melissa pointed at Angie. "You set me up, didn't you?"

"I have no idea what you're talking about," Angie said.

"Miss, you really have to go." Mary Ann stood in front of Angie. She spoke into a walkie-talkie. "We need security at VenuShell, store A7."

"You ruined my life!" Melissa cried. "Don't you get that? Why won't you leave me alone, Angie?"

"That's enough." A stern woman's voice commanded. Melissa looked up to see the woman who had given her the cream, standing next to Mary Ann.

"What did you do to me?" Melissa demanded.

"The cream worked as it should," the woman said.

"Are you kidding me right now?" Melissa wanted to rip the woman's tongue out of her mouth. "*Look* at me!"

"The cream only works to bring out the beauty that's inside you," the woman said. "And what is truer than beauty that resides in our hearts?"

"I don't... this isn't me!" Melissa screamed. "How can you call this beauty? I'm turning into a monster!"

"You are seeing yourself the way that you think others see you," the woman said. "But it doesn't have to be this way."

"I... I..." Melissa didn't know what to say. She wasn't... she surely wasn't... Melissa had never met this woman before in her entire life. How could this woman know?

"You don't know what you're talking about," Melissa said.

"Oh, but I think *you* do."

Whispers surrounded Melissa. She couldn't tell what they were saying. Then they got louder. Angry, mean voices spoke out around Melissa.

"It's not right."

"Marriage is between a man and a woman."

"They should just keep it to themselves."

"Shut up!" Melissa covered her ears, trying to stop all the nonsense. She looked around the sea of faces, staring at her.

"I'm a monster." Melissa's own voice boomed around her. She pushed her hands harder against her ears in an attempt to block out the voices.

But it was no use.

***

"We can do this." It was Angie. She and Melissa were in her room a few months ago.

"I'm... I'm scared." Melissa said.

"Don't be scared." Angie had tried to tell her. "We can do this together."

Together. It felt nice. No matter what anyone else told her, she had never felt this way about anyone else before, not even Tony.

Angie felt like warm sunshine. She was the one that Melissa imagined holding hands with at the altar. But her mother and the people at her church... they wouldn't allow it.

Angie held Melissa's hands.

"Melissa, I love you."

"What is this?" Melissa's mother had walked in on them then. Her mother's rage was nothing that Melissa had ever seen before. She threw Angie out and turned to Melissa.

"You can't see her again, Melissa."

"We go to the same school, Mom," Melissa said. "Of course, I'll see her."

"No. What I meant was you can't see her like *that*."

"I don't understand."

"I just want the best for you, okay?" Melissa's mother softened. "Any parent would want a good future for their child. And this... *thing* with Angie won't get you that good future. Can't you understand that?"

"I... I guess." Melissa couldn't figure out the feelings swirling and buzzing inside her chest. Was she angry? Upset? Mad?

At who?

"Promise me you will *never* see that girl again and that you'll stop this monstrous behavior."

"Okay, Mom."

Melissa's mother pulled her into a tight hug. "It is for your own good, Melissa."

But Melissa *had* to see Angie again, at least to explain what happened. The next day at school, before everyone got there, Melissa met up with Angie one more time.

"It was horrible what we did," Melissa told Angie.

"Melissa, I don't think you're the one talking to me right now." Angie stepped closer, but Melissa stepped back, keeping that distance between them. "Melissa, I love you."

"I..."

"Tell me you love me, too."

"I..." Melissa wanted to say those words Angie so desperately wanted to hear. But her mother's angry, red face prevented her from saying it. "I can't, Angie."

"Why not? Why can't you say it, Melissa?"

"Because it's not right. My mother, she... she says it's wrong. That it's monstrous. That I have a good future ahead of me and I can't ruin it."

"How would you ruin it?" Melissa saw the hurt in Angie's eyes. How red they were from being on the verge of tears.

"Angie, please," Melissa said.

"I don't care what your mother or anyone else thinks. What do *you* think, Melissa? Do you think you would ruin your 'good future' if you said you loved me?"

"I won't have one if I'm with you." Melissa knew that what she said came from her mother, and that swirling, buzzing feeling inside her chest was suffocating. "I..."

"Forget it," Angie brushed her off. "Maybe your mother is half right. Maybe you are a monster."

***

Monster.

Monster.

Monster.

The word ricocheted inside Melissa's skull. She opened her eyes and scanned the crowd gathered around her. People stared at her, whispering to their friends behind their hands.

Melissa stopped at Angie. Mary Ann's arm was still wrapped around her shoulders, and Angie looked like she had seen a ghost. This was her fault. Melissa knew what she had to do now.

"Please, Angie, you have to help me," Melissa dropped to her knees. She looked up at Angie, who had stepped out from Mary Ann's arm. "I'm sorry! Okay? I shouldn't have... I'm sorry."

"I..."

"I didn't mean to hurt you because hurting you hurt me. I listened to voices that didn't matter and never will. The only ones that will matter are yours and mine. And I'm telling you now, I'm sorry, Angie."

"Get up." Angie helped Melissa to her feet. "I'm sorry, too. I didn't realize that you were under so much pressure. But I hope you know now that it's going to be okay. As long as we have each other, we are going to be okay. More than okay."

"I know that now," Melissa nodded. "You're the one I've always wanted." She pulled Angie in close. "I love you, Angie."

"I love you, Melissa. You're not a monster. You never were."

When Melissa looked into the mirror in front of her, a rash-free face stared back.

About Whitney Trang

Whitney Trang graduated from the University of California, Santa Barbara where she double majored in English and Communication. She has always loved books. She began writing her own stories at age seven and hasn't stopped. She published her first short story in 2014. You can find her on Twitter @wctwrites.

First Day of School
Dawn Winters

"Echakcclachhh!!!!"

I reeled up from a dreamless sleep, choking on my own spit. After an epic coughing fit, a large glob of reddish-brown phlegm dislodged from my throat and onto my lap.

I startled, staring at the messy wad while trying to wake up and not freak out. Why was it that color? Is this the start of some nameless disease that will soon end me? Not wanting to be like my hypochondriac mother, I decided to avoid Googling.

Sighing, I picked up my phone and swiped up. The screen lit up from the movement, showing me 8:30 AM on Monday, August 18, but it wouldn't unlock. Fuck. It didn't matter anyway... I was late on the first day of my senior year at Little Haven High. I threw my phone back on my bed and crawled out from the covers, my legs cramping slightly from the sudden movement. I stretched up on my toes, feeling stiff from sleep.

"Ughhhhhhh," I moaned and dragged myself to my closet. At least I could see I had picked out my outfit the night before: jeans and an oversized retro band shirt of my mom's. TLC wasn't the same after Left Eye died, but "Crazy, Sexy, Cool" was going to be the vibe of this school year. I pulled on my Doc Martins and stuffed my wallet in the back pocket after attaching its chain to a belt loop.

In the bathroom, I hit the switch with the heel of my palm and looked in the mirror. A pale, slightly puffy version of myself stared back at me. I scoffed, which caused another coughing fit, this time with nothing three-dimensional exiting my throat. With only time to do either skin or teeth care, I chose the former, groping through the drawer for the moisturizer my dad bought me as a part of an ill-conceived beauty gift basket assembled for my 17th birthday in an effort to help me be more femme. Ironic—he knew more about beauty products than me.

Slathering on the moisturizer, I tried to pinch some color into my cheeks, but none would come. Welp, I thought, the Wednesday Addams aesthetic would have to do for the day. I ran my fingers through my hair, happy I had chosen to cut it all off after watching the first season of the original *L Word* and seeing Shane's shaggy locks. I slapped the light switch again, glad my mom's early shift at the plant had her leaving hours before. She wouldn't be there to yell at me to do things properly.

I headed downstairs, stumbling over my feet on a middle stair. Clutching the banister, I slowed down a bit—no need for a bloody nose to add to the attention of me walking into first period late. Stopping in the kitchen, I briefly considered breakfast. The bowl of fruit on the counter was not calling my name, and there was no time for protein, which is what I really wanted. I grabbed a banana and shoved it in my bag. The clock on the stove read 8:45. At this point, I was going to be late to second period, and Ms. Paré was not going to be happy, even though I was her favorite.

I took out my phone to text Oli that I was on my way. When I swiped up, it still wouldn't unlock. Great. I could see that she had texted me a few times, but there was nothing I could do. Turning on my heel, I started to jog toward the door. My boot immediately caught on the edge of its toe, and I keeled forward. Instinctively, I reached out to brace myself, forgetting everything I had learned about falling in intermural volleyball, and heard the distinct crunch of bone against bone as my palms made contact with the floor, followed by my chest.

Groaning, I laid there for a second. With my right hand, I pushed myself up to roll over on my left side. Glancing at my hand, I saw my middle finger bent back at an unnatural angle. It must have taken the brunt of my fall. I felt no pain, though. Shaking my hand out, I thought I probably severed a nerve when I sprained it. I pushed myself onto my knees and without thinking yanked the finger as hard as I could. Again, I felt no pain, and the finger looked oddly frozen in place, but at least it was pointed in the right direction. Standing up with no time to take further stock of my body, I pulled the front door open and headed outside.

I got in my car—a bright blue Pontiac Sunfire my mom had driven through college. Unlike my t-shirt, the vintage had no appeal, but it was a free car and at least it had a working sunroof. I had to pay for the insurance and gas, and my job at the state's last remaining movie theatre paid enough to cover both. I turned the key, and the sounds of Our Lady Peace covering "Tomorrow Never Knows" filled the space. Mom's soundtrack to *The Craft* has been stuck in the CD player since her senior year of college. It wasn't the worst, but I needed something from this decade to power me to school. I switch to the radio, and the baseline of Doechii's "Bullfrog" pumped out the speakers. Perfect. I threw the car in reverse and sped toward school.

The heat was so bad I could see it in waves over the cars parked in the student lot of Little Haven. They made us park in the very back by the football field. At least seniors got the front ten rows. I fumbled with my seatbelt—probably another thing broken in the car—and got out. Making my way slowly through the crowded lot, I thought I would get to the building covered in sweat, but fate gave me one break and I arrived dry. Pulling open the door, I was too much in a rush to feel the sweet relief of the air conditioning.

Without stopping at my locker, I headed to second period English. When I peeked in the classroom, I could see Oli in the back row, her head lolled back, staring at the ceiling. Their hair was slicked back in its usual ponytail, and they were wearing their trademark basketball shorts and baggy t-shirt. She hated school as much as she loved reading, so I knew she would at least be half paying attention to Ms. Paré, but her heart and mind were already thinking ahead to after the final bell rang and she could be on the court. Basketball was their first love, but I didn't mind coming in at a close second.

I slowly opened the door, trying unsuccessfully to sneak in, when Ms. Paré stopped what she had been discussing and swiveled her head toward me with the rest of the class.

"Nice of you to join us, Ms. Maiani," she said, flatly. "We were just discussing 'The Epic of Gilgamesh'…I'm sure you're familiar?"

No. No, I wasn't familiar with "The Epic of Gilgamesh." I shrugged, attempting to exude an unmatched coolness (a 'la Shane) and the right amount of contrition for Ms. Paré. She was my favorite, too, and my top choice for the letter of recommendation I would need to get into a good journalism program next year. As for the epic poem, Ms. Paré was known for starting the school year with a lesser-known ancient text, both to challenge us and get us to avoid relying on the internet for a good summary. She cleared her throat, breaking my brief paralysis, and I began clunking back toward the empty seat next to Oli.

"Where were you, B?" she hissed, her consummate spearmint gum shoved to the corner of her mouth. I could tell she was frustrated, but that didn't stop her from using her nickname for me. She called me "B," which to most people was short for my middle name, Beatrice, but we both knew it was also short for other sweet names, including Boo, Bae, Babe… Her not using my first name, Zoe, was a good sign that she wasn't that mad. I called her Oli, which was technically short for Olivia but also recognized that Oli's gender was fluid most days.

I mouthed, "Slept in…phone wouldn't work!" to her and showed her that my phone would not unlock. She snatched it and swiped up, entering my passcode effortlessly. Shooting me an exasperated but bemused look, she handed the phone back to me as Ms. Paré shouted "phones away" mid-sentence without breaking stride in her pacing or the lecture.

"Without Gilgamesh, we would not have Katniss Everdeen. Without Gilgamesh, we would not have Harry Potter. And, without Gilgamesh…" she paused dramatically, and I knew she was about to say something provocative. "We would not have the story of Jesus."

The half of the class that was locked in frowned in thought collectively. If she didn't have a cult following among students and alumni, Ms. Paré would have been unceremoniously asked to resign about once a week. I loved her for it.

The rest of the period we learned about how the five Sumerian poems about Gilgamesh and King Uruk survived from the ancient world and were assigned the 4,000-year-old text for reading that night. The bell rang, and chaos ensued as everyone gathered their stuff while trying to check their phones, desperate for the content missed in the 55 minutes of class.

I looked at Oli; she was waiting expectantly for me to get up.

"What happened to your finger? It looks a little purple."

"I tripped on my way out the door. I don't know what happened this morning. I set, like, three alarms on my phone. It must not be working... I can't wait to get the 20." Oli knew I wasn't the best with technology, and my mom's old iPhone 11 was on its last leg. Mom was raised by her great-grandmother who survived the Great Depression, so buying a phone when my current phone technically worked was not something she was willing to do. If I wanted a new phone, I'd have to put in extra hours tearing tickets and cheerfully repeating, "Enjoy your show," to every ancient Boomer who still went to the movies. The only reason she had a newer phone is because the cell company had basically given her one for free.

"Your phone is fine, B. You just suck at tech," she said, pulling me in for a kiss when Ms. Paré's back was to us.

"Woah. B. Your breath is KICKIN'!" Oli listened almost exclusively to 90s hip hop, so most of her slang was courtesy of Warren G, Missy Elliott, other mainstream artists, and a handful of underground artists she found in my mom's stash of tapes. Mom had inexplicably saved her tapes and had recently bought a boombox from eBay. She and Oli had bonded over the lo-fi sounds of songs recorded from the radio onto a tape. Mom was unphased when I came out to her, but she still had high standards for anyone who dared to ask me out. Oli passed the test when they walked in the house wearing an original Notorious B.I.G. shirt.

"I didn't have time to brush this morning," I mumbled, my hand reflexively moving to my face. She slipped me a piece of gum as I hurried from the room, not wanting to be late for the next class.

Third period was trig with Mr. Dingle, whose name inspired dozens of nick-names. Maybe if he made math more interesting, he wouldn't be such a target. The minutes on the ancient wall clock slowly ticked by. All I could think about was lunch. I wasn't sure what the cafeteria would be serving, but I hoped it would involve red meat. My mind wandered, thinking about a rare filet (which would never be served at Little Haven), racks of ribs, or at least a burger.

The bell rang, and I was out of my seat before anyone else. The hallways were too crowded to run—students lingered at lockers that were relics from the past, and I had to push against the throngs of juniors and seniors who could leave school for lunch. As a senior, I could also leave, but my weekly lunch allowance went farther at school. As I neared the cafeteria, I couldn't smell what was being served. The usual pungent smell of mass-produced, reheated food usually permeated the corridors near the room, but today my singular focus on getting meat saved me from distraction.

I got in line without stopping to claim a spot at our usual table. Craning my neck to see what was on the warming table, I heard and felt a soft pop. I instinctively rubbed my shoulder and neck without feeling pain. Weird. I quickly glanced down at my finger, which had gone from a light purple to more of a light gray, and I shoved it under my tray. When I was next in line to order, I saw that cheeseburgers were one of the options.

"Can I have a cheeseburger with three patties and no bun?" I asked. "And, no vegetables!" The thought of eating a vegetable made me feel a little ill. The lunch worker looked at my wryly but said nothing.

After I paid, I grabbed a seat next to Oli and our friends Daryl, Shaun, and Alice. I glanced at Alice to see what she was wearing. She was never without her harness and black knee-high boots—both had become her brand—and she didn't disappoint on the first day back.

"New harness, Alice?" I asked, through a mouthful of burger. I had shoved half of the first patty in my mouth as I sat down.

"You like it?" she replied, sniffing slightly. "What's that smell?"

"Oh, B didn't brush her teeth this morning," Oli said matter-of-factly.

Before I could protest, a piece of macerated meat lodged itself in my throat. I began coughing and trying to swallow simultaneously. Daryl, always ready for action, began pounding my back to help prize it from my throat.

Ignoring the havoc and in a raised voice, Alice said, "No… it's more like rotted meat."

"Maybe it's the hamburger," said Shaun, mostly to himself. Shaun was a quiet kid who was absorbed into our group by happenstance. He wasn't particularly charismatic, but he also didn't bother us, so he just kind of hung out.

The meat finally slid down my throat, and I sipped some water. Oli glanced at me and asked, "What's that bump on your neck?"

I reached for my neck for the second time that hour and felt a hard bump toward the base of my head near my ear.

"I don't know? I think I just overextended it seeing what was for lunch."

"You're tripping, B. You should have your dad check it out."

I took another huge bite of burger and shook my head. My dad was a nurse; I didn't want him worrying about yet another problem caused by my clumsiness.

Daryl had gone back to his pile of fries. He declared himself to be a vegetarian last year, which was a challenge because he hated all fruit and vegetables except potatoes. Alice had given up on trying to figure out the source of the smell and was trying to convince Shaun to dye his red hair an even deeper shade of red to match hers. Oli tilted their chair back and sighed; they were used to my stubborn streak.

I grabbed the last of the meat patties and took another sizeable bite. As I chewed, I thought about what happened this morning and if any of the injuries were related. Deep in reflection, I suddenly crunched down on something hard.

"Acchhkkkk!" I opened my mouth and rooted around inside to grab the offending piece of cow bone that was clearly left in the ground meat. My fingers found the hard object, and I pulled it out. Staring down at my hand, I yelped.

It was a molar. My molar. I swallowed and moved my tongue around my mouth, finding the void in my gums. What. The. Hell. My mom was going to kill me. Years of checking to see if I'd brushed, regular dental checks even when money was tight, and a lifetime ban on soda unless it was a special occasion. Cavities were enemy number one, and I just lost a whole tooth.

"What the FUCK is that?!" The front legs of Oli's chair clunked on the linoleum, and she leaned toward my open palm.

I closed my hand in a fist and snatched it away from her. "NOTHING!"

"It looked like a tooth. B, did you just lose a tooth?"

"No! It was just a piece of gristle in the burger." I was suddenly full, the meat sitting heavy in my stomach. I abruptly stood up.

"I'm going to head to AP bio. I heard Weidmann is going to have us dissect an earthworm to show that we're good enough to be there. I want to be ready." My friends blinked up at me, unsure about how to respond to my clearly erratic behavior. Silently, Oli passed me another piece of gum before I walked away.

As I left the cafeteria, my tongue worried at the gap in my back molars. I had expected to taste blood, but the only sensation I felt was the empty socket that once held my tooth in place. I unwrapped the gum and shoved it in my mouth. I barely registered the mint taste as I walked into the bio lab.

Weidmann was sitting at her desk. She glanced up as I walked in, "Hey Zoe! Good summer?"

I nodded with a quick, closed mouth, "Mmmmhmm," and moved toward the back of the room to a table in the corner.

"Why don't you sit up front? I might need to monitor some students who are less dexterous with sharp objects."

I sighed heavily and pivoted. Weidmann wasn't wrong, but did she have to be so blunt? I stomped up to the front and dumped my bag in a chair.

"Grab an apron and an instrument kit—we're dissecting earthworms today!" Weidmann's enthusiasm for biology was not as infectious as she thought.

I donned the apron, whose questionable stains I chose to ignore and sat in my seat waiting for the others to get to class. While I waited, I tried my phone again. Weidmann was only a few years out of college, so she was not as salty about us having our phones out in class.

That didn't matter, though. My phone again lit up with movement and again would not open. I scoffed and went to slam it on the table without looking. It slipped from my hand before it hit, my palm made contact with something cold, and I heard metal crashing against metal—all within milliseconds of each other.

"Zoe," Weidmann's voice came out a bit shaky when the clatter died down.

"WHAT?!" I didn't mean to yell, but by then I was done. I looked at Weidmann's ashen face and looked down at my hand.

The tray of dissection tools had toppled, and a scalpel was sticking out of my palm, its blade an inch deep in my flesh. For a few seconds, I just stared at the metal protruding from my palm. Then, without thinking, I grabbed the instrument. As I yanked it out, I hear Weidmann scream, "ZOE, DON'T TAKE IT—"

Too late. With the scalpel gripped in my right hand, I gawked at my left palm, expecting blood to be pouring out of the sliced wound. Instead, a thick, red-tinted black substance began to slowly ooze from my hand.

"Zoe," Weidmann whispered. "Are you feeling okay?"

I wasn't. I wasn't feeling okay. I felt nauseous, the burgers still sitting undigested in my stomach. I gagged, heaving doubled over. With effort, I started coughing. In my woozy state, I thought throwing up might make me feel better. As I hacked, I could see Weidmann slowly backing up toward the door, her hand over her mouth.

Finally, I felt a piece of meat in the back of my throat. With one final cough, it flew out and hit the floor. Weidmann stopped retreating and gazed at the meat on the floor. But it wasn't meat.

It was a lump of spongy pink lung, streaked with black. It glistened on the floor in a small puddle of the same brownish-red, viscous fluid I had coughed up this morning. I covered my mouth and looked up at Weidmann.

"Zoe, do you remember what you did yesterday?" Weidmann voice was stronger and more leveled.

From behind my hand, I mumbled, "Why does that matter?"

"It's just the same outbreaks that Troy and Franklin experienced last year have been rumored to be here now," she said gently, still keeping her distance from my oozing hand and marble-streaked chunk of lung.

People didn't like to talk about the outbreak. It tore communities apart. Families with infected people were ostracized, the neighbors moving away immediately. Most people followed the guidelines hastily published by the government—keeping distant, only being in contact with known individuals, wearing masks—but a loud, passionate group took to Reddit and other platforms, vehemently denying the outbreak's existence and refusing to do anything the government said. Luckily, my parents followed the guidelines to the letter, and we were kept safe.

"Zoe?" Weidmann said, breaking me from my thoughts.

"I can't really remember what I did. I guess I got ready for school, hung out with Oli, had dinner with my parents, went to the park for a walk after..." I trailed off. I couldn't remember what happened in the park. I couldn't remember coming home. I couldn't remember going to bed.

"I think we need to call the principal," Weidmann said, moving toward the classroom intercom.

"NO!" I yelled, grabbing my bag off the chair. "I'm okay! I wasn't infected. I'm just not feeling well."

"Zoe, if you've been infected, you need to be quarantined. It's for everyone's safety," Weidmann said loudly, reaching for the intercom button.

Without thinking, I reached down and grabbed the hunk of lung from the floor, gripping it so tightly it squished through my fingers. I ran from the room, stumbling over my feet. When I reached the doors to the parking lot, I paused. I wasn't out of breath. I should have been out of breath, but I wasn't. I shook my head to make the thought disappear and pushed open the doors.

I started down the five concrete stairs leading from the school to the parking lot but tripped on the second one. Falling down the last three, I again fell with my hands outstretched. The left side of my face hit the sidewalk, and I let out an involuntary "oompf."

Lying on the concrete, I could see my middle finger lying on the sidewalk, a few inches from my right hand. Ignoring the severed digit, I pushed myself up to a standing position. Looking down, I saw my left foot was at a ninety-degree angle, the toes facing my right ankle. Fuck.

I started toward my car, slowly dragging my foot along the sidewalk, leaving my finger and the now unidentifiable lung lump splattered on the sidewalk. Grunting, I wiped at my mouth. Sweat poured down my face—I had finally started to feel the heat, but when I looked at my hand, I didn't see sweat. My hand was coated in sticky black liquid that had seeped from wounds on my cheek.

I tried to walk faster. If I could get to my car and get home, I'd be fine. All this could be explained. I'm sure Mom would know what to Google when she got home. I couldn't wait to be home. We could have dinner and just relax. My thoughts involuntarily shifted to dinner, and I realized what I wanted most for dinner was Mom. Or Dad. Or Oli. Or any human.

I violently shook the thought from my head. "No!" I said out loud, pulling my left foot along.

I finally made it to my car. Turning it on, I punched the CD button. Matthew Sweet's "Dark Secret" sounded from the speakers. I sat back in my seat and closed my eyes, listening to the lyrics.

"You are sickened by the weakness/Of a heart that's filled with fear/And if the world won't understand you/You can make it disappear..." I finished the song, letting the sound of the music flow through me.

I was suddenly calm. A sad sense of resolution washed over me. I knew what I had to do. For mom, for Oli, for all of them.

I reversed my car from the spot and as best I could, steered it out of the parking lot.

CENTERVILLE TEEN DIES FROM SINGLE-CAR COLLISION

August 19, 2028

Zoe B. Maiani, 17, died yesterday when her vehicle struck one of the columns holding up the Route 725 overpass on I-275. Maiani was alone in her 2002 Pontiac Sunbird when it collided with the column, and doctors say her wounds were primarily to her brain, as the car's airbags failed to deploy. Investigators estimate the car was traveling at a high rate of speed when it impacted with the column.

This story is breaking. More information will be released as we receive it.

About Dawn Winters

Dawn Winters lives in Alvaton, Kentucky with her wife, Sarah, and their brood of animals, including two dogs, two cats, and a flock of unruly chickens. She has MAs in Literature and Criminology and an EdD in Educational Leadership. She teaches English and Criminology at Western Kentucky University where she is also actively involved in living and learning communities and first gen student initiatives. She is an avid reader, true crime enthusiast, and occasional traveler. While she has published and presented on various pedagogical topics and has been writing and enjoying bad poetry, personal essays, and fanciful stories her whole life, this is her first piece of published fiction.

Inside Outside
Leon Lavender

"Bye!" I turn to wave, but Erin's long gone. She'll be off to work; she's a "mature" student at thirty-three, and has a mortgage to pay. I'm still washing up brushes and palettes in the sink, the porcelain stained fifty shades of everything. It turns out art students in college are just as messy as they were in grade school. Perhaps even more so, with the freedom and experimentation college brings. Finally, I dry my hands on the useless blue paper towels, stuff my sketchbooks into my own bag, and head for home.

My backpack is weighing me down today—my current project on gender dysphoria is several sketchbooks long already. I suppose I should have expected it; with the work being so personal, its like it just flows out of me. Although sometimes that "flow" is more akin to tearing a bandage off a wound and leaves me feeling like I've been bleeding out on the page.

Despite the heavy backpack making the walk home harder, I still take a detour into a corner shop to buy some sweets. I'm watching **The Substance** tonight, and I can't watch a film without snacks! I grab some Sour Gummy Blobs—my favourite— and something called "Devil's Breath" just because the name makes me laugh, and head to the counter. The man checks my items, chewing his gum thoughtfully.

"That'll be $5 young lady," he says.

I watch the wad of gum bounce around his open mouth, feeling my face flush. "I'm—"

I'm not a young lady, is what I want to say, but the words are as sticky in my throat as the chewing gum still bouncing around his mouth.

"Here," I say instead, placing the money in his hand and leaving the shop as quickly as I can without looking rude. I stop, leaning against the wall of the neighbouring building, pressing my fists against my eyes until colors flash under my eyelids. I thought the haircut would change things. I guess I thought wrong, again.

"Hey there."

I startle, opening my eyes to find a short, slender man in a charcoal suit and pristine white shirt. Way overdressed for this dump; he must be lost. "Can I—" I pause. Clear my throat. Try again, lower this time. "Uh, can I help you?"

The man smiles. "On the contrary," he said. "I thought *I* might help *you*."

I take a step back, but meet the wall. "Uh...How? Why?"

The man's smile widens, almost too much. "You seem troubled."

I shake my head, taking a sidestep instead. "Uh, no, I'm good. I'm fine, really. Uh, thanks for asking."

The man grasps my hand. I try to pull away, but he only places something in my palm, closing my fingers over it.

"If you change your mind, you can call me," he says, nodding down at my closed fist. Then he reaches down and plucks the "Devil's Breath" sweets from my hand. "Ha. Funny," he says, before tossing them back to me. I scrabble to catch them. "Remember," he says as he turns to leave, "you only have to call."

I run home after that. I don't know who that man is or what he wants from me, but I'm not hanging around to find out. I reach my house, fumble with my keys until the door falls open, run up the stairs—ignoring my parents greeting me by the wrong name—slam my bedroom door and sink against it.

Panting for breath, I finally uncurl my clenched fist. The paper falls to the ground. Not a phone number but instructions, and a symbol.

A pentagram?

Oh, you've got to be kidding me.

I toss it into the bin beside my desk.

***

I stand in front of my full-length mirror.

I know it's unhelpful, like my therapist says, but I always find myself returning to it. Taking in my soft face, soft arms with skinny wrists, the unwanted curves of my hips and chest. My new haircut—the one I was so pleased with two days ago—seems softer now, effeminate; could it be seen as a pixie cut? Why does nothing I do make people see me any differently? Why can't my outside match my inside?

I lash out, kicking over the bin. Rubbish spills out, the note from the stranger fluttering to land almost purposefully on top.

I pick it up, snorting in amusement. Sure. What the hell. Let's summon a demon or whatever this is supposedly for. The instructions tell me to paint the symbol on the floor in blood. Scribbled beside that in different handwriting are the words "can just be red paint" and "doesn't have to be directly on the floor."

I ponder this, then ransack my art supplies, pulling out a tube of red paint and a roll of cheap newsprint paper. I pin one end of the paper down with my art toolbox and the other with my desk chair, then set about painting the symbol. There's something almost meditative about painting those sweeping lines. By the time I'm finished, I'm calm again.

I stand back to admire my work. It looks like something out of a horror film; a cheap, shoestring budget one that came out in the mid 80s, capitalising off the success of those that came before it while adding absolutely nothing of note to the genre. Of course, I'd be lying if I said I didn't love those terrible films.

Next, the instructions call for a candle on the topmost point of the symbol. That's simple enough; I grab the scented candle from my windowsill, and set it down on the still-wet paint. Ugh, maybe I should have let that dry first. I hesitate with the lighter in my hand. Lighting a candle sat on a piece of paper, which is sat on a wooden floor… My parents will kill me if they find out.

I go to my door, and flick the lock into place. There. Less chance of being caught now.

Carefully, I hold the lighter's flame against the candle wick. It catches, a gentle flame taking hold. I stand back, quickly, and—

Nothing happens.

Yeah, I'm not sure what I expected. It was clearly a prank, and I obviously knew that, but a small part of me is disappointed. I'm about to lean down and blow out the candle when the flame leaps from the wick and onto the paper, igniting along the entire painted symbol. I scream—but clamp my hands over my mouth almost immediately. I can't let my parents find out I've set my room on fire! I dance on the spot, looking for something to put it out, but the flames grow taller and I'm forced to back into the wall.

Something—some*one*?—is emerging from the flames. Small horns sprout from their head, but otherwise their face is human, and somehow familiar. They're short, slender, and—

They're completely naked.

I flush, trying to look anywhere but below their waist.

"Ahh," the person—demon?—says, stretching his arms wide. Wings unfold behind him as he does so. "You *called*." He gives a satisfied smile that sets me on edge.

"You...You're the guy from earlier?"

The demon pauses, tapping his fingers on his lips. "It's more like the guy from earlier was me, rather than me being him," he says. "If you catch my drift."

I don't, but decide to ignore that. "What do you want?" I ask, backing up only to find I'm against the wall again. I'm getting tired of having my back against a wall. Something flickers in the demon's eyes.

"What do *I* want?" He shakes his head. "This isn't about me, it's about you. What do *you* want, Travis?"

"I—how do you know my name?"

"Again, this isn't about *me*, it's about—"

"Me," I say. "Okay. What if I don't want anything?"

The demon smiles, wider than looks comfortable. "Oh, I think you do." His eyes glitter. "Aren't you tired of having your back against a wall, Travis? Literally, and metaphorically?" He waves at my desk chair, still holding down the paper with the symbol on it. "Have a seat."

I hesitate, but figure if he wanted me dead he'd have already done it. I sit down.

"There," the demon says. "Nice and comfy. Now." He claps his hands together. "What can I do for you? What do you want most of all? Your deepest, most desperate desire?"

I shake my head. "Look, you really need to keep it down, my parents—"

"Can't hear a thing." The demon smiles. "All part of the service."

I glance at the door, but no one's come running yet.

"Fine. You're going to grant me a wish?"

The demon nods, then shakes his head. "Yes, but no. I'm not a genie."

I twist my hands in my lap. "But...You said you can give me what I want most."

The demon nods again. "Yes."

I swallow. "I... People don't see me as who I am."

The demon sighs, tilting his head. "That's not much for me to go on. That could mean you're a dog person but everyone thinks you're a cat person, or they think you like horror books when you really like romance, or—"

"They don't see me as a boy!" I snap, then sigh. "Sorry," I say. "I just wish my outside matched my inside, you know?"

The demon looks into my eyes with an intensity that's hard to pull away from. "And that's what you want? For your outside to match your inside?" he asks.

I nod. "Yes, more than anything."

The demon claps his hands together. "Then it's done. The deal is sealed."

I stand up. "Wait, what do you me—" My voice breaks off into a scream and I fall to the floor. My skin is burning, my organs are pulsating, moving around inside of me. I'm dying—I must be dying. It was a trick; this demon never wanted to help me—I've seen enough horror films to know that—and now he's *killed me* and I'm dying.

Something tears, I think—it's hard to tell one pain from another—something's wet against my skin; blood, or something thicker. I think I'm still screaming, but I can't tell where my mouth is. I can't tell where any part of me is. There's one final, heaving, rupturing burst of pain, and it stops.

I'm dead.

I must be.

There's a rasping, wet sound nearby. I open my eyes.

The demon is sat on my desk chair, watching me, and I realise the wet sound is my own breathing.

"Am I—still alive?" I manage, though my mouth feels far away somehow. Misplaced.

The demon laughs. "Of course! I'm not allowed to kill people, even if they ask me to. Well, not directly anyway, but that's a whole other—"

I try to sit up, but I can't find my legs. "What ...have you done to me?" I ask, my voice rasping in a throat I can't locate.

The demon looks affronted, placing a hand on his chest. "Exactly what you asked for: I made your outside match your inside," he says. "If you're dissatisfied, maybe you ought to have phrased your request more... *accurately*." With that, he disappears in a small burst of flame.

My heart pounding so hard I feel it in every artery, I heave myself towards the floor-length mirror. It's so hard to move any individual limb that it feels as though my body has become one useless slab, and I keep catching glimpses of raw, red flesh. Eventually I find it's easier if I shuffle and slide along the floor, and I manage to drag myself to the mirror.

I scream—but the sound is weak, rasping, almost silent.

The mirror reflects not a boy, but a writhing blob of flesh and muscle. Veins and arteries cover my surface and here and there I spot one of my organs, just visible beneath a translucent layer of flesh. I don't have limbs, or a head, or a visible mouth either—just a pair of lidless eyes staring out of the gore.

I'm—I'm a monster. I can't stay here.

I slide over to my door, but have no hands to open it. I force myself against it, my writhing mass squelching against the wood until it splinters and falls away, and I move for the stairs. Someone will have heard that, but if I can just get out of the house without being seen—

A scream and the sound of ceramics smashing.

My mum stands in the doorway to the kitchen, a shattered mug at her feet. "Harold!" She shouts, running back inside. "Harold, there's a monster in the house! What has she been *doing* up there?" Mum hollers my deadname from the kitchen. I hear Dad's footsteps from the living room.

No time. I half slither, half roll to the front door, smashing my way straight through this time.

At least I'm strong. I make my escape down the road, passers-by screaming at the sight of me.

"Oh God what is that?"

"Did it come from the sewer?"

People scatter at my approach, staring wide-eyed from behind bushes and bus stops. Someone falls to the ground as I pass and begins praying fervently for the forgiveness of mankind's sins.

I never should have painted that summoning circle. I can't believe I trusted a demon.

***

The sun sets as I flee. Under the cover of darkness, I feel safer. There are certainly less people around, and less screaming. I squelch onwards on autopilot until I find myself outside a familiar house. I'm not sure why I came here—I belong deep in the woods, or the sewer, or some other secret place where no one could find me.

I pause before the door, unwilling to break through this time. With effort, I congeal myself into a taller shape, and bump against the doorbell. It rings, and a few moments later, the hall light turns on.

The door opens, and Erin's mouth opens too.

"It's me!" I cry before she can scream. I force my voice to sound as human as I can, but still it rasps wetly. "It's Travis!"

Erin leans against the door frame, clutching her chest. "T—Travis...?" For a moment I'm worried she's going to faint. She pushes her glasses up, then looks past me into the darkness. "It's really you?" she asks, her eyes settling on mine.

"Yes!" I cry, and she must hear the shake in my voice because she steps forward as if to embrace me—like she has every morning of college for the past year—only to stop as I pull away. "Don't," I warn her. "I'm...sort of wet all over, I think."

Erin pauses, looking behind her, then back at me. "Well," she says, "at least wooden floors are easier to clean. Come in, quickly, and tell me *everything*."

***

And I did tell her everything.

I told her about the stranger, the summoning circle and the demon. How the demon twisted my wish to make me this... this *monster*. I was crying as I told her, I think. It's hard to tell when your whole body is wet all the time, but I think my eyes were watering. She's let me stay in her basement—says I can stay as long as I want to.

There's a mirror down here, which Erin apologised for and said she'd move, but I didn't want her to move it. After we talked, after I was finished crying and we sat quietly deciding what to do next, I had time to think.

As I was fleeing my home, worrying about people seeing me as a monster, worrying about scaring people, I'd overlooked something.

No one, not a single person, had thought I was a girl.

Yes, they'd thought I was some harbinger of evil, or some terrible experiment dredged up from the sewers—but not one of them had thought I was a *girl* harbinger of evil, or a *girl* terrible sewer experiment.

I'd lost my parents, of course. Though they'd always seen me as a monster, of a sort. Truthfully, I think I lost them a long time ago. At least I still had Erin.

Now, I crawl along the cool concrete of the basement towards the cracked mirror Erin left behind. I squelch myself up to my full height, and take in the rippling red meat and muscle glistening in the glow of the single lightbulb. I watch my heart beating visibly beneath a thin sheet of flesh. My arteries pump along my surface, and I meet my lidless eyes in the mirror.

I may no longer be human, but I am strong. I am beautiful.

And, despite everything, I think I could be happy.

About Leon Lavender

Leon Lavender is a queer trans creative from the UK. His work focuses on reinterpreting common tropes, often with a queer spin. In both writing and art he is fascinated by what it means to be a monster, what it means to be human, and the line between. You can find his writing in Ghost Orchid Press's 'Cosmos' and 'Rock Band' anthologies, 'There's More Of Us Than You Know: A Queer Horror Anthology Benefiting The Trevor Project', and in 'With Teeth' an anthology benefiting the Lakota Wolf Preserve from The Radical Book Co. His work in other mediums can be found on Instagram, @leonlionman

Mirror Girl, Hungry Gods

Solstice Lamarre

THEY CALLED ME *BEAUTIFUL* again.

Oh, Callendia, you are the most beautiful young girl in the whole city. Oh, Callendia, you will make the prettiest bride one day. Oh, Callendia, what is it like to look at the mirror and see a face blessed by the gods?

I look in the mirror now, and I can see it. What my mother brags about, what her friends fawn over, what her friends' children envy, the reason why I cannot go down the street alone without anyone bothering me.

Callendia, she's a beautiful girl, yes. She has everything: perfect curls, perfect delicate button nose, perfect clear-blue eyes, the perfect amount of freckles, perfect soft curves. She's the talk of the town, she's the one every eligible young merchant, and even some young *lords* are fighting over. She's the promise to her parents, that despite being their only child—just a daughter—she'll bring them prosperity, she'll slide them up the ranks of society. Callendia, she's a beautiful girl, and, as she's been told, the best thing a girl can hope to be is beautiful.

She's just not *me*.

Looking in the mirror feels like looking at a stranger, copying my every move out of pure spite. I wait for the straight line of her mouth to turn into a smug smirk. I wait for this reflection—not mine, never mine—to mouth the words *got you good, didn't I?* I wait for any sign that this has been a decades-long trick of the gods, and that this stupidly, horrifyingly beautiful girl isn't *me*. But the girl in the mirror keeps up the charade. Moves exactly when I move. The line of her mouth stays flat.

I've never seen her smile.

***

My mother is a little too doting this morning. She fusses over my hair for far longer than usual, and insists I wear the newest dress she bought me. She has our breakfast served in the garden by our mechanical servants and she then spends time putting daisies in my braids while singing slightly off-key, but in a way that is comforting nonetheless, the strange tune of happy childhood memories.

"What is all... this for?" I can't help but ask, gesturing vaguely at her, and her strangely cheerful mood.

"Oh!" She giggles, like a girl with a secret. "I didn't even tell you!" She kisses my cheek, and a cold shiver of dread slithers down my spine before she even starts uttering her next words. "Your father and I finally agreed on a suitor."

Beautiful girl. Perfect bride. Suitor.

The words don't seem real. I don't know why I thought my parents' quest for an advantageous match was a distant, future thing. It's been months of young men kissing my hand and calling me the Jewel of Garrelia, kissing my parents' feet in the hopes of getting to kiss *me* someday. It all felt like it was happening to the girl in the mirror. Not *me*. Never *me*.

I look down at my hands. There's jam on the corner of one of my nails. My fingers are long and thin—*perfect for piano, sewing, and embroidery,* my mother once said. I try to recall, for a second, what the girl in the mirror looks like. The girl they're marrying off. The details of her face keep escaping me. I couldn't draw her if I tried. This is one of the many reasons I have to believe that she's not me.

When away from a mirror, I can't seem to remember the face these hands are attached to.

***

My mother drags me through the city to the first official meeting with my betrothed. Garrelia is, as usual, bustling with activity. Women in colorful ornate dresses walk arm in arm and laugh loudly, followed by copper humanoid servants carrying their belongings. Carriages pulled by mechanical beasts with glowing eyes pass us by. Young boys race each other on the street and mothers pretend not to be bothered when they jostle them—*boys, you know*. Men in bright tunics and breeches walk so fast they're almost running, looking either impressively busy or distressingly late. Above us, the occasional hot air balloon flies through the sky, runes painted on its flank as a prayer for safe voyage to the wind gods.

I love the city as much as I hate it. The noise, the activity, the wonders of the human mind coupled with the power of the gods, it all used to amaze me. Of course, that was when I was a child and I got to run through the streets with my childhood friend, and I hadn't yet taken notice of the girl in the mirror and her twisted games. When it didn't matter what my reflection looked like and I got to be a wild, joyful thing. Now, it all feels smothering. Everywhere I look I see the women I'm supposed to be and the men I shouldn't envy. And everyone seems perfectly fine being a cog making the city run perfectly, as usual.

I can tell by the sheer size and extravagance of the house that my parents settled on a young lord. I am not surprised. What else would be the purpose of an only daughter?

What I don't expect is the actual young man waiting for me in the sitting room arranged for our meeting, his mother standing proud next to him. Lord Niccolo Assavia gives me his most charming smile, and I let out a hysterical laugh, which our mothers seem to interpret as delight, but we both know.

My father, as a merchant and inventor, is fairly influential in the city. Influential enough to be invited to plenty of noble garden parties, where I used to run wild as a child, and then be exposed as a pretty thing of value, in the hopes of setting me up for this kind of union.

I remember Niccolo growing increasingly friendly towards me, and being there for me when my childhood friend and neighbor, Emilien, disappeared mysteriously right as I began being seen as a woman rather than a child, at the tender age of thirteen. I remember looking forward to these parties and getting to laugh with a friend again. I remember a specific night; drinks being replenished endlessly even as we drew away from the rest of the noise. I remember jokes and compliments and being called *beautiful* and it *almost* not feeling as bothersome as it usually did. I remember everything feeling fuzzy but coming back into sharp focus when his hand settled on my thigh. *"Don't."* I remember him sighing deeply and leaving me alone as his final words rattled around in my mind *Fine. It's okay. You'll probably change your mind soon enough.*

I feel like a deer facing the dark end of a rifle and wondering why its legs won't move when it needs to run more than ever. Niccolo smiles, and I laugh, and I should turn around and run and never look back. But where would I go? So, I sit down as prettily as I know how, and I let our mothers chat about wedding plans, and I smile emptily at Niccolo's compliments, and I laugh every time I'm supposed to. There are no mirrors in the room, but it's as if I swapped places with my reflection. The girl in the mirror is acting as the perfect bride to be, and I'm watching, stuck inside the wall, screaming at her to run.

She smiles so, so sweetly, a trusting lamb not understanding that what the soft-voiced farmer is holding to her throat is a knife.

***

I tell my mother I want to go to the Temple district to pray to Asira. She lets me go easily, too easily. I've never gone to pray to Asira on my own before. When she lets go of my arm, it's as if she's letting go of a stranger. *Oh mother, when did you stop knowing who I am?*

Asira's temple is one of the biggest ones in the district, a white building covered in scenes painted in red and framed by intricate flower designs. Depictions of weddings, births, kisses, sex, and inspiring muses beckon people in to wish for good matches, fertile wombs, and romantic connections.

I imagine going in and kneeling at the goddess' feet, wishing for a happy marriage. A few years ago, being married to Niccolo might not have been a dreadful thought. It still shouldn't be, really. He never did anything truly untoward. His worst crime was being rude and entitled, but then again, was it entitled if he was right?

Yet, if I picture him laying a hand on me, the feeling of being a hunted deer takes over again. Would it be different if it was anyone else? Is it just slowly sinking in that this is what my life is supposed to be? Any faceless husband with his hand on my thigh, and the girl in the mirror smiling back at him, because that's what daughters do. The constant feeling of needing to run but being unable to.

I take a deep breath and enter the temple. Its layout is as straightforward as most temples. A long alley paved in intricate mosaics leading to a huge statue of the goddess looking down at us like the ants we are. Smaller statues representing different aspects of the goddess frame the alley, and people elect one to deposit their offerings and prayers to.

I make a beeline for the ten-foot-tall statue. She's fully painted, draped in colorful silks, holding a fruit in one hand, halfway to her mouth, and a contract in the other. A songbird sits on her shoulder. Her traits are supposed to be severely beautiful—a wife, a mother, a spurned lover—but she only reminds me of the girl in the mirror and the smirk I imagine she'd wear if she let herself show her true colors.

I kneel among the offerings and lean forward, laying a hand on one of the goddess' feet.

Why did you make me beautiful? What's the point? What is this supposed blessing of yours I've been praised for? What if I don't want it? Not the compliments from my parents, from neighbors, from older men, from boys my age even. What if my reflection feels like a twisted stranger? What if the girl in the mirror isn't me? What if I'm not a beautiful girl? What if I'm not a girl at all?

The last question doesn't come as a surprise to me. It's not a new discovery. The girl in the mirror is a stranger, not only because she's so beautiful it's a curse, but because she's a girl at all. But it's not like pondering the situation helped find a solution. Running away to live as a boy? I don't want that either, and who would ever believe this annoyingly delicate, pretty face belongs to a guy anyways? I just don't want any of it. The softness, the smiles, the godsdamn freckles.

"Ah, here for young love, aren't you?" An older lady kneels next to me. "I've heard about you. They call you a jewel, don't they? They're right. You're lucky, you know? Love comes easy to pretty things like you."

Something in me snaps. I always thought the day I would finally break it would be in sobs. But that's not what happens.

I bare my teeth at the old lady and growl. *"Fuck you."*

Her gasp is loud, but not louder than the silence in the temple as my curse echoes against the high ceiling.

The anger, the resentment, it all crawls under my skin and breaks the surface all at once. I should apologize immediately. I should press my forehead to the floor and beg the goddess for forgiveness for my disrespect. That's what the girl in the mirror would do.

But I don't. *I* don't.

I raise my gaze to the goddess' unforgiving face. "And fuck you too!"

I stand up, hitch up my skirts higher than what's proper, and *run*.

***

The Old Woods are the pride and plague of Garrelia. They flank the western side of the city and give it this breathtaking postcard look when looking up from the Eastern Port, a city of vibrant colors and mechanical progress, lined by a horizon of wild forest.

What they don't tell the tourists is that the city is constantly fighting the woods back. Garrelia used to be ideally located between the sea and the woods, natural resources present left and right. But the city grew, and in turn the woods grew bitter. The Western districts are constantly overrun with plants trying to grow back where they were uprooted. The locals call it the Curse of the Dajan, the old gods. Affected households send people up to the old temples deep into the forest to pray to half-dead, old, deeply angry gods. Sometimes they don't come back.

Emilien and I used to dare each other to go into the woods. The one who'd go farther would get their afternoon snack paid for by the other's allowance. When our parents found out about the game, they were furious. *This is not what children of your breeding do. You are lucky you do not have to go into the woods, so just don't go.* It felt like folk stories to us. The woods are hungry. Some children never come back. As if.

Emilien never came back, though.

His parents said he ran away and was never found again. I always had a feeling he ran to the woods. When we ran through the city, we always, always ended up here. The path retraced by many pilgrims, the path that plunges into the forest's dark maw. For the first time, I look at the thick spruces and oaks, and I feel it. Hunger. Teeth waiting to tear me apart. Claws sinking into my flesh. I take the time to let it sink in. The fear of pain, loss, *being hunted*. But it always comes back to this. My face being torn apart by something dark and ancient and ravenous, and all I can think is *yes, take my face away from me, even if it hurts.*

Is it how Emilien felt when he stood here years ago?

I try to go back to Niccolo's sitting room. Remind myself of propriety, duty, and what I *should should should* do. Marriage, beauty, *hands everywhere.* The deer looks down the barrel of the gun again.

I crouch and tear my most expensive dress apart until my knees are visible.

And the deer runs into the dark, dark woods.

***

The foliage is so thick that it gets dark quickly. Not enough that I stumble around, but enough that it's not difficult to jump at moving shadows that may or may not be real. The pilgrimage path is thin and easily overrun by bushes and thorns. Time slips out of my hands. It's impossible to gauge how long I've been walking by the position of the sun and I don't have a pocket watch on me.

My resolve doesn't last long. Walking over old, rusty mechanism that lost the war against the forest doesn't set my spirit at ease. Hunger churns in my stomach, and I taste sour fear on my tongue. Would I even manage to go back before dark? What am I doing? All to avoid losing myself to the girl in the mirror? Would it really be so bad, the path my parents set me on?

When I stumble upon a small stream, it feels natural to kneel next to it and try to catch my reflection in the water. It's distorted and wild, but it's still her. The incredibly, awfully beautiful girl who doesn't smile. The stranger that everyone sees when they look at me. *Beautiful, so pretty, a porcelain doll of a girl.* I plunge my hand into the stream to mess with the reflection.

"I can't, I can't, I *can't.*"

My anguished plea only gets answered by wild, high-pitched laughter. When I look up, there's a girl sitting on a flat rock on the other side of the stream. She's wearing a white dress —though it looks more like a piece of fabric artfully wrapped around her body—over tight brown pants that have seen better days, as well as sturdy boots covered in dirt. Dark brown hair flows down her back, and a makeshift crown of antlers sits on her head. She's strange, but more than anything else, she's familiar.

"What's so funny?"

"Oh, I don't know, how long it took you to get here, probably. That you let it get this far. That dress looks ridiculous on you."

My eyes widen, and I go to say her name, but it feels wrong. Like the girl in the mirror feels wrong. She grins at my opened mouth, stuck on a name that no longer belongs to her.

"The forest named me Holly, if you were wondering."

"The forest named you?" There's a sneer in my voice, I'm not sure why. Because hiding behind skepticism feels safer, despite the heavy hunger rumbling under my feet, almost palpable in the air.

Holly raises an eyebrow, unimpressed. "It'll name you, too."

The repulsion I feel is immediate and overwhelming. *No.* It takes me a while to notice my lips are curled in a snarl, showing teeth.

Holly's second eyebrow goes up. "Or maybe not, we'll see. You should follow me."

She gets up and leaves without any other words. My first instinct is to stay there, out of spite. *Don't tell me what to do. I'm so tired of doing what I'm told. Screw you.*

But I imagine spending the night by the stream, the ghost of the girl in the mirror lying next to me, and the decision isn't that difficult.

Holly leads me through the forest, and it seems to bend around her. The thorns I would've tripped on subtly get out of our way. The path that seemed uncrossable becomes easy enough to tread through. Shadows darken our path in a way that feels comforting instead of menacing. A wild fox stops to watch us go past but doesn't spook away from us. Holly inclines her head towards it in a show of respect that I could swear the fox acknowledges.

The temple doesn't look like any other temple I've ever seen, but I know immediately. The hunger is so strong here. *Teeth tearing flesh apart. Claws digging into my face.*

Holly leans against the mouth of the cave and smiles, foxlike. Nothing about the cave entrance indicates a place of worship, except maybe that it gets dark immediately, and I can't see even a few feet inside.

"I'll tell you what I tell the pilgrims I guide here. You'll only get one chance at striking a fair deal, and if you're not fair to the forest it will not let you out alive."

I frown. "Care to be more specific? What deal?"

She shrugs. "You'll see."

"What if I don't go in?"

Her grin spreads wider. "You will. Some don't, but you will. I don't think those who turn back ever make it home, but I haven't checked that thoroughly. Take the risk you want to take, that's all."

"I don't like how cryptic this is."

She shrugs again. "You ran away from the clear-cut gods to plunge into the mouth of the cryptic ones. Deal with it or take your chance alone in *very* hungry woods."

"What did *you* do?"

She bows slightly, a smirk still tugging at the corner of her lips. "Freedom against service. Being a forest daughter is easier than being a merchant's son by a long shot."

"Freedom against service seems quite contradictory to me."

"It's not." She gestures vaguely at the mouth of the cave. "I'll let you make your choice in peace." Shadows lean towards her and when I blink, she's not there anymore, but I hear an echo of her wild laugh.

***

Stepping inside the cave is easier than I would've thought. I try to reason with myself for a while. Going back wouldn't be so bad, no? But Holly said I wouldn't be able to without going inside the temple, didn't she?

And despite everything I tell myself, I don't really want to go back. I want antler crowns and wild laughter. I want to know what deals ancient gods offer to runaways afraid of their reflection in the mirror.

It's deeply dark in the cave, but I keep walking across the uneven floor. After a while, despite the absence of clear sources of light, I seem to get used to the complete darkness. The mouth of the cave goes down, down, down. The darker it gets, the easier it gets to see the details of the rough stone, the water dripping down from the ceiling, and the *bones*. Animal, some, probably. But human, mostly. Despite my best efforts, my breathing gets erratic after the third full skeleton.

The cave rumbles with deep, unearthly laughter, but I keep walking, until I come across the first drawings. Etched in the stone, or painted in rich shades of russet and ochre, scenes in common modern styles decorate the wall alongside depictions that are clearly ancient.

The forest and its beasts. The forest as a maw, eating humans that walk into it, oblivious. A strange stag with too many antlers. A fox with a devilish grin. A girl with blood dripping from her mouth. A fish with too many eyes. A king sitting on a throne, a tree sprouting from his empty eye socket.

The one that really stops me is an ancient, indistinct human silhouette. As the mural progresses, it bends over in pain, and starts changing. Spikes explode from its back, and an animal maw full of sharp teeth replaces its human face.

Before I can stop myself, my hand brushes the last drawing.

Tell me what you want.

The voice doesn't come from anywhere but rumbles deeply inside of my skull. I gasp, unable to breathe properly under the strain of the overwhelming presence. It's everywhere now. Shadows in the cave, a rush inside my body. And it's still *hungry*.

The answer comes to me easily. In my mind, the girl in the mirror looks back at me.

I want her <u>dead</u>.

Ancient laughter makes my bones shake inside of my body.

Easy enough. But what do you want as a replacement?

I've never entertained the thought long enough to have an answer prepared. If I could choose my own reflection, what would it show? A less beautiful girl? Certainly not. A handsome, self-confident boy, another version of Niccolo? A shiver of disgust travels down my spine.

My fingers stay on the last drawing. Something in me longs for it.

This? This would hurt, child.

"It already hurts," I whisper.

And what would you give me in exchange, little one?

A fair deal. Freedom against service. Only one chance. What could I give for a different reflection? *Hunger, teeth, claws.*

"I'll… stay. Eat for you. Feed for you. Bring you more worshippers. Get back the city for you. Destroy trespassers for you."

The laughter feels softer inside my bones now. *Oh, foolish child. You promise too much.*

Fear seizes my body. I failed. I didn't manage a fair deal. The girl in the mirror, she's still here. She'll always be here. They'll always miss their beautiful daughter, a jewel of Garrelia, *such a pretty thing*. I'll die looking like her.

That last thought is what makes my eyes tear up. That breaks me enough that it doesn't feel shameful to beg.

"*Please*. Please, at least change me before you kill me. I can't do it anymore. I can't."

Such dedication. Such fear. It's almost a waste to get rid of that delicious, delicious feeling. But it's been a while, you know, since I've had someone willing to take on a bit of my old-days appearance. So, fine, I'll give it to you. Men will scream when they see your face. Children will be scared of the stories they tell about you. And you will bear a part of my hunger, and it will consume you forever, unless you can feed us.

I don't get to thank the presence or answer it. It disappears as brutally as it came, and leaves me weak and trembling, unable to move towards the exit.

When the first bone breaks, I scream.

What the drawings don't show is that the change is slow. Bones break suddenly one after the other, until my throat is so hoarse from screaming that no sound comes out anymore. Breathing feels like a feat against the hot, blinding white pain. I can't see, I can't speak, I can't beg it to stop happening to me. All I can do is feel, until my body breaks under the pressure, and even then, when I *should* pass out from the sensation, it just keeps going. Like the presence is keeping me awake for this. Like feeling the pain is a part of the price.

The feeling of bones elongating and rearranging within my skull makes me throw up, and it tastes like blood. My hands grip the stone of the floor, and it feels tender under my sharp bones—claws?

Teeth tearing me apart. Claws digging inside my face.

Can't see, can't scream. Blood in my mouth, on my face, flowing inside and outside my body.

Bones pierce the skin of my face and elongate outward. There is wind and water against flesh that should never have been exposed to the elements.

No, no, no, no. This is wrong. This shouldn't be happening.

When my spine breaks in three distinct, brutal *klacks* everything *finally, finally* goes black.

***

When I come back to myself, I am running. Running like I have never run before. Everything is a blur around me. Am I dizzy? Am I going that fast? There is blood in my mouth and my teeth are so unusually sharp that they cut into my tongue with each stride. The wind feels like knives against my face. I see differently than I used to. Everything is sharper, brighter, more detailed. My eyes follow every movement in my surroundings. When something small and fast runs past me, an instinct I didn't use to have kicks in, and my rear legs launch at the prey and my teeth lock around soft fur and tender muscle and snap the rabbit's neck in half.

I keep running. Something rumbles from my stomach and spreads to my whole body.

Hungry.

Yet, the thing that stops my wild run isn't food. It's water.

The pond is small and still. I can tell from the smell that a herd of deer was here recently, but I made them run.

When I lean over the water, the girl in the mirror is gone. I let out a long, relieved groan. It doesn't sound like noise a human could make.

The *thing* that stares back is strange and horrific. It's covered in dense black fur from the neck down, with huge wolf legs and arms that go past its knees and end in sharp bone claws. Its face is grotesque, a deer skull still shedding human flesh in places, with glowing yellow eyes and sharp teeth. Bone horns curl on top of its skull instead of ears, and bone spikes protrude out of its spine.

It's not beautiful. *I'm* not beautiful. Not a pretty girl, not a handsome boy. A nightmare thing no one will lay its hands on. A creature so wild that it cannot bow to a puny human's expectations.

My reflection grins, sharp white teeth exposed threateningly. I see myself in the water, and for the first time, looking at myself, I smile.

***

Holly strokes the strangely sensitive bone of my forehead. She looks towards the girl we escorted to the mouth of the cave. Her with carefree laughter and promises of freedom, me with the fear of my teeth against her throat and the hope of becoming something *other*, something *powerful*.

No matter the deal she makes, the forest will feast, and the bottomless hunger I feel will be eased, if only for a few days.

Freedom for service. I get it now. It comes out as a low, haunting growl. Holly understands anyway.

"Took you long enough. I haven't asked yet. What did it name you?"

I remember the offer of a name. I remember rejecting it without a thought. There is no name given by anyone that I will bear. Freedom, to me, means this. An unknowable body, and a nameless soul. I don't say any of this, but Holly nods anyway.

Out of the cave comes out a fox with a knowing grin. She darts into the forest without a word to us.

I leave Holly to go hunt. A rabbit, a deer, a pilgrim who will get lost and eaten, or a child wanting to shed their skin for another. It doesn't matter. I'm hungry enough for all of them.

About Solstice Lamarre

Solstice Lamarre is a French, non-binary aroace writer. They write queer, neurodivergent stories in various genres, but always come back to themes of monstrosity, found family, and all sorts of queer love. Their work has previously appeared in *Unthinkable: A Queer Gothic Anthology*. When they're not writing, they work as an English teacher for French teens, read an unholy number of books, play video games they never finish, and cuddle with their cat.

Monsters
Valerie Hunter

You've come to see us, I know you have. You're all alike. Maybe you'll claim your motivation is different—you came because a friend insisted, you came with an interest in science, you came out of pity—but the end result is still the same. Your slack jaw, your wide eyes, the way your heart speeds up. Deep down, no matter who you are, you've come for a thrill, and we don't disappoint.

But I know, too, that as soon as you leave the carnival—maybe even before you leave—you're convincing yourself we're all fake. Only young children and simpletons truly believe. It's 1896, and you're too smart to think God or nature could ever create the likes of us. This is just clever costuming and greasepaint. Monsters aren't real, and that's the fun of a freak show—to pretend for a few moments that they are, goosebumps dotting your arms and the backs of your necks, and then leave the tent and never have to think of us again, or, if you do, to believe we're nothing more than frauds.

Would it alarm you to know we're real? Oh sure, there are a few embellishments—the wolf girl's tail, the greenish tint to the skin of the human alligator, the way the conjoined twins always speak in unison—but we're not some two-bit operation having to scrape by on pennies. Dr. Canning may not be a real doctor, but he is a man of means, and he scoured the country for his attractions. It's easy enough to find freaks if you go looking. Orphanages, asylums, hidden attic bedrooms—he rescued us from all sorts of places, even lesser carnivals.

As for me, I found the carnival myself, but it was still a rescue. Dr. Canning says I'm the best bearded lady he's ever had, and I don't bother reminding him I'm hardly a lady, just a girl of sixteen.

You might think that the beard doesn't make me a freak, that I could just shave each morning, wear a bonnet to obscure the shadows of my fast-growing whiskers. That might work, but it might not, and it hardly seems worth the risk. People don't like what they don't understand; they don't like deviations from their expectations. Freaks are expected in a carnival, but not passing you on a sidewalk or in a shop. Despite keeping my head down and my bonnet deep, men might still notice the shadow of my beard and insist I must be a man, insist I must prove my denial.

The carnival is safer. If you want to believe I'm a man here, you can accept it as entertainment rather than perversion. Here I can wear a low-cut dress to show off my ample and very real bosom, but no one's allowed to touch me. Here you can accept that I'm a woman, and assume my beard is fake.

You think we're not real, but I know you also invent your own realities for us. You think that if you stare at us long enough, you'll know everything about us. You think Paul the lion man is a brute, so ugly and oafish under all that fake hair. You think Clara the dwarf is a tiny child, unable to understand anything you say. You think I must be some pitiable young widow, willing to don a lustrous fake beard in order to support myself.

In truth Paul is kind and calm, Clara erudite and well-spoken, and I am neither a widow nor pitiable. I am the most monstrous freak here, even if I shaved my beard clean off, but you can't tell that by looking at me, can you? No one sees my curse.

If you knew, you might think the beard is a byproduct of that curse, but it's not. The beard came first, around the time of my first monthly bloods, though admittedly it's become thicker and harder to conceal this past year.

I was an orphan. (I don't know why I say that in the past tense; I still am one, of course, but somehow it no longer seems relevant.) I was raised by my aunt and uncle, made to work for my keep, but once the beard appeared, they cast me out. It disturbed them; they didn't like to think they were related to something like me.

They sent me to an orphanage, but the matron there called me an abomination, said I might corrupt the other children. She sent me to a workhouse, and then I ended up in an asylum. That's where it happened. The curse. Anna, my roommate, turned me. She tried to warn us—me, the doctors, everyone—about what she was, but no one listened. We should have listened. On the first full moon after her arrival, I watched as she became something else. It was both terrifying and fascinating to watch her transformation, all that hair sprouting across her body, coarse and thick.

I didn't try to run; they always locked us in at night. I should have cowered, attempted to hide, but I didn't. I watched as Anna became a wolf, watched as she battered herself against the door, desperate to get out. I tried to stop her—stupid, I know, but I didn't want her to hurt herself—but she knocked me aside, her claws grazing my shoulder. She howled, and when an attendant opened the door to see what the commotion was, Anna tore him to pieces, devoured him, then bounded off. I took advantage of the open door and scurried away, too.

I didn't realize I had the curse in me until the next full moon, when I awoke naked and filthy the following morning. Luckily, I was on my own, sleeping rough at the edge of a forest, so I didn't seem to do any harm, but I worried that I might someday. That's when I sought out Dr. Canning. I told him what I was, and he believed me, looking intrigued instead of horrified. I suppose a man who makes his living with freaks isn't scared of monsters.

He asked me if I'd consider transforming for an audience each full moon—safely caged, of course—but when I declined, he didn't push the idea. He was fine with taking me on as a bearded lady, and locking me away in a cage when the moon was full. The carnival included a small menagerie; he had cages available.

I was grateful, of course. I *am* grateful.

But I'm starting to wonder. I don't remember myself when I'm changed. Or rather, I don't remember afterwards what happened when I'm the monster. The wolf. I remember entering the cage, the terrible anticipation, and then the next thing I know it's morning and I'm shivering and wrapping myself in a blanket.

But lately there's been blood. Smudged on the bottom of the cage. Smeared across my skin. Coating my tongue and throat.

When I ask Dr. Canning, he says, "It's only rabbits," smiling like this answer should relieve me. "You howl something terrible. If I feed you, you settle down."

I want to vomit. "Please don't do it again," I tell him.

"I have to," he insists. "Your howls upset the other animals, and I'm worried a worker might start poking around and discover you. You don't want your secret to be revealed, do you?"

I shake my head as his words echo in my ears. *Other animals.*

The morning after the next full moon, I awake to more blood, but also a spectator. Ida the wolf girl stands outside the cage, her expression wary. I shrink back into a corner, pulling the blanket tighter around me.

"Sorry," she says. "I didn't mean to startle you." She's around my age, her entire face and body thickly downed with ash brown fur. We've never exchanged more than hellos before.

Words come rushing out of her mouth now. "I watched you, last night. Does it hurt?"

"I don't remember." How long had she watched? What had she seen? I don't like the thought of her seeing me like that, the me that isn't me, but I also recall my own fascination in watching Anna transform.

"It looked painful. The changing." She stares at her furry hands. "You were more wolf than me."

"You shouldn't have watched," I say.

"I'm sorry," she repeats, still not looking up. "He charges people to see you, you know."

The words jolt against me like an electric shock. "What?"

"Dr. Canning. He gathers the richest men in whichever town we're in, and they pay to see him toss you a rabbit. You devour it. It's..." She trails off, as though unable to put into words just what it is. "You didn't know?"

"No!" Fury courses through my veins.

"He made me watch last night. Said I have a lot to learn from you." She looks over her shoulder furtively. "He'll be coming to let you out soon. Don't tell him I told you." And with that, Ida darts away.

Dr. Canning does come soon, letting me out with his customary smile as he solicitously asks how I feel. I answer him automatically, frantically planning my escape. But there's nowhere else for me to go, nowhere to protect me when I'm a bearded young woman, nowhere to protect the world from me on those nights when I'm a monster.

I seek out Ida later that day. "What does he want you to learn from me?"

She won't look me in the eye. "To be wilder. More frightening. He thinks I'm not sufficiently wolfish for the guests."

I snort, not because it's funny but because it's so absurd. I can't get used to the ridiculousness of this place, all its shadows and paradoxes.

Ida and I talk a lot in those next few weeks, as the moon wanes and then waxes again. She's been at the carnival since she was a child, as long as she can remember. Like me, she knows she belongs here, knows she can't escape, accepts her freakish appearance and all that comes with it, realizes there's no use in wishing for anything different. She used to love Dr. Canning like a father, but now she thinks that's not what fathers are, that her devotion shouldn't be given so easily. He gets rid of people frequently, and where would she go if he got rid of her?

I tell her my story, too, and how it scares me to lose myself in the monster. I want to ask her to watch over me when I transform, keep Dr. Canning from using me, but I know Ida can't prevent it. She is not a monster, just a slight young woman unused to confrontation and desperate not to lose her place here.

But we talk of other things. Our hairiness. Our differentness. Our hidden selves that no one bothers to wonder about. All the likes and dislikes we have developed as freakish girls in the wide world.

I let her stroke my beard. She lets me run my hand over her furry arms, and then her face. We kiss in the quiet of an empty tent, the hair of our faces mingling. Is this freakish behavior? Monstrous? I find I do not care. Ida makes me happy, and there is little enough happiness in life.

The day before the next full moon, I watch every single man that enters my tent to gawp, and I wonder which of them are rich enough to see me the following night, whether I will haunt their nightmares forever after or whether they will convince themselves I was never real at all.

But the next night it rains, and the carnival is canceled. I let Dr. Canning shut me into the cage and try to take solace in the fact that there will be no onlookers tonight.

When morning comes, I am no longer in the cage.

I am naked in the damp prairie grass, covered in blood. It's matted in my hair, my beard, under my torn fingernails, more blood than half a dozen rabbits could ever contain—

I run. I don't know where I am, don't know where the carnival is, don't know what I've done or what I should do, so I just run. Maybe if I run fast enough, far enough, I will catch that other part of myself, the part I was last night.

Instead I run into Ida. She wraps me in a blanket and holds me tight, and then she tells me what happened last night until I can almost imagine I was there.

Dr. Canning wanted Ida to be cursed like me. Said that the curse would improve Ida's nightly performance in the freak tent. Said two of us would be better than one, would bring in more money at a full moon.

He strong-armed Ida, holding her against the bars of my cage, but I didn't cooperate, wouldn't come near her. Ida struggled and cried, and Dr. Canning got angrier and angrier, finally opening the cage to throw Ida in. If I killed her, so be it; it would serve the sniveling fool right.

"But you didn't kill me," Ida says, as though this isn't already obvious. "You leapt straight over me and pounced on him."

She pauses, and I picture Dr. Canning locked up in a cage each month, turning into a monster for the enjoyment of an audience. But Ida goes on, as I knew she would.

"You tore him apart. He's dead."

I try to feel horrified, and I am, of course I am, but I'm also thinking of Anna. How I attempted to stop her, but she only pushed me aside. How she devoured that attendant, a horrid man who always leered at us and let his hands linger in places they shouldn't.

Had anyone been around to tell Anna what she'd done, afterward? Had she been sorry?

She shouldn't have been.

"Did I scratch you?" I ask Ida.

"No."Is it possible that even in monster form, we know who is good and who is evil? Is it possible the real monsters are brought to justice by those of us who don't deserve our curses?

I know that's too simplistic. Surely no one deserves to be killed in such a manner. But I remind myself it wasn't me who did it, that Ida is fine, that maybe some things aren't meant to be questioned.

The carnival continues to tour. No one questions that Dr. Canning died suddenly in the night; surely some of them must have heard something, but they pretend they didn't. Our secrets are our own here. No one asks to see the body, including me.

Paul takes over daily operations, though he lets one of the veteran roustabouts make all the arrangements with the folks from each town. No one wants to see a lion man unless he's in a freak tent. Ida reinvents himself as a dog girl, much more fitting than a wolf. She is the one who shuts me in the cage on each full moon, watches over me until the sun rises, reassures me that nothing has gone wrong. Every night when the moon is not full, we are still together, but there is no cage. She tells me I'm beautiful, and I tell her the same, and it feels real because it is.

Perhaps you've come to see us, or perhaps you will soon. I'll puff out my bosom and smile demurely while stroking my silky beard, and you'll gawp and wonder why a woman would debase herself like that, and then you'll forget me as soon as you leave the tent. You won't recognize my beauty. If you happen to visit on the night of a full moon, you won't see me at all, but you might hear my howl, which I'm told is full and wild.

But it's all right. You know I'm not real, and I won't try to convince you otherwise.

About Valerie Hunter

Valerie Hunter teaches high school English and has an MFA in writing for children and young adults from Vermont College of Fine Arts. Her stories have appeared in publications including *Cicada*, *Paper Lanterns*, and *Inaccurate Realities*, as well as multiple anthologies.

Pearls for a Swine
Jude Deluca

DNA COMICS' *I CAN'T BELIEVE IT'S NOT CHRISTMAS HOLIDAY SPECIAL!*
SPECIAL!
DECEMBER 30TH **1998** – <u>BACON DAY</u>
LI'L GUTS IN: *PEARLS FOR A SWINE!*

HAVE YOU CHECKED THE CHILDREN: Think of all the children in the world and the horrors they go through every day. When a kid says there's a monster under the bed or the Boogeyman's hiding in their closet? Those are the lucky ones. Then you've got the cursed ones. The dead ones. The survivors. Which is why GUTS & GLORY, the gun-toting super team that defines the 1990s, began THE LI'L GUTS INITIATIVE. A place for all the transformed, traumatized kids and teenagers to work out their aggression and be given a home to make sense of their weird, wondrous, and wretched new lives.

Mentored by the immortal warrior witch HONOR until the day they get to join the GUTS team or the GLORY team, the LI'L GUTS are gonna find the things that go bump in the night and teach 'em that payback is a total "B" word!

ACTIVE ROSTER: ASTRONAUT, AWE, **BACON**, BUZZ, CHAMPION, CHIROPTERA, CUCKOO, HARROW, MITE, MOTE, RIPPER, SHOCK, ~~TADPOLE~~

***

Maybe it was destiny, me ending up the way I did, considering what day I was born on. I didn't even know it was a holiday until recently. Not, like, a really important holiday, the kind they let you stay home from school on. One of those gag holidays they use to fill up a calendar so adults have an excuse to act stupid at their office and department stores can sell junk.

Because I was born on December 30th, my parents decided I could celebrate my birthday five days early on Christmas. They could've let me celebrate it on New Year's Eve, that's a holiday too, but I think they were looking for an excuse not to buy me two sets of presents. Though looking back, I never particularly felt stiffed in the gift department.

Or, come to think of it, I'm beginning to suspect those gifts that said "From Santa Claus" might've really been from Santa Claus. I'm surprised I haven't had a run-in with the man in red yet. With the sort of life I'm living, anything's possible.

God knows my brother always complained about how many presents I got to open.

...I try not to think about my brother too much if I can help it. I'm reminded of him every time I look in a mirror and I see what I've become. I've tried to feel more comfortable looking at my reflection, but now my problem isn't so much how I look, it's what my appearance reminds me of. All because I happened to splash some mud on the woman who lived down the road from my family's farm.

I need to stop blaming myself. That's what everyone on the team tells me. Rocky, my brother, he's the one who got mud on Ursula while he was arguing with his best friend. I tried to stop them before they landed in that big puddle just as she was about to cross the street, but, I think she would've cursed us all anyway. Ursula never seemed to like kids.

"If you're going to rut in the mud like a bunch of pigs, then by all means."

It's years later and I still hear that cold voice in my head, clear as day. Those words changed my life forever. Changed all our lives.

"Earth to Connie! We are awaiting your return! Come in Connie!"

Harrow's voice cut through my thoughts, making me wonder how long I'd been staring at myself in the bathroom mirror. She's the oldest of us in the group, our unofficial leader, and it's only a matter of time before she joins the older teams. That's where all the action is. It was kind of funny, considering she didn't have any superpowers yet she was the one the rest of us deferred to when Honor or one of the others, like Warden or Super-American, weren't around. You'd never guess from looking at her. So ordinary.

"If you make us wait any longer, your birthday's gonna be over before you know it!" Harrow warned me.

"Sorry, must've spaced out," I said.

"What were you doing in here?" Harrow asked.

"I was thinking of trying out a new hairstyle, maybe a French braid, but I'm having trouble doing it myself," I revealed.

"You should've asked for my help, I could've had it done for you ages ago," Harrow said.

"What, and have you try to pass that off as your gift to me? As if!"

"Come on, let me help or by the time we get into the common area everyone will have helped themselves to the birthday cake," Harrow warned as she pulled in a chair from the massive bedroom us girls shared.

"Please tell me you guys didn't really get me a bacon cake," I said as I sat down to let Harrow braid my hair. I saw her eyes dart from side to side in the mirror. "Are you serious? That's so gross!"

"Well, it's not like the bacon's actually IN the cake," Harrow pleaded. "It's a chocolate maple cake that just happens to be decorated with bacon on the side."

"Bacon is not a dessert!" I argued.

"C'mon, the guys were just having some fun," Harrow reasoned, looking apologetic in the mirror as I glared at her reflection. "They really did go all out. Some of them are pretty jealous since they don't have their own holiday."

"I knew this was a bad idea as soon as Shock told us what sort of holiday today was," I huffed. "I really didn't need a theme party. We're not little kids anymore. Well, I'm not exactly little anyway, am I?"

"To Honor and all the others, they still think we're kids until we pick between Guts and Glory," Harrow sighed as she twisted several strands of my long red hair in her fingers.

"...some of us didn't have to pick."

I saw Harrow let go of my hair, and then looked down at my hands resting in my lap.

"I miss Tadpole as well," Harrow finally said.

"She's not Tadpole anymore, is she?" I bitterly laughed. "She's 'Frog Princess' now. She didn't have to worry about being old enough to join a new team. Now she's thousands of years ahead of the rest of us with the Power Paladins."

"More like a thousand and a couple of hundred," Harrow specified as she got back to work on braiding my hair. I said nothing in response, causing her to add, "I know she was your best friend."

"We weren't best friends," I corrected.

"Sure seemed like it to the rest of us," Harrow figured.

"It was... more than that," I finally said.

"No!" Harrow gasped, a smile of excitement on her face.

"Well, we weren't like that!" I stammered. "I mean, we could have been, if she hadn't left!"

"Oh my God did you have a crush on her?" Harrow laughed as I felt my face blushing as red as my hair. "That's amazing!"

"It's not so amazing now that she's gone, is it?!" I angrily shouted.

"I—I'm sorry." Harrow immediately stopped smiling. "I didn't mean to make fun, honest. You know I'd never tease you for liking another girl, Ruby."

"...yeah, I know." I buried my face in my hands.

"None of us would."

"I know."

Harrow continued to braid my hair in silence as I sat and thought. It was weird, hearing my birth name said out loud. I couldn't recall the last time someone called me by that name. Most often I was addressed by my codename, or as "Connie," the shortened version.

Or "pig."

Or "monster."

Or some combination of the two.

When Ursula said that thing about us rutting like pigs, I thought she was referring to my parents keeping pigs on our farm. She must've known Rocky and I were the ones who had to feed the pigs every day. We always complained about how much we hated doing it. How we hated pigs in general because of how loud and messy and disgusting they can be.

Turned out I was more right than even I expected.

The changes happened slowly, but painfully. First came the fur. I can't tell you how much blood I lost trying to shave it off, until I was practically cutting off patches of my skin thinking that would make it stop. Then came my toes fusing together, hardening, becoming hooves. My bones snapped and stretched. Muscles tearing apart and then regrowing. My teeth grew bigger, faster than the rest of my jaw was growing to match. Eventually, the pain got so bad I don't... I still don't remember exactly what I did during my rampage. I just remember waking up to find a bunch of superheroes standing over me, surrounded by destroyed buildings in the remains of what was once my hometown.

They were able to get to me in time, but it was too late for Rocky.

No one would tell me what he did to our parents, who must've been too close to him when his own transformation finally finished.

They never found Ursula, but Honor assured me they're still trying to find her to see if she can undo what she did to me. It was Honor's magic that brought me back as closely as I am now. I've been like this for so long, I have a hard time imagining what I looked like before all this.

To be honest, I don't look much like a pig. I'm more of a boar. If I were to be really accurate, I kind of look like the Beast before he got changed back into a prince. The Disney version, I mean. But "Boar" didn't have enough "oomph" for a codename, they said. And apparently "Beast" is trademarked by some comic company I'd never heard of.

Between "Bacon" and "Piggy," I figured, at least people like bacon. I didn't know at the time someone came up with a Bacon Day.

"You know," Harrow cleared her throat, snapping me back to reality. I really do have a bad habit of spacing out. "I've always been jealous of your hair. It's so red and shiny. I've never seen anyone with red hair this shade. You're lucky."

"There was this old lady who owned the general store in my town and she'd say the same thing," I recalled.

"Oh yeah?"

"She used to think I'd become a model someday just from my hair alone," I said. "I don't know why it's so shiny. I never did much for it when I was younger except brush and wash it."

"Sometimes that's all it takes," Harrow laughed.

"If I followed Tad—I mean, Frog Princess, into the future," I suddenly found myself asking, "if they'd let me join the Power Paladins with her, I wonder what my new name would've been? Someone told me the Power Paladins all took inspiration from classic literature. Maybe I could've gotten something based on *Animal Farm*."

"You really miss Brilla that much, huh?" Harrow asked.

"It's hard not to," I said. "I get why she had to leave. Anything to get away from that freak of an older brother she had." Harrow's face scrunched up at the thought of Brilla's abusive brother, and I felt my blood boil at the memory. I could never forget about her saying how many times he tried to kill her until she sought help from a witch. I still wasn't entirely certain of the chain of events, but Brilla ended up turned into a frog monster for her troubles. Guts & Glory tried to change her back, but, like me, she was stuck with physical reminders. Between the two of us, she lucked out with green-tinted skin, webbed toes and hands, and a prehensile tongue.

The two of us bonded over our shared transformations. There were others on the team who had animal-based forms, like Buzz and this new girl Ripper. Brilla and I, we had something a little deeper. A lot more pain that, I now understand, we didn't do anything to deserve. It felt like we both understood each other in a way the others didn't. Thanks to Brilla, I started to feel more comfortable with my body despite the torment I went through. I've reached a point where I'm not entirely certain I really need to go back to the way I was.

I thought I was able to help her, too, but, her brother's bullying ran deeper than I was able to understand. The fear of him coming after Brilla again was too great, and I genuinely don't blame her despite so many people willing to stand between him and her.

But it's hard not to miss her. Does that make me selfish?

"Finished! What do you think?"

I stood up, turning to see myself with my hair now neatly styled into a sleek braid going down my back.

"I love it!" I said.

"It goes great with your dress," Harrow complimented. I was happy to hear it. After making some peace with my appearance, I decided that didn't mean I had to limit my wardrobe. Honor's helped me a lot with clothes shopping since we're both over seven feet tall. I've also gotten some styling types from Gaza, the sizeshifter on the Glory team. Shoes I need to have custom made for my feet, though. I had on a flowing, pale pink dress I'd gotten myself as a Christmas gift for special occasions. I was happy to have an immediate chance to wear it, though I doubted anyone else was going to dress as fancy as I was.

Sure enough, most of my teammates on Li'l Guts, and some of the heroes from Guts & Glory who decided to stop by for the occasion, were in full costume.

"Just in case of an emergency," Paragon reasoned. He always attended the birthday parties for us in Li'l Guts. "The year's almost over but crime doesn't take a holiday off."

Speaking of holidays, most of what my friends had done for Bacon Day thankfully, or maybe not so thankfully, was concentrated solely on the food. There was bacon in practically everything, and I could only imagine what all that grease was going to do to our complexions. I made sure no one saw me picking off the pieces of, ugh, Canadian bacon from a slice of pizza because I didn't want to hurt anyone's feelings.

"Isn't this a little weird though?" Astronaut, a newer member I hadn't gotten a chance to know very well, asked her fellow newbie Chiroptera. "Like, she calls herself 'Bacon.' That'd be, like, if they threw a party for you and served fried bat."

"Fried bat's actually an excellent source of protein," the bat-winged girl said to the alien abductee. Neither one of us could tell if she was joking, but it made me lose my appetite until it was time for cake. Sure enough, I was served chocolate and maple cake decorated with maple-glazed bacon bits. Someone said it'd been baked by that bomb girl who recently joined Guts, Pineapple, I think was her name. She's the granddaughter of an old school villainess with a Carmen Miranda theme (you know, the dancer who wore the fruit hat). A few weeks ago, she'd done this huge prank for Cupcake Day on the 15th which, I heard, almost resulted in someone dying. I'm surprised they let her supply the cake, but it was better than I expected.

All in all, it was a nice birthday party. Kind of like the ones I had back home, but a little kiddy. It reminded me how all of us are still kids to Guts & Glory, even though most of us were already teenagers and a couple years away from becoming adults. Maybe this was their way of telling us to enjoy it while we can, before we grow up and become part of the world. Fight deadlier threats. Put our lives on the line.

And I'm as tall as the adults already!

After cake it was time for gifts. Thankfully, no one really minded having to shop for birthday gifts despite Christmas being a few days earlier (for those who celebrate it). Someone must've really not minded when I opened a box to find the most gorgeous pearl necklace I'd ever seen in my life. One long strand of shimmering white pearls, each barely bigger than a dime.

"This is, I don't..." I could barely comprehend how beautiful the pearls looked as I held up the necklace for everyone to see. I couldn't take my eyes off them. I heard someone asking me who they were from. They were mesmerizing, the light almost radiating from them. I wasn't even sure who said the box didn't have a name on it when I immediately draped the pearls around my broad, furry shoulders.

I do know it was me who started screaming.

Then everyone else started screaming.

Pain, a familiar pain I hadn't felt in years, assaulted every inch of my body. I fell to the ground, convulsing, agony radiating up from my feet to the top of my head. It was so many sensations at once. Snapping, burning, twisting, melting. I was so lost in the sea of my own pain I couldn't recognize the pain everyone else in the room was feeling at the same time. I'd learn later about our shared suffering.

The worst of the pain came from my feet. It was as if they were simultaneously being crushed and ripped apart. I worked up enough focus to get my shoes off, but that only managed to stop the crushing feeling. Through tears of pain I could see I no longer had hooves. Likewise, the fur on my legs was slowly receding back into my body. My body bled and for a moment I couldn't breathe as the rest of my body was gripped with an even worse crushing sensation. I was shrinking, I realized. My bones being forced back into the shape they once were.

"GRAAAAAAAAAAH!!!!"   I   howled.   I   screamed. "*AAAAAAAAAAAAAAAAHHH!!!*"

And then finally it stopped with a popping sound.

I lay there, huddled on the ground, sobbing, hugging myself, bleeding everywhere even though I had no cuts. Opening my mouth to cry caused me even more pain as my teeth and gums throbbed. I used to fantasize about returning to my old body, but nothing so violent as the nightmare I just endured.

These hands I now had. I didn't recognize the hands I held out in front of my face, with pale skin and clear nails. Softly I placed these alien fingers on my cheeks, wincing, hiccupping from my sobs. My face's angles were familiar but unknown to me, as I ran my hands down my face, to my neck. Down my chest. I was so small and weak.

I hated it.

But before I could further comprehend my situation, I heard sounds of destruction. Trying to stand, I almost tripped on the dress which was now too big for me. I found myself caught in the eye of the storm. Everyone in the room, my friends, teammates, mentors, they were destroying everything.

All of them monsters, just like I'd been.

Only these monsters had powers I didn't.

I wasn't even sure why they were ignoring me as they destroyed the common area or fought each other in their frenzied states. I couldn't even tell who was who from all the torn costumes and general chaos.

Reaching my neck again, I felt the pearl necklace and tried to rip it off. It didn't take a genius to guess the necklace was responsible, but even a genius wouldn't have guessed that as soon as I tried to get rid of it, the pearls tightened around my throat like a noose.

Even as the air was choked out of me, I tried to dig my hands into any space I could find between the necklace and my skin.

"I see you're still the rude little girl I remember you as," a cold voice said. "You didn't even say 'thank you' for my gift."

The necklace loosened just a little for me to whisper, "*You!*"

"You will address me as Miss Ursula if you wish to keep breathing," my former neighbor said as she materialized before me wearing the same dark green dress she'd worn when she cursed me and my brother. She didn't look a day older, her face still made of some unknowable substance which made it impossible to guess how old she was. Her hair was still the same dark color, a green that was so deep it almost seemed black. Her eyes still the same poison green, the same cold stare.

I saw a smile form on her dark green lips as she said, "Ruby, my dear, you've become such a beautiful young woman. You have impeccable taste in fashion. I'm certainly happy the pearls go so well with your dress."

"W-why?" I gasped, still feeling the necklace tighten around my neck.

"Why what? Why did I punish you? You know why, dear," Ursula clucked while ignoring the destruction around her. "Youngsters today. So rude. I had to punish you and your brother for your roughhousing in public. It's obvious your parents didn't do a decent job of instructing you on how to behave outside of the house, so I needed to—"

"No!" I screamed. "Why this?!" I gestured to my friends, my family, fighting each other now that their humanity was gone. Was this how I acted when my transformation ended? I started to imagine the sort of fight I had with my brother when I was suddenly lifted off the floor.

"Do NOT interrupt someone when they're talking!" Ursula shouted as I gagged. An invisible hand held the pearl necklace up in the air, pulling me with it. I was then dropped back on the floor, crying out as I landed on my foot and felt something break.

"You see? You see what I'm talking about? You haven't changed at all!" Ursula scowled. "All of the children I've needed to punish, but you, my dear, have been the most stubborn. The most obstinate! I thought you and your brother had taken care of each other when my spell ran its course. That was my mistake. I should've stayed long enough to see it through to the end."

I looked up at her, silently glaring at her, when Ursula said, "You may speak now."

"Then why didn't you just finish me off if you knew I was still alive?" I said, keeping my voice low even though I was trembling. Somehow despite the shrieks and screams, Ursula still heard me plain as day.

"Because you needed to understand something first," Ursula calmly explained.

"What did I need to understand?"

"THAT YOU WERE BEING PUNISHED!" Ursula screamed so loud it drowned out every other sound around me. "YOU WERE SUPPOSED TO BE MISERABLE! I WASN'T PLAYING A GAME WITH YOU WHEN I WORKED MY MAGIC! I TURNED YOU INTO A MONSTER AND THAT'S HOW YOU WERE SUPPOSED TO STAY!"

Ursula moved quickly, her green dress swishing before her, when she grabbed me by my neck and held me up by herself instead of using the necklace.

"How could you ever find happiness as a monster?! You weren't supposed to become a, a, a superhero, of all things!" She stammered with rage. "This was supposed to teach you to be respectful and mindful of others. You weren't supposed to be happy. You weren't supposed to find any sort of joy in what you are! That's not how punishment is supposed to work!"

"You don't have the slightest idea of the things I've seen since you cursed me!" I shouted back. "I've had to fight supervillains, save the world—"

"And do you have any idea how many other children would kill to be in your position?!" Ursula shouted. "Look around you! You see what your selfishness has brought upon these people?! No, no you don't. You still haven't gotten the lesson. When you do something wrong, you deserve to be hurt. If you'd shown any contrition, maybe, maybe I would've forgiven you. But you flaunted your curse. Took pride in it. You accepted it, despite being a hideous freak!"

"I learned to live with myself!" I countered. I shouted loud enough to make sure her attention was on my face, and not my hands as I bunched up the loosened pearls I still wore. "I was with people who didn't care. People who finally convinced me I didn't do anything wrong just because you're a vindictive, evil piece of—"

"So they had to be punished too," Ursula replied. "If they couldn't recognize you for the ugly thing you are, they deserve punishment too. For making you think there's anything worth looking at in the ugliness I brought out of you."

"YOU'RE THE ONLY THING THAT'S UGLY!" I yelled as I wrapped the pearls around Ursula's own throat and squeezed. "YOU'RE THE REASON MY PARENTS ARE DEAD! YOU'RE THE REASON I HAVEN'T SEEN MY BROTHER IN YEARS! YOU'RE THE ONE WHO NEEDS TO BE PUNISHED! *YOU'RE WHAT'S UGLY!*"

My vision went as red as Ursula's face as I squeezed the necklace tighter around her God-awful throat, remembering the pain I felt as a child. The pain I felt waking up to all those dead people. The pain of learning to love myself all over again thinking I could never go back. Finding happiness as I was. Helping the world. Helping myself. So much pain I wanted to, to—

SNAP!

The pearls fell before me, fell from my fingers as I suddenly fell back once the necklace broke apart. The last thing I caught sight of was Ursula's eyes rolling into the back of her head as she collapsed on the floor.

***

"—by? Ruby?"

A voice I thought I'd never hear again brought me back to the waking world. The last thing I saw was red, but now the world was green.

"Brilla?"

"Hey, birthday girl," my friend said in a tear-stained voice. "You started the party without me, huh?"

"How, w—what...?"

"You didn't think I'd forget your birthday, did you?" Brilla asked. "I got Prom Queen to let me come visit you for your big day, but when we arrived, everything was a mess."

I struggled to look around, seeing unfamiliar heroes cleaning up the wreckage of the common area and the remains of my birthday party. The last time I'd seen some of these people was when they took Brilla into the future. My teammates, my other friends, were being treated for wounds. Some of them were unconscious and unresponsive. I didn't see Ursula's body anywhere.

I held up a hand to wipe a tear away from Brilla's face, gasping a little to see the fur was back. I don't know why I was surprised, considering everyone else was back to their regular forms, too.

"Too," I suddenly said.

"To? To what?" Brilla asked.

Looking down, I could see the dress I bought was torn up. Reaching a hand to the back of my head, I felt my braid had come undone.

"Too bad you didn't get here earlier," I laughed despite the pain I was in. "I thought time travel was your thing now."

"I wanted to be fashionably late," Brilla answered.

"I had my hair done special for the occasion. And I just bought this dress. Didn't even save the receipt."

"Well, you look good in everything," Brilla chuckled.

I laughed.

I laughed until I cried.

We cried until we kissed.

Despite everything, this was the best birthday I ever had.

About Jude Deluca

Jude Deluca's a nonbinary aegosexual Capricorn (he/she/they). She's a professional detective of horror media who has rediscovered several lost and unpublished stories, such as Goosebumps: Dead Dogs Still Fetch by R.L. Stine and Braden Gardner. Her areas of interest are magical girls, slasher fiction, YA horror, 90s nostalgia, superhero dads, and big beautiful men. She's got her first novella coming out from Mad Axe Media in 2026, and is currently co-editing a charity anthology of 2000s horror and is working on a collection of superhero horror for From Beyond Press.